Rein‹

Path of Lazy Immortal Book 1

A.P. Gore, Patricia Jones

To
my lovely Family!

Copyright
@ A.P. Gore/Patricia Jones

ISBN:

Sign up for my Cultivation sect to get latest update, and sneak peeks.

Contents

1. Reincarnation Mistake   1

2. Alive?   6

3. Dream or Reincarnation?   12

4. Blood Essence Body Cultivation Art   19

5. Sneak Attack   25

6. Dead young master?   32

7. Blood Nourishing Powder   35

8. Heart Blood   43

9. Blood Essence Body Layer one   50

10. Danger   58

11. Ancient Ruins   65

12. Escape   71

13. Du clan   79

14. Beast Subduing Pill   88

15. Blood Essence Body   97

16. Rapid Breakthrough   104

17. One Sword Strike   110

18. Three-Fold Strength Defense Array   119

19. Inconceivable Strength   127

20. Blood Pearl   134

21. Desperate Struggle   140

22. Soul Stone   146

23. Golden worm   153

24. Strange Power - Dantian repaired?   159

25. Five Elemental Way Qi Cultivation Art   166

26. Divine Refinement City   171

27. Dilemma   177

28. Strength Array   182

29. Danger   189

30. Yin Yang Threads   196

31. Yin Yang Hand Divine Art   200

32. What!   206

33. Supreme Inheritance   212

34. Fei'er in Danger   220

35. Back to Old Martial City   226

36. Lesser Isolation Array   231

37. Green Fang Dagger   238

38. Schemes of Du Clan?   245

39. Dao of Arrays   252

40. Treasure Map   258

41. Murder   264

42. Du Lufang's Rage   270

43. Godly Liquid   278

44. Daughter in law   284

45. Shocking Breakthrough   290

46. Qi Initiation Fruit Upgrade   296

47. Qi Initiation Layer   303

48. Li Guan   310

49. Forbidden Technique   317

50. Stepbrother?   326

51. Trap or gift?   333

52. Du clan barge in   339

53. Tier 4 clan?   346

54. Essence Burning Pill   351

55. Li Wei's master   358

56. Du Su   366

57. A rare hope   373

58. Forbidden Technique   378

59. Fire Beast Explosion   384

60. Still Alive?   391

61. Third Choice   396

62. Heaven's Suppression   403

63. Fire and Ice   410

64. Path of Immortality   418

65. Cultivation Realms   427

Chapter 1

Reincarnation Mistake

Heavenly winds rushed through his long fluttering hair as he descended onto the Paramount God Palace, his workplace with all the heavenly screens installed. He was known for his handsome and smiley face, but today his demeanor had turned vile. His sky-blue silky clothes imported from the Godly Silk Palace a few days back pricked his skin, and he itched to get out of the filthy clothes.

That was a terrible choice of clothes.

As he descended onto the top platform that housed the Seven Divine Juncture Lotus, the usual tranquil wind swirled into a whirlpool of fierce north winds.

"My lord. Why are you in a foul mood today? This lowly servant doesn't dare to ask, but concern forces me to ask about your bad disposition."

"Shut up, Shrug. I'm in a particularly vile mood today. Experiment T2459's timeline is screwed because of a bad girl and I've got to send everyone back two hundred years."

"My lord. If you move the Time Law back, it will impact your date with Dao Princes Ridhana tonight."

"What if I destroy T2459? They are just six universes. Yes, let's do that." His face broke into an ear-to-ear smile. It was just an experiment that had run for 50,000 years. It wasn't something precious like a date with Dao Princes Ridhana.

"My lord, let this lowly servant carry the task out for you. I can't manipulate time laws, but I can destroy an experiment easily."

"Just make sure no reincarnations are ongoing through Hell's Granny Wheel. That can cause trouble."

The lowly servant bowed with utmost sincerity and the lord's felt a surge of happiness. As his mood changed, fierce winds that had plagued the area turned into docile sheep and started nourishing the plants, and his servant breathed a sigh of relief.

Ten minutes later, his servant sprinted into Heavenly Dao Palace where all the experiment nuclei were stored. Finding T2459 wasn't a tough job. Destruction was always easier than creation.

As easy as destroying a measly god from a universe.

"Dao Destruction." Azure energy flew out of his palm and wiped out all six universes included in the T2459 nucleus.

"That was easy." He chuckled as the universes folded into themselves and the nucleus collapsed. "Wait . . . no." An awful premonition occupied his heart. He had forgotten something important.

Hell's Granny Wheel. He'd forgotten to check that. It was the second thing on the list of things out of his control, beyond his capabilities to interfere with. Even his master couldn't do it.

"Dao Energy Interface. Condense."

A thin film of azure energy formed in front of him, listing all the reincarnations going around the whole experiment nucleus.

"In the name of Holy Dao, what a blasphemy have I done?" Ten names appeared on the list, and one of them belonged to nucleus T2459. It was a pest named Li Wei. He was a low-level wastrel that had lived for 200 years and died at the hands of a girl. He was in the reincarnation cycle, and out of the T2459 nucleus. Where should he put that pest now?

The lowly servant couldn't think of a solution, so he looked around to find someone dying right at that moment.

There was one Li Wei that had died a few minutes before in T120. Without thinking, he transferred Li Wei's soul into the already dead Li Wei.

Clicking on the Dao Energy Interface, he quickly accessed nucleus T120. The old Li Wei had died from a nanobot attack, and his brain was fried.

But it was just a brain. Fixing it wasn't an issue. Another azure energy streak flew out of his palm, and the already dead Li Wei recovered 30% of his brain. Enough to survive.

And then dead Li Wei opened his eyes.

"Done." The lowly servant sighed, cold sweat breaking out under his dark blue robe.

"Error. The era of reincarnation doesn't match."

An error popped on the Dao Energy Interface, and Li Wei's soul flew out of the old Li Wei that he had just restored.

"Holy Dao. What should I do now?" The lowly servant sweated profusely. It was insane, and he didn't know what to do now.

"Searching for another suitable era." A new line popped up on the Dao Energy Interface.

"Nucleus T2460 found. Same era found. T2459 Li Wei is dying right now. Do you want to transfer T2459 Li Wei's soul to T2460 Li Wei?"

"Yes, please." The lowly servant shouted and watched a sixteen-year-old boy getting up in the backyard of a small house. The era looked the same, and the boy looked fine.

"Holy Dao. This has settled." The lowly servant closed the Dao Energy Interface and moved out of Heavenly Dao Palace.

By rushing out quickly, he forgot to check Li Wei's current soul condition. He didn't realize the soul had moved with the nucleus T2459 consciousness and had encountered a foreign object in nucleus T120.

Chapter 2

Alive?

Li Wei opened his eyes, taking in the shabby roof above his head. Fist-sized holes riddled it like someone had practiced a fist martial art on the roof. It looked exactly like his own childhood room, and he could even see the bright sun shining in the fair blue sky through the holes.

Pain crept under his skin as his senses became clear. Under his bare back, stones pricked his skin. Something wet and sticky flew over his chest, but he couldn't lift his hand to wipe it clean. Trying to lift his hand sent a bout of pain through his head and very core.

The pain. It shocked him fully awake, and he realized he was in a small room that looked like his own room two hundred years ago. The ten-by-ten-foot room had nothing but a small black ceramic pot that stored water and a bed roll made up of his old clothes. Surprisingly, the room had dust scattered over each and every thing other than a beautiful female's painting that hung on a wall.

That was the only painting of his mother that he had, and he always cleaned it and nothing else.

Was he in a dream? He must be. It had been two hundred years, and he still remembered this room vividly. His days of eating dog shit were spent in this room, at the back of his father's courtyard, before he ran away.

He still regretted not taking that painting with him. For many years, he'd thought of coming back to look for the painting, but he never got the chance. Because of his circumstances, by the time he came back to Old Martial City, the Li clan had vanished from the State of Zin. Completely.

Yes, this had to be a dream. A dream coming to him a moment before his death. So, the bitch succeeded in killing him. All his life, he'd loved her, but in the end, she'd killed him like a slaughterer killing a chicken. These must be memories coming back to him before his last breath. But why would he remember this shitty place instead of the many beautiful memories he'd made later in his lifetime? Why would his death trigger this particular memory?

And this pain. Shit, it felt like his entire body was being torn apart by something and he was losing all his blood. The metallic taste in his mouth and the smell of his own blood confirmed he was bleeding.

Lifting a small mirror at arm's length, he looked in it. Two bright blue eyes accompanied by a plump youth's face stared back at him.

Blue eyes. How could it be true? After practicing fire type body cultivation, his eye color had changed to red. Quickly, he checked his right shoulder and it had an old scar. Was it a dream? Even if he dreamed about his young days, why was he bleeding everywhere? He'd never had bled like this in his room. One time, Chang Wu beat him half dead, but it wasn't this bad.

A warm breeze rushed through the holes in the rooftop, covering his bare body and providing him the tranquil feeling he needed right now. Through a hole, he spotted the Azure Dragon Tree that towered above his small room. His childhood was spent around that tree. As far back as he could remember, he had never seen his mother. Later, he learned she had died when he was one year old. After her death, his stepfather had hated him and married another woman. From his earliest memories, he'd always spent time near this tree.

Well, Li clan members used to call it Big Piper Tree. After spending one hundred years in the sect, he saw this precious tree again, growing in the herbal garden of Senior Brother Jiang Jai. One day Senior Brother Jiang told him about the usefulness of this tree while drinking Seven Herb Immortal Tea below the vast expanse of the tree. That tree was awesome, and he could still feel the sweet taste lingering on the back of his tongue.

Too bad no one had known how rare this tree was. These tree leaves could be sold to a sect for a lot of money.

Seeing the tree leaves once again, he remembered little Fei who always ran around him. After leaving this place, he never went back. Maybe he should have, just for the sake of little Fei who always looked after a wastrel like him.

He should have come back. Regret ran deeper in his heart than he thought, otherwise why would he see this scene before his last breath?

A sweet smell suddenly covered his senses, giving him much needed calmness. It even reduced the immense pain he felt for a moment.

"Young master, I'm back." A tiny girl's beautiful face appeared before his eyes. She had two big blue eyes, and a dimple on her right cheek. She wore a long maroon robe that wrapped around her small fifteen-year-old body.

She carried a bowl bigger than her waist, and it exuded a medicinal smell. By the smell, he guessed it was the Regenerative Powder that every second store sold in Old Martial City.

She was Ki Fei, his servant. The only other person that spoke nicely to him in the Li clan compound other than Li Chi, his stepsister.

He sighed. Regret slipped through his meridians. He should have come back to check on her before the Li clan vanished from the city. For a mortal like her, living sixty years was tough. With his status in the sect, he could have helped her to live another hundred years at least.

"Fei'er. I'm sorry. I ignored you. I wish I had acted differently. But a dead person can't regret or cry, can he?" A lone tear escaped from his eyes.

The girl dropped on her knees and clasped his mouth. "Young master. Please don't speak like this. Fei'er will die if you talk like this." Sob after sob slipped out of her mouth, but then she halted. Her eyes turned to steel before she started wiping his bare chest with the liquid she'd brought in the small ceramic pot. "Wait for me to reach layer two Refinement Realm, and I'll teach those bastards a lesson."

Her soft hand brushed against his chest, and he could feel the low-level regenerative liquid entering his veins and a smooth feeling spreading through his body. But how could this dream be so vivid? Was it really a dream?

Then there was another issue. Fei'er was talking about Refinement Realm. Why was she talking about cultivation? Her Spirit Root was damaged when she was a child, so she couldn't cultivate. What a strange dream.

But before he could say anything, a formless aura swept through the room followed by his stepfather, Li Sua, entering through the small door.

"You wastrel, you even got beaten by a layer one Refinement Realm trash. I truly despise you . . ." A formless attack assaulted Li Wei, and he lost his consciousness.

But he couldn't confirm if it was a dream or not.

Chapter 3

Dream or Reincarnation?

Dripping water woke Li Wei from a bizarre dream. A shiver passed through his mind when he recalled it. In the dream, he'd faced a strange, inconceivable artifact that could talk in his head. It was called an AI chip. When he opened his eyes on a battlefield littered with other strange metal artifacts, the AI had spoken in his head, telling him some weird information like his injury condition, life percentage and whatnot. Before he could react, another strange thing happened. An azure light broke from the skies and pulled him away.

A cold water droplet fell on his eyelid, shaking him awake. A tiny hole in the roof was placed right above his face, and it was raining outside, enveloping the room in the unique, tranquil fragrance of soil. He used to live in a country covered by year-round rainstorms, so this smell wasn't something unknown. In fact, he'd missed it after running away from his home. And having a room with a roof full of holes, he'd practically lived in the rain.

Wait, wasn't this a dream before him dying? Why was he back in the same dream again, and was this a different part of it?

No, something was amiss. The rain, the cold air slapping his face, and this unique fragrance. How could he experience this all over again? Then there was the pain of a rough surface below his back, and now a gray robe covering his body.

Who had put a robe on his body? His stepfather?

No way.

He tried to move his head, but a lingering pain opposed him. If this was a dream, this pain wasn't possible.

What was going on? Had he reincarnated into his old self?

How was that even possible?

Of course, reincarnation was possible. A decade ago, he had even met a reincarnated beauty in his sect. She was as cold as ice, and other disciples called her Ice Queen behind her back. But she'd started as a baby and later gained her memories.

However, the reincarnation he knew of required one to born in a new body, not go back to one's old self. Time manipulation wasn't possible in his world.

"What the heck is happening?" he whispered, and in agony he raised his hand to slap himself awake. Suddenly he realized he could move his hand. Albeit with lots of pain. It wasn't crippled like it had felt previously. Even his injuries seemed a bit better.

Using his divine sense, he probed his physical condition.

A sharp pain shot into his mind when his divine sense spread through his body, but ignoring that, he went ahead with probing.

Five feet, ten inches. Youthful appearance. Sharp nose, square jaw, and fat protruding out from everywhere humanly possible.

He was sixteen years old again, and his bone age confirmed it. If this was reincarnation, then he was back at his sixteen-year-old self. Strange. Ice Queen had only evoked her memories after she reached a certain martial realm, and she'd remembered her past life that occurred a hundred and fifty years ago.

Strangely, he had traveled into his past, and with all his future memories and divine sense intact.

Damn, that meant his dantian—

He quickly poured his divine sense into his dantian. Although he couldn't inspect it like he could his other body parts, he felt qi leaking through it. A small leaky dantian. So, he couldn't cultivate. He couldn't even reach layer one Refinement Realm with this dantian. He had to fix his dantian and find a Dantian Strengthening Fruit to expand its size.

If he compared it with his old life, this was same.

If he wanted to walk on the same path he'd previously walked, he would have to wait two more months for his fortuitous encounter with senior sister Wang Zia.

But he would not dare. Nor would he accept it. That bitch had killed him in the end.

Hatred blew in his head when he thought about that bitch. She was his life. When he lay in the depths of a crevice, waiting for Ferocious Beasts to eat him, she'd arrived like an angel. Lifting him up from the depths of despair, she'd given him a way to walk forward. With her help, he'd transcended cultivation realm after realm. Only to die at her hands in the end.

Hatred rode through his meridians, pushing him to the brink of madness. If only he hadn't met her, he would be dead. Well, he couldn't blame her for helping in the first place, but then why did she kill him in the end?

Calm down, Wei.

Taking a deep breath, he controlled his emotions. Being an Array Master, he knew patience. Once he'd had to spend ten years in a puny place to carve an array to get out of a secret realm. Comparing this to that, this was nothing.

Anyway. That was then, and this was now. Somehow, he had another chance at his own life, and that too with his memories intact.

His lips moved, spreading in a wide smile. With all his memories intact, he was almost an Array Master. He could direct his life again from the start. This time he would change his destiny.

For the better. He would become a lazy immortal in this life.

What should he do next?

When senior sister Zia found him, he was a wastrel beggar and whatnot. He'd lain at the bottom of the deep crevice, waiting to get eaten by a Ferocious Beast.

But he didn't die. Two beautiful gray eyes had saved him and looked at him with amusement. It was senior sister Zia that carved a Three Beast Sealing Array in his leaking dantian and repaired it. She'd also given him a cultivation method for his attributeless qi, Three Vein Metal Qi Art. It was a mid-level cultivation art, and with that art he'd cultivated quicker and soon joined a mortal sect. In the end, he'd even had time to join senior sister Zia's sect, Firmament Sect.

If he wanted to run on the same track again, he would be called a dog by the heavens. This time, he would choose his own path.

First thing first, he had to fix his leaking dantian. But where would he find another Array Master to carve a high-level array like Three Beast Sealing Array in his dantian? This State of Zin had no Array Master. And even if he found one, why would an Array Master carve an array for him? And even if he somehow convinced an Array Master to help him, would he or she carve an array on his dantian?

No, they would think it suicide. Even senior sister Zia wasn't sure at first and asked him to think one hundred times before agreeing to it. That time he was desperate enough to not die, so he'd agreed.

If he wanted to cultivate, he had to carve an array into his dantian himself. With his divine sense, he could carve the Five Direction Sealing Soul Array that he had learned in his previous life. It required one to have strong divine sense and soul power, and he had both.

Excited, he poured his divine sense into his dantian and tried to check the leaky part, but a headache overtook him, and he was quickly thrown out of his dantian. Something was wrong with his divine sense, and his gut told him not to use it unless he needed it badly. He would need to reach layer one Foundation Realm to stabilize his current divine sense. Right now, he could only gauge its condition, couldn't pinpoint its location. His stronger divine sense wasn't useful until he broke through a whole realm.

There was another issue. His current body might not withstand the overbearing method of array carving on the walls of his dantian. Sister Wang Zia had used a different method, but he didn't want to go with that low quality method again. So, carving an array he wanted would be nothing but suicide.

Depression hit him. Was he going to end up a wastrel even after gaining a reincarnation advantage? Would he have to run away and wait to meet with senior sister Zia?

No way. He would die rather than meet her again. This time, he would ignore her and become a lazy immortal.

Chapter 4

Blood Essence Body Cultivation Art

Someone entered his room, disturbing Li Wei's thought process.

The six-foot-tall boorish figure bending his way through the five-foot-tall open frame door wasn't Fei'er but his stepfather. It was pitch dark and cold, but in the flickering candlelight he spotted his father's rage filled eyes. His long fingers held a leather whip, and Wei knew what was coming for him.

Wei looked around, longing to avoid the upcoming beating, but with his tattered body he couldn't move from the ragged bedroll he slept on. Even moving slightly on the rough cloth made him feel like someone scrubbed a mountain top with his bare body. It left a bitter taste in his mouth because it was similar to the body cultivation art he'd practiced in his previous life.

Cold wind rushed through the open door. It was broken the last time his stepfather had smashed it in rage.

Ever since, when it rained, he'd faced the assault of cold wind and mad rain.

When his father bent down over his fragile body, he looked like nothing less than a demon looming over its prey. Wei's first memory of this man was when he'd beaten Wei's ass red for some miserly reason, and it sent shrills through his soul.

Li Sua was an arrogant asshole, and Wei hated him through and through. It might seem an extreme opinion for a stepfather, but he wouldn't bother trying anymore. After Wei's mother died, Li Sua had completely ignored him, marrying more concubines and making children with them. He not only ignored Wei but beat him at every possible occasion.

"Please forgive this Wei for not being able to properly greet father." Wei spoke first, clutching the ragged bedroll with his fingers. The man least deserved respect from him, but he didn't want to add fuel to the fire. The old him was a stubborn fool and always went against his stepfather, receiving beating after beating.

But no more. On this new path, he had to tread carefully and enjoy his life.

"You can already talk . . ." Li Sua replied, his eyes red. His quivering hand betrayed his intention to beat Wei. Lashing out with his leather whip, he attacked Wei's abdomen.

Wei cried out in pain. That bastard treated him like a dog. But Li Sua was still Wei's father, and that's why he'd never gone back to the State of Zin because he feared he would kill Li Sua at first sight.

Another attack landed, and his soul almost jumped out of his mouth.

"Father!" Wei shouted in pain. His body was still recovering from the beating he'd received from Kang Tan, and now his stepfather was adding to it. Blood spurted from his body whenever the whip touched him, and soon his gray robe turned into shredded rags stained red.

"Why did you come back alive, wastrel? If you've guts to fight, why didn't you die instead of bringing shame to my Li clan?" Li Sua's whip moved like a snake, biting Wei in various places.

"I have a Foundation Refirming Pill, father," Wei somehow shouted, and suddenly the whip stopped an inch short of him.

"What did you say?" Li Sua's face flushed red. He definitely wanted to continue, but he stopped, as Wei had told him something precious.

Li Sua had been stuck at layer two of qi Foundation Realm for years, and without a costly pill he couldn't advance. In the State of Zin, Alchemists were rare, and every pill cost a huge amount of gold coins. Being a measly elder of the Li family didn't provide many resources to Li

Sua, and he could only bitterly try to absorb heaven and earth's energy to reach the next level. But with the poor heaven and earth essence levels of the State of Zin, it was nearly impossible to advance through cultivation levels without a pill.

"I've got a Foundation Refirming Pill. That's what I fought with Kang Tan for. This little one had only one thought, to get it for you. With my blood, I found it for you, father."

Li Sua bent down, his face flashing with delight. "Wei'er. Tell me, where is the pill? Give it to me now."

Wei snickered in his mind. This bastard changed his colors faster than a chameleon. In Wei's whole sixteen years, he'd never him Wei'er, and now he was trying to get cozy.

How presumptuous.

But what could he do? Wei sighed in his heart. This was a pill he had gotten his hands on a couple years back and saved for himself, but now he had to give it to his stepfather. This pill was his ticket to finding a peaceful month so he could cultivate peacefully. Otherwise, this man might beat him to death. In his current condition, any more injuries might push him to death.

Damn this body. He hated it right now. If only he could cultivate.

"Father, it's in the right corner of the room. Under the ceramic pot." He coughed, spitting blood. He had many injuries, but that barely fulfilled the requirements to cultivate Blood Essence Body Cultivation Art.

After waking up in his sixteen-year-old self, he had thought this through. Every cultivator had two paths of cultivation. Qi cultivation and body cultivation. In the State of Zin, only a few knew about body cultivation, but outside of it many people walked on this path.

Qi cultivation used heaven and earth essence energy and converted it into qi that could be stored in one's dantian. Body cultivation didn't convert essence energy. Instead, it stored it inside one's flesh.

While qi cultivation depended on one's Spirit Root attribute, body cultivation solely depended upon one's Physical Root. It was a mysterious organ present in one's body that determined the person's cultivation, talent, and aptitude.

Well, he had a flop there as well. He had a Bronze Grade Spirit Root and Earth Grade Physical Root.

Everything in this world was divided into grades: Bronze, Silver, Gold, Earth, Human, and Heaven. Bronze was the lowest grade, and Heaven was the top grade. In the mortal world, Silver Grade root was of paramount importance, and even in the Firmament Sect that ruled over the mortal world, Earth Grade root was a rare sight.

Because he had an Earth Grade Physical Root, senior sister Zia had taken a fancy to him.

Unfortunately, his Earth Grade physical root was of the lowest quality, so he couldn't cultivate Firmament Fire Body Cultivation Art to the higher realms.

That wasn't important. That art was tyrannical and required one to constantly temper their body with fire, and he hated getting burned. After a day's session, he would have blisters all over his body, and everyone would treat him with disgust.

But in this new life, he wouldn't cultivate Firmament Fire Body Cultivation Art. Instead, he would cultivate Blood Essence Body Cultivation Art. He had found it in the secret realm where he was trapped for ten years. He didn't know the Grade of the art, but it was absolutely above Gold Grade, so he wanted to cultivate it, but he couldn't before, because he had already cultivated another art.

But in this life, he could, and he remembered the steps and incantations to reach the first few realms of cultivation with Blood Essence Body Cultivation Art.

It was just that he needed to drink the blood of other people.

Chapter 5

Sneak Attack

Li Jia sneered at Li Tang's proposition. In the darkness, he was trying to hide his devilish smile. That old brother of his was trying to push him, the mightiest son of Li clan's patriarch, to a lowly branch city. Did he think Li Jia had just come out of his mother's womb?

"Senior Brother, just because you're an eldest son doesn't allow you to rule over others. The Patriarch position is yet to be decided, and I've already reached layer four of Foundation Realm, while you've been stuck at layer five for many years." Li Jia refuted his Senior Brother's idea of stationing him in this city. The Patriarch wasn't pleased with the current elder, Li Sua, and his way of ruling, so he had sent the three of them to re-prime Li Sua and decide on the next actions.

"Jia'er, you don't know the might of the heavens. Until you reach layer five, you're beneath me," Li tang replied in a stern tone.

Li Jia snorted in his heart. Wait until the Heavenly Firmament Sect opened their recruitment for outer sect disciples. Once he was admitted into the sect, he would definitely get his hands on the Foundation Refirming Pill and reach layer five quickly. With his talent, he might even get another pill and reach layer six soon after. That would put him in line with their father, Li Shua. He might even become the next patriarch.

An intense smell rushed through his nose and enthralled his senses.

"A Foundation Refirming Pill. Someone has taken out a Foundation Refirming Pill." The youngest son, Li Ti spoke. He had been trifling with pills for some years, and he was said to have some knowledge about them.

Even Li Jia recognized the fragrance. He had seen a Foundation Refirming Pill in the clan treasury by accident —their father treated it like a profound artifact. How could he forget the way his father had beat him after he touched that pill?

"Let's see who's in possession of the clan treasure," Li Tang said in a calm voice, but even the darkness couldn't hide the greed in his eyes.

"Yes." Li Jai quickened his pace. He had to get his hands on this pill and make a breakthrough. With this pill, his chances to get in the Heavenly Firmament Sect would be doubled.

≫≫ ≪≪

A sudden laugh pulled Wei out of his ruminations.

"A Foundation Refirming Pill. My Li clan is surely blessed by the heavens." Someone spoke loudly, and Wei squinted to take in the scene unfolding in his room. Three people had entered his small room, and suddenly it felt like they were all chickens stuffed inside a small cage.

Wei recognized the trio that had barged into his room. They were his uncles: Li Jia, Li Tang, and Li Ti. They were sons of the current patriarch, Li Shua, his maternal grandfather, and had a tyrannical attitude. They all wore dark blue martial robes baring the symbol of the Li clan on their chest. It was an axe, because the Li clan mainly performed wood cutting on their large pieces of land.

They had their eyes fixed on the small bean-sized pill in Li Sua's hand. It was the Foundation Refirmation Pill Wei had hidden a few months back. He had found it in an ancient ruin near Old Martial City, where they lived. For two years, he had hidden it from everyone else, saving it for himself. Originally, when his old self had left Old Martial City, he'd lost the pill to a group of bandits. Now, Wei used it in a way that would benefit him.

Squinting, he watched the trio carefully. The eldest uncle, Li Tang, had a huge body, a monkey face, and a boorish appearance. He looked after the main business. The other brothers, Li Jia and Li Ti, were stationed in other important cities. What were they doing here?

He had to stop them from snatching the pill from his father. If they succeeded, his father might vent his frustration on him, killing him in one go.

That must not happen.

Wei sent a divine transmission to his stepfather. "Eat it already, you fool."

Li Sua jumped on the spot, looking around.

"Li Sua, what are you waiting for? Give me the pill," Li Jia said impatiently, taking a step forward.

"Li Jia, the pill will come to me." Li Tang ferociously pushed his hand in front of Li Jia.

"What are you looking at?" Wei transmitted. "I'm the pill spirit, and I've taken a liking to you. It was destined for you, fool. Eat now. If you eat it, you'll gain immense benefits and might even become the next patriarch." Divine transmission was a skill that came when one's divine sense awakened, and for the first few realms of cultivation it was impossible to know about divine sense or divine transmission. So, Wei was sure his stepfather wouldn't know where it came from.

A headache overcame him as he used divine transmission, like his body was telling him not to use it.

Damn, that bastard was hesitating while looking at the pill.

Wei sent another message, venting a bit of the hatred from his heart. "Bastard. If you wait any longer, they will snatch me and then you can only wipe your ass with your empty hands."

Li Sua stared at Wei for a moment.

Wei sent another message. "What are you looking at? That crippled kid? That fool didn't even know what treasure he looted from another fool kid." "Don't even think about anything else. I, the pill spirit, will squash them once I enter your body. You don't have to worry about anything." As Wei boasted, he could see the hesitation from his stepfather's eyes vanishing. Divine transmission was a soul-to-soul message, so his physical body didn't make a single movement, and that was enough to fool his stepfather.

Li Sua once again stared at the pill and then gulped it down.

"Li Sua . . ." Li Tang, the tallest and oldest son of the patriarch, dashed forward and slapped Li Sua, but the pill had already entered Li Sua's stomach. There was no turning back.

"You bastard. You defied an order from me, and that means punishment," Li Tang bellowed in rage as he punched Li Sua twice, back-to-back.

"Elder brother Tang, please stay your hands." Li Ti stepped forward and held Li Tang's hand. "Let's arrest him and take him to father. He has betrayed our clan and stole the pill from treasury."

"Treasury?" Li Sua howled, his face grimacing in pain. The pill contained a huge amount of pure qi, and one had to refine it as soon as possible, otherwise it would endanger the user's life. "It was mine from the start, and I ate it."

"Li Ti, let's just kill him." Li Jia howled in rage. "He ate my pill, and I must kill him."

"Elder brother Jia, don't do something that will anger our father." Li Ti once again stepped in. "We have to take him back. We can't kill him. We should ask the patriarch to kill him by throwing him in Thousand Hell Valley and make an example of him." Li Ti spoke softly, but his ideas were quite cruel.

Li Sua's face turned grim. He opened his eyes and gawked around himself. "Senior, please save me. You said you'd help me. Now, please come forward and take action and kill these wastrels."

Li Jia chuckled, his left eye twitching slightly. "You're going to die, and you still dare to call us wastrels? You and your son are wastrels." His gaze jumped to Wei for a moment and then vanished.

Wei snickered in his mind. For an arrogant fellow like Li Jia, a cripple like him was nothing but a fart, so he wouldn't pay attention to him, and that was good. And with them taking his father away, he would be gone and punished heavily.

That fit his plan perfectly. At first Wei didn't want to give his pill to these ants, but he wanted a peaceful period to concentrate on his recovery and body cultivation, and when he spotted this trio nearby, a plan had formed in his mind, and he'd exposed the pill. The pill had a unique scent, and he'd expected it would attract attention from this trio. If he hadn't, then he would have used divine transmission to draw them.

His plan would have failed if his stepfather hadn't eaten the pill. But everything went perfectly in the end.

"Let's take him." Li Tang pulled out a thick rope and wrapped it around Li Sua and dragged him out.

"Wastrel." Li Jia suddenly raised his leg and stomped it on Wei's abdomen. A sharp pain shot from his stomach, and he felt his whole-body convulsing before he lost conscious.

System: Host body is in danger. Activating...

Chapter 6

Dead young master?

Ki Fei hummed a folktale as she passed the back of the Li clan compound. From the time the morning dew appeared on the wildflowers, she had lined up in front of old Lou's store in Old Martial City's north market. She didn't even get to enjoy her morning tea because of this, but she didn't regret it even a little bit. The Pink Rabbit's Breath old Lou sold was a miraculous regenerative medicine. People even joked that it could regrow an immortal's heart. Jokes aside, she had seen its usefulness when she had suffered a heavy injury, and if it could alleviate a little of the young master's pain, it would be worth the fifty silver coins she'd spent on it.

Lost in thought, she kicked a large stone lying in the road and tore her long gray gown. It had nearly cost her whole month's salary, but she was more afraid of the young master's reaction. He liked cleanliness, and he would despise her if she looked like this. Cursing over her carelessness, she first checked the broth she had bought. Thank goodness, it hadn't spilled. It still emitted the heavenly fragrance of Pink Rabbit. She licked her lips, remembering the sweet taste of the Pink Rabbit meat she once ate when she was a kid. It tasted heavenly.

With the back of her hand, she checked her face, and thank goodness there was no dirt. After that small blunder, she increased her pace cautiously and headed to the young master's room. In less than ten minutes, she reached the open doorframe of the young master's lone room at the farthest corner of the Li compound. Seeing the ruined door in the broad daylight, she sighed in her heart. A few months back, old master Sua had smashed it in pieces after getting angry at the young master. Since then, her stubborn young master had refused to repair it, although he suffered from the rain and cold wind. If he could cultivate, rain and wind wouldn't mean anything to him, but with his mortal body he couldn't resist the effects of the cold.

"Wait for me to get stronger, young master. I'll help you take revenge for your punishments," she whispered as she stepped through the open door.

"Young master . . ." Her heart stopped when she spotted young master Wei sprawled on the floor in a pool of blood.

"Master." She dropped the pot and rushed ahead to check on young master Wei's pulse. Tears streamed from her eyes, and she couldn't focus on his pulse for a few breath's time.

"No . . ." she cried when she got no pulse. Her heart sank to the pit of her stomach. "Young master, how could you leave me like this . . ." There was no pulse coming from young master Wei's body, and she couldn't believe he was no more. This was impossible. Last evening when she fed him chicken soup, he even joked around with her. He'd looked so good in the evening light. His face had even gained back a little of the color he had lost after the fight with that bastard Kang.

This must be the old master's doing. That devil of a man always beat the young master for no reason. It must have been him again.

She touched her heart. It was in pain, and there was no remedy for this. It only knew revenge. "Old master Sua . . ." She dropped on the young master's chest, wrapping her tiny hands around his neck. "I vow to the heavens today that one day I'll get strong and kill you for killing my young master."

"I don't know if you can kill him or not, but if you don't let me go, I might die right now." A familiar voice shook her soul.

Chapter 7

Blood Nourishing Powder

Li Wei didn't know how much time had passed since Li Jia nearly took his life. When he regained consciousness, the dark had vanished, replaced by sunrays stretching through the hole-ridden roof, bringing a refreshing chilly aroma with them.

He was alive, or so his throbbing body and the rough ground under his back told him. On top of that, the cold wind brushed against his wounds, sending chills through his body. It had rained the last time he had his eyes open, and the chill still hung in the air. Even his blood smelled cold and icy.

A bout of coughing took over his body, and he almost lost his life again. Li Jia's kick had destroyed his abdomen and the meridians nearby it. The last thing he remembered was blood spurting from of his mouth and stomach, staining his shirt with red color.

At least that bastard didn't hang around and mutilate his corpse. He would have been dead if that had happened. Truly dead.

Wait, there was another thing. Something popped in his vision, like an overlay. It was called . . . system?

A headache overtook his brain, and he couldn't remember anything about that mysterious thing. But he had a gut feeling that it had saved his life.

But was his life completely saved?

Sending his divine sense into his body, he checked his condition. A bout of pain shot from his head, like someone was splitting it into two parts.

What was wrong with him? Why was he getting these headaches?

But wait. They only came when he used his divine sense.

Suddenly, he realized the issue.

This was happening because his divine sense carried his experience and intuition along with it. And that was the crux of the issue. If it were only memories, it shouldn't be unstable, but memories differed from experience. Memories could only teach him theories about things, but experience taught him the working of an art or a technique.

Although his divine sense was reincarnated with his soul, his current body couldn't support it—he didn't have soul space. All his previous life's experience lay inside the divine sense while his memories became merged with his soul. He could feel his divine sense weighing with heavy experience, but it wasn't connected to his soul. It was a kind of a third-party entity for him, and his own divine sense hadn't formed yet.

Basically, he was a clean paper with lots of memories and an extra piece of experience that didn't belong to him, but to his previous life. If he wanted to store these experiences, he had to form a soul palace and assimilate this experience in his own divine sense. But how could he form a soul palace at his current realm?

The divine sense lived in soul space formed after a cultivator reach a certain realm. But he was too fragile to have a soul space, or even a hint of a soul space. If he overused his divine sense, it would crumble, and along with it all the experience of his previous life.

He couldn't use his divine sense anymore. If it crumbled, he would lose his intuition, and that would be like life without vigor.

Ignoring his divine sense for a moment, he assessed his body's condition.

The situation was grim. Only ten percent of his blood remained in his body. The meridians around his stomach had been ruptured, and blood still leaked from his gut.

But this was good. Really really really good.

When he decided to choose Blood Essence Body Cultivation Art, he planned to use his previously injured state to start cultivation. Blood Essence Body Cultivation Art cultivated one body in Blood Essence Body, and the initiation required one to lose as much as blood one could, so the new blood formed with the cultivation art would be vigorous and full of essence. This was a pragmatic art that could leave one careless about one's body. As long as a drop of blood and soul remained, one could regenerate their whole body in the higher realms. Loss of blood, injuries, and regrowing one's limbs would be nothing once a person reached mid-level realms of Blood Essence Body.

Of course, it couldn't regenerate one's dantian, as it wasn't part of one's physical body, but a mysterious entity. Then this was all in the future. Currently, he could only wish to reach Foundation Realm quickly and gain the first power bestowed by Blood Essence Body. Once he reached Foundation Realm, he would know the details of that power.

Currently, he only had ten percent of his initial blood flowing in his body. Barely enough to keep him alive. Thanks to his divine sense, he could perfectly gauge his own body's condition.

In a normal condition, he would have never achieved this low blood percentage, as he would never dare to exhume his blood to such low levels. When he decided to cultivate Blood Essence Body Cultivation Art, he'd planned to exhume fifty-one percent of his total blood and start cultivating—the bare minimum amount required for cultivating the first level. But now, he had achieved a ninety percent blood loss, and that would be extremely beneficial for his future cultivation.

He was about to recite the cultivation method when something dropped near his head and two tiny hands wrapped around his neck, almost crushing him. A sweet fragrance emitted from the owner of those hands and he knew it was Fei'er. Her body always emitted this unique fragrance. Like an Ice Orchid Flower. This fragrance could calm one's mind.

But that didn't mean he could indulge in this fragrance for long. With only ten percent of his blood remaining and a mortal body, he would surely die if this assault continued even for a few more breaths.

"I vow to the heavens today that one day I'll get strong and kill you for killing my young master." Fei'er's determined voice struck in his mind. This girl was the last tie he had left to this mortal world. She was a servant in his house, but he had never treated her like one. He'd always treated her like a little sister, and no matter what, she always stuck with him, in thick and thin. He even paid her salary by earning money himself. Although he could only provide her a bare minimum salary, she stayed with him.

"I don't know if you can kill him or not." Opening his eyes, he gasped for a breath. "But if you don't let me go, I might die right now."

"Young master!" Fei'er released him in a jiffy and sobbed hard. "I thought . . ." She wiped her eyes with the backs of her tiny hands and then a beautiful smile bloomed on her face. "Forget it. As long as you are okay. But this blood . . ."

"Fei'er, I'm fine. Tell me, have you reached Refinement Realm layer one?"

Fei'er nodded, her eyes still misty at the corners.

"Good. Go to the corner and dig a foot deep, and you will find a money pouch."

Fei'er arched her brows, her small mouth pouting.

"Go, I need you to buy me some herbs." He coughed, pain radiating through his nerves with every movement of his throat. It made him realize how fragile a mortal body was. After cultivating to the peak of Refinement Realm, one would get years added to their life and get rid of common sickness or small injuries that normally happen with every mortal. Unfortunately, most of the people never reached that stage. They remained in the first few levels of Refinement Realm and gained only small benefits. Only geniuses with Silver Grade Spirit Root or Physical Root were selected in the sects for cultivation. Others remained at the bottom. They could never reach the apex of the Mortal Realms.

In the path of cultivation, the first stage was called the Mortal Realm, and it matched with the realm he currently lived in. It contained Refinement, Foundation, Bone Baptization, Marrow Cleansing, Boiling Blood, and Heart Blood Realm. These realms were further divided into nine layers.

"Young master, please drink this Pink Rabbit broth first. It will help you restore your energies."

"No, get the herbs first," Wei said firmly. "Get me Blood Flower, Bone Protruding Fruit, and Red Ginseng." These were all low-grade herbs that could be crushed together to form a simple Blood Nourishing Powder. A common recipe known among commoners. It didn't require any alchemy knowledge or a furnace. But it was an excellent life saver in tough situations, so many people carried these things with them. "Also get a White Cicada Fruit."

"These . . ." Fei'er's eyelashes fluttered. "Young master . . ." She hesitated and looked at the money pouch hanging at her gray dress's waist. "They will cost at least ten gold, and the quality will be quite low."

"I have thirty gold saved in the pouch. Buy three sets. Don't worry about quality." All he cared about was these herbs' blood replenishing power, and he didn't need a

Gold Grade herb to replenish his current blood supply. A low-tier Bronze Grade herb would do. Like a Root, everything else was divided into grades. Bronze being the lowest and then Silver, Gold etc. But for herbs and certain things, these grades were further divided into low, middle, and high tiers. All three herbs he'd asked for were low-tier Bronze Grade herbs and quite cheap, available even in an outskirt city like Old Martial City.

Although he knew a better recipe that didn't require any alchemy knowledge, those herbs wouldn't be available in this city, nor he could afford them for now.

Fei'er dug at the corner and five minutes later she came back with a shabby black pouch. After burying it in the soil for nearly two years, it had already lost its luster and showed signs of decay.

"Young master. I'll get the herbs you asked for, but why do you want White Cicada Fruit? That smells horribly. It's not part of the Blood Nourishing Powder."

So, the lass had a basic knowledge of alchemy. Good. In this life, he had a goal set for himself. He was going to become an Alchemy Master and to do that he had to visit Alchemy Comprehension Tower first.

"You'll find out when you bring them back." Wei sneered.

Chapter 8

Heart Blood

Fei'er walked through the sun-illuminated door and smiled at him with her beautiful blue eyes. Wei heaved a sigh in his heart. She had come back in just two hours, and the way she held her pouch close to her heart give him assurance that she had gotten all the herbs.

He'd been waiting for this and couldn't hold it anymore. Taking the risk, he sent his divine sense into his body. As he sent his divine sense through his body, he realized he had lost more blood, and his blood percentage hung around just nine percent.

"Did you get the White Cicada Fruit?" he asked in a tattered tone.

She nodded, spreading her lips in a faint smile as she sat next to him. Her body exuded a unique fragrance that calmed him down a little. Something he needed badly right now. It reminded him of the time he'd met this lass for the first time. He was badly hurt, lying in the street, and a little girl came forward offering him a fruit she was eating. Her clothes were tattered and her face dirty, and yet she offered the fruit upon seeing his condition. That touched his heart, so he recruited her as his servant, as she wouldn't take money without working for him.

"Good." That was his only option for survival.

But before that, he had to perform a step with her help.

"Fei'er, help me get up." After she left, he had tried to move his hand but failed as pain took over his consciousness, and he almost lost it.

"Young master, please let me crush this into a paste and apply it to your wounds. You don't need to get up for that." Fei'er put down the herb pouch and brought a stone crusher near him.

"No. Help me get up first." He coughed, and his lungs almost jumped out of his throat. All his organs were in turmoil, and if this continued, he might not make it to tomorrow.

Fei'er gritted her teeth and slid an arm below his back. Her soft touch eased his pain, but he spurted a mouthful of blood out.

Water droplets fell on his face, and he spotted Fei'er crying silently.

"Young master, please let me apply the paste first."

"No. Do it." He gritted his teeth and gulped down the next bout of blood trying to jump out of his mouth.

After a minute of vicious pain and two mouthfuls of blood, his back rested on the stone wall. The cold penetrated through his tattered shirt and into his back, sending a shiver through his spine.

"Now . . ." His chest heaved. "Squeeze the White Cicada Fruit into a juice and create Blood Nourishing Powder in another pot." The room swirled around, and he almost lost consciousness again.

He couldn't lose it.

Not yet.

For the next ten minutes, Fei'er worked as per his instructions, and two pots, one filled with white juice that smelled spicy, and the second with Blood Nourishing Powder, were ready in front of him.

"Bring the juice forward, stab my heart with a knife, and put my Heart Blood in the juice."

Fei'er's face twisted, her eyes spanning wide. "Young master, what are you asking?"

"Get my Heart Blood out and pour it into the White Cicada Fruit juice and then feed me that."

Her eyes spanned wider than humanly possible, and her face turned grim. "Young master, do you want me to kill you?" She suddenly slapped herself hard. "How can I think like this? Young master, I can't do this."

Wei pushed the next bout of blood back in his stomach. "Fei'er, this is the only way for me to survive. Don't worry, I won't die. The White Cicada Fruit will replenish my blood."

Fei'er shook her head and stepped back.

"If you don't do it, then I'll die," he said, and he surely would. His blood level had reached rock bottom, so just the Blood Replenishing Powder wouldn't save him. Unless he got a high-tier Silver Grade medicine, nothing else could save him.

This was his only choice right now. If he forty-nine percent of his blood had remained, hell yes, he would go with the Blood Replenishing Powder, but not now. The White Cicada Fruit had topmost importance to him right now.

White Cicada Fruit was a common fruit and had little use in alchemy. Even commoners discarded it, as it smelled horrible. It was known for its dilution property and used by many small sects to dilute heavenly elixirs and poisons. The diluted liquid would have some percentage of the original elixir or poison and could be used in large quantities.

White Cicada Fruit had another version called Three Leaf White Cicada Fruit. It had better properties and could maintain a better percentage of the original liquid's properties, but it was quite costly. White Cicada Fruit retained fifteen percent of the original liquid's properties, while its big brother retained thirty percent.

Of course, the one Fei'er bought was the normal one and would only make the juice keep twelve to fifteen percent of his blood's properties. That's why he needed the purest of his blood, and that was his Heart Blood. Every human produced a drop of Heart Blood once in a year, and it was stored in one's heart. It was a super blood drop that contained the power of thousands of blood drops. It wouldn't be useful for common people, but high-level cultivators had many uses for it.

"Young master, how could you . . ." She sobbed, stepping backward.

"Fei'er." He coughed. "Let me show you. Get a small pot and pour a drop of your blood and some White Cicada Fruit juice in it."

Fei'er's eyes gleamed and she followed his instructions. When the white juice mixed with the blood, it turned dark red at first, then the color faded and settled on a faint red. It even carried the faint fragrance of orchid.

"Taste it, and you'll know."

Fei'er hesitated for a moment and then drank the juice. "It tastes like . . ."

"Your own blood. I've lost a lot of blood, Fei'er and I need to replenish it. But I need my own blood to do this," Wei replied, but it wasn't entirely true. There was another method. He could use another's blood too.

Blood Essence Body Cultivation Art was a tyrannical art. It lay in the gray area of the righteous and demonic path. One could cultivate it faster by drinking blood from others, but that was a superficial method—and a demonic one too. Although he didn't believe in being the most righteous guy in the world, he didn't like demonic ways either.

The other way of cultivating Blood Essence Body Cultivation Art was using one's own blood. One could drain oneself and then regenerate new blood using the cultivation art. Despite being slowest, it brought many benefits.

If he had only lost fifty-one percent of his blood, he could have stabbed himself and guided the knife using his divine sense to take a drop of his Heart Blood, but now he had to rely on someone else, and whom could he trust other than Fei'er?

"But young master, you've already lost so much blood. If I make a mistake, you might die."

"Fei'er. I've lost ninety-one percent of my blood, and there's no other way to gain blood. Don't worry, I know a secret method that will help me replenish my blood using this method."

"But . . ."

"Just do it. It's an order." He hardened his face.

"But I'm afraid."

"I'll guide you."

After five minutes of hesitation, she pulled a small knife out and put it on his chest, but she shook her head the next moment. "No, I can't do it."

"Fucking do it already." With all his might, he pushed himself forward and let the knife pierce his heart. Pain withered through his fragile body as the metal tip entered his skin first and then muscle. It was excruciating, and he couldn't take it, but he had to.

"Young master, you . . ." Fei'er was about to pull her knife back when he pushed himself to the extreme and grabbed her hand.

"Do it."

"This . . ." Fei'er closed her eyes, gritted her teeth, and pushed the knife into his chest.

Inch by inch, a marker of agony closed on his heart. As he had lost most of his blood already, no blood came out of the wound.

That was a good thing, as he didn't want to pollute the heart blood.

"To your right," he cried through his teeth as the knife headed for his ribcage.

Fei'er sobbed and moved the knife to her right a little.

"Little more . . ." A loud cry slipped out of his mouth as the knife stabbed in the wall of his heart. He couldn't take it anymore and lost consciousness.

Chapter 9

Blood Essence Body Layer one

Li Wei was roaming through the dreamland when cold water splashed over his face. The moment he opened his eyes, a thick speck of sunlight blinded his eyes. His eyes failed to bear even that much sunlight.

Things were grim, and even his divine sense seemed to turn dull and hazy.

"Where . . ." A pair of pretty moist eyes stared at him in the backdrop of his shabby room that became blurry as he glanced at it.

"Young master." Fei'er grabbed his chin and pushed a small ceramic cold bowl to his lips. "I've extracted two drops of your Heart Blood and made this juice." She sounded hurt.

"Thanks . . ." He couldn't say anymore. All he wanted was to lose himself in the unique orchid fragrance she exuded and sleep for an eternity.

No. Li Wei, wake up. You have to do better in this life.

A sharp voice came out of his subconscious, thrashing into his mind and obliterating the degenerated thoughts. No, he couldn't lose himself. In this life, he couldn't make the same mistakes.

With all his might, he forced himself awake. With half-open eyes that felt like tons of weights were attached to them, he stared at the thick red blood in the white ceramic bowl with a blue dragon painted on it. Inhaling deeply, he smelled the blood. It smelled like nothing. It was his own blood. Every person had a unique smell to their blood that depended on their Spirit Root attribute, but his Spirit Root had no attribute, so his blood smelled like nothing. A blank sheet that he was re-writing with his own script. This blank sheet would get to the apex.

Not the Earth Grade Physical Root, but his blank sheet Bronze Spirit Root would carry him forward this time.

For his own life, he had to remain awake.

Pressing his lips on the bowl's cold edge, he gulped the first sip of his own blood. It tasted awkward.

"Blood Essence Body Cultivation Art. Initiation." Shouting in his mind, he directed the blood he just drank into his first meridian, the meridian that connected to stomach: Yangming meridian.

Blood Essence Body Cultivation Art was peculiar in its cultivation method. Unlike the old art he'd practiced, Firmament Fire Body Cultivation Art, that required him to consume fire-attributed things, Blood Essence Body required him to baptize his own meridians and revive himself. Essence energy he absorbed from nature would revive his meridians at lower levels and bring forth his body's potential.

Revive in oneself. Form the ultimate Blood Constellation. Blood above all.

It was the first line written on the jade slip he'd obtained in the strange secret realm. Once completed to a certain level, it would pack all the knowledge the body experienced in each drop of blood, allowing one to revive oneself from a single drop.

It worked on one principle and disregarded everything else.

It formed the ultimate Blood Constellation.

Blood above all.

Well, he didn't believe in it completely, nor had he the jade slips to cultivate this art to the peak levels. He didn't need them. He only had to reach Foundation Realm to sustain array carving using his divine sense and then cultivate qi. This was a special Soul Array he had learned in the later part of his previous life. It was different from the array Wang Zia had carved in his dantian using beast blood. It was far superior to the method Wang Zia had used.

But he had to reach Foundation Realm to try that. Right now, his divine sense was weak and flickery, but it might stabilize once he reached Foundation Realm. Even in all professions like Alchemy, Arrays and Artificers Foundation Realm was the least stage of cultivation one needed to reach before starting one's journey on that path.

The first drop of White Cicada Juice mixed with his blood passed through his throat and entered his Yangming meridian. It was a large meridian that connected with thousands of small blood vessels surrounding it. The initiation of Blood Essence Body Cultivation Art required him to circulate his blood through a certain path along with a specific chant. It was like qi cultivation, where he circulated heaven and earth essence through a special path inside his body. Once initiated, he would be able to absorb heaven and earth's essence energy and store it inside his blood and body.

One drop, another drop, and then multiple drops started moving through the blood vessels and reappearing in his Yangming meridian, but a strange thing happened. For every one hundred blood drops, only fifty would come out of the connected blood vessels. Thanks to his divine sense, he could watch every blood drop passing through his meridian.

They were disappearing in the middle.

What was going on? Where did the blood go?

Bewildered, he spread his divine sense to the other parts of his body.

What he saw left him in shock. Before this, his body was devoid of any blood, like a blood-drained corpse, but the condition was changing. New blood started appearing all over his body. Shiny red blood drops drove through his meridians and blood vessels, rejuvenating them with strong vitality. In comparison, his old blood looked like dogshit. It had a faint black color, while the new blood had dark red vitality. If he compared it to the Foundation Realm in his previous life, it was way better than that. And this was even before he reached the first layer of Refinement Realm.

This was a heaven-defying cultivation art. Now he realized why this cultivation art required one to bleed to death and drink another's blood to initiate it. It needed space in the body so it could replenish the blood using this strange phenomenon. It actually multiplied the blood through some means. If one tried recycling one's own blood with one hundred percent blood force, they might explode from too much blood.

That made sense. The less blood one had in their body, the better the cultivation art worked. And this new blood had an incomparable vitality when compared to the blood he had.

Maybe this was a good thing. With an elated heart, he drank the juice faster, sending it through his Yangming meridian. The best part, it didn't hurt at all. When he'd cultivated Firmament Fire Body Cultivation Art, he'd had to put his body through so many hardships. One time he even had to step in an alchemy furnace. A hot, bubbling alchemy furnace. That was more than brutal, and he'd had nightmares for months after that experience.

This was much better.

Time passed slowly, and he drank the pot full of White Cicada Fruit juice mixed with his Heart Blood in six hours. It took six hours, but he felt like only a moment had passed in between, and the result was astonishing.

When the last drop of White Cicada Fruit juice moved out of his Yangming meridian, he noticed it had changed color from faint black to a throbbing red. It had gone through the qualitative change, and if he had to measure his blood quantity, he had replenished sixty percent of his total blood.

He felt a lot better.

But the initiation wasn't over. Two more steps were needed to complete the initiation. First, to draw out the old blood, and second, to refill the rest of his blood. Suddenly, he felt good about having only nine percent old blood remaining in his body.

Thanks to his divine sense and the color of the new blood, it was easier to spot the old blood. As he had bled profusely, his body had pushed all the remaining blood to two organs: his brain and heart. That made sense. If any organ had failed, he would have died already.

"Fei'er." He opened his eyes and stared at the little lass sitting next to him with her head on her knees. In the darkness, she looked so sad, and he had an urge to tousle her hair and tell her everything was all right.

"Young master." Her head snapped up, her eyes teary.

"I'm fine, but I need you to stab me again, just above my ears, and next to my heart. Stab it until it bleeds."

"Young master . . ." She cupped her small mouth.

"Don't you see I'm doing better than before?" He asked, smiling faintly. Although his wounds hadn't healed, his vitality had undergone a tremendous transformation, and he could force his muscles to act on his will.

Fei'er scanned him through her beautiful eyes. "Yes, but this . . ."

"Do you want me to do it myself?"

"I'll do it." Bringing the knife up, she first stabbed it in his heart under his guidance, drawing a lot of blood out.

It hurt like hell, but his heart was in overdrive, pushing new blood through his Yangming meridian and producing new blood everywhere.

"Brain now." Out of the nine percent old blood, his heart had five and his brain had four remaining.

Crying, she stabbed above his right ear and pierced a hole in his brain, rupturing a small meridian.

Blood oozed out of his skull, and he felt his consciousness fading in and out. As the blood flew out of his brain, his thought process became muddy, and he stopped sensing things around him.

But it lingered only for a few breaths, and soon everything become clear. Clear unlike before.

He had reached the final stage of initiation, and was on the verge of reaching layer one of body Refinement Realm. Now he could finally absorb heaven and earth's essence energy.

Chapter 10

Danger

In an isolated room in the Li clan compound, a bloodied man lay on the ground. His clothes were tattered, and various wounds could be seen on his whole body. In all, he was beaten like an animal.

Two men entered the room, and one of them kicked the bloodied man as soon as he stepped in.

"Li Sua, are you still not talking? Don't blame me for not showing mercy for a thief like you." Li Jia punched with his right hand and sent Li Sua's wounded body flying away. Because of this bastard, Li Jia had lost a golden opportunity to step into layer five Foundation Realm. If he had eaten the Foundation Refirming Pill, he would have reached layer five Foundation Realm easily and entered the Heavenly Firmament Sect in the next month's recruitment.

But this bastard had to eat that pill like a pig.

"Tell me, how did you steal that pill?" His next punch landed on Li Sua's nose, breaking his already bloody nose.

But no matter how he hit this bastard, the rage flowing through his heart wouldn't subside.

"Li Jia, wait." Li Tang entered the room and spoke in a loud voice. A golden talisman lay in his hand, and it emitted a strange mysterious light. It was a Far Distance Sound Transmission Talisman. Li Tang had used it to converse with their father, Li Shua. They were afraid if Li Sua had stolen the pill from the clan's treasury, they would face wrath of their father.

"What did father say?" Li Jia stopped his kick in midair.

"The pill is not from the treasury. It seems we underestimated this junior brother of ours. Either he squandered money from our clan, or he obtained it from somewhere else." Li Tang's eyes glittered like a hungry pig.

Li Jia turned his head to stare at the blood-laden Li Sua on the ground. That bastard was telling the truth. He got it from somewhere else, but how could he arrange so much money? The Li clan branch in this city only worked in the nearby mountains, cutting trees. They could never accumulate this much money. Li Ti handled the accounts, and it was impossible to cheat him. Even Li Jia didn't dare to squander any money from the arm of the business he took care of because of their younger brother.

"Li Sua, if you tell us the source of the pill, we might let you live." Li Jia stomped his foot on Li Sua's right knee, crushing it a little.

"You motherf—" Li Sua cried out in pain. "Pill spirit, you've betrayed me. Come and help me, else you'll die a horrific death."

Li Jia frowned. This bastard kept calling on an unknown pill spirit. Either he had lost his mind, or he was fooling them.

"Tell us the truth. Else I'll pull your tendons out and feed them to dogs." Li Jia used his qi to push his leg on Li Sua's knee. A cracking sound came out of Li Sua's leg, and he broke out with another loud cry. This degenerate brother had no shame. He cried like a girl.

"I'll— Let me go, please. I'll tell you the truth. It was my son, Li Wei, who gave me this pill. He stole it from somewhere. Go and ask him, but please spare me."

Li Tang's forehead broke out in black lines. "Isn't that the kid you killed yesterday?" He stared at Li Jia.

Li Jia broke out in a cold sweat. If this proved to be true, then he had stepped on a scorpion's tail.

"Don't worry. He is alive. There's a girl feeding him Blood Nourishing Powder." Li Ti spoke for the first time. This younger brother of theirs was a silent person, but he had a terrifying degree of perception and a massive information-gathering network. Because of him, their clan business had flourished for the last five years.

Fortunately, Li Ti did not aspire to the patriarch position. His goal was to join the alchemy sect of the region, Divine Fragrance Palace, so Li Jia didn't have to fear his extraordinary gifts.

"Then let's go and capture this kid," Li Tang said. "Li Ti, stay here and look after Li Sua. Make sure he doesn't run away."

After Li Ti nodded, they stepped out of the room and headed toward the lone cabin at the corner of the Li compound.

·»»»⟩ ⟨⟨⟨⟨·

Evening light passed through the doorframe, illuminating young master Wei's tranquil face. Ki Fei changed her position so the bright light wouldn't disturb young master's sleep.

The restless day had passed, bringing hope and peace. It was most brutal day of her life. Watching her young master waver between life and death had stressed her to the limit. She felt like she had aged ten years at least in a single day.

However, it had ended well, and the young master had passed into a calm sleep. His face was devoid of any pain, and what more could she ask?

While staring at his peaceful expression, she remembered the strange White Cicada Fruit juice the young master made for himself. It was a bizarre method she had never heard about. Where did the young master found about it? Thinking about it, the young master had hidden so many things from her. This weird method, money buried in the ground . . .

The strangest thing, he even knew the path of the knife when she'd stabbed it into his chest.

A bout of emotions jumped into her throat when she thought about how she'd stabbed her young master so ruthlessly. When he'd bled, she felt like stabbing herself for the inhuman thing she'd done.

But he'd survived, and that was what was important. After he went through all that, his injuries had healed from the inside out, and now only shallow cuts remained. If he wasn't sleeping peacefully, she would have changed his bloody clothes. Seeing those bloody clothes on his fair body made her heart squeeze in fear.

Did he lose some fat?

She stared at the young master's figure. He looked a little thinner. It must be because of the injuries. Going forward, she must feed him well enough to regain all the fat he lost. If he became thin, he wouldn't look handsome anymore.

"Fei'er." The young master's eyes popped open, a shade of red and green peeping at her. Wait, when did the young master's eyes became a little red? They were always green. Was he bleeding in his eyes? "Go and hide. Whatever happens, don't come out. I'll solve this matter myself." Raising his palm, he patted the back of her hand.

Bewildered, she stood. What was going on? She wanted to ask, but instead she moved out of the room and stepped into the darkness. Tracing her palm over the stone wall, she moved behind the home. The fragrance of wet grass haunted her nose when she stepped on it. The area behind the young master's house was covered in weeds. She made a note to clean it up once the young master regained his health.

Two figures rushed from the well-lit buildings and headed toward the young master's room. In the dim light coming from a nearby street lantern, she spotted their fierce faces.

"The heavens are smiling on us. This trash is still alive," one of them exclaimed after entering the room.

Ki Fei clenched her fist. She wanted to dash in and punch that bastard who dared to talk rudely about her young master, but then the young master's words reverberated in her ears. He'd said he would solve it. And after seeing him miraculously surviving the brutal ordeal of blood loss and injuries using a weird fruit, she believed him.

"Uncle Li Jia. Please forgive this little one for not being able to properly greet you. This little one is injured." The young master's fragile voice drifted out next.

Her heart shuddered in fear. Was he injured again?

No, that couldn't be. A minute before, he had spoken with vigor. Was he pretending?

"Brat, if you want to live, tell me where you got that pill."

"Uncle . . ." A long silence prevailed. "Okay, this little one will tell you. No, I'll show you, uncle. I found it accidently, but this little one was afraid to go in there. There might be more of those heavenly pills."

A greedy laugh echoed through the room, and then the two men walked out, one carrying the young master over his shoulder.

She was about to follow them when a sound echoed in her mind.

"Dig three feet down in the middle of my room, and bring the ring you find to the Ancient Ruins outside of the city." That voice sounded like her young master, but how could he speak directly into her mind?

She didn't understand, but she went back inside five minutes after the men left the room to do his bidding.

Chapter 11

Ancient Ruins

Fierce wind blew against Li Wei's face as they made their way through the long lanes of Old Martial City. He had grown up on these streets, and seeing them again made his heart flutter. Two hundred years. It was a long life to live, and he realized he hadn't enjoyed it much. In the mad pursuit of power and love, he'd lost the reason of being a human.

Li Wei enjoyed piggybacking on Li Jia's back. Being cared for by someone, he loved this, and he should do this more. In his last life, he'd wasted too much time working hard and cultivating. Most of his years in his previous life, he'd spent a few hours with senior sister Zia, and rest of the time he cultivated and cultivated.

But in this life, he would walk a different path. With the knowledge he had about the future, he would live a lazy life.

Yes, that was his goal. To become a lazy immortal.

Closing his eyes, he enjoyed the free ride.

His being shook as Li Jia jumped over a large pit. At some point, Li Jia's leather shoes stopped smacking paved city street, and Wei opened his eyes and found himself surrounded by pitch dark night and dirt road. Five minutes into the wild, the city's urban smell vanished, replaced by wild grass and fresh soil. The last of the city lights vanished as they delved further toward the Ancient Ruins.

Did Fei'er followed them? He hoped she would, otherwise his efforts might be in vain. If he couldn't lure these bastards with a few Body Refirming Pills, they might not let him go, and right now he absolutely couldn't go against them.

Licking his lips, he savored the bitter taste of the Blood Nourishing Powder Fei'er had fed him before sleeping. With the Blood Nourishing Powder and the innate healing capabilities of Blood Essence Body, his deep injuries had already vanished, and only shallow cuts remained over his skin.

There was one more thing he'd gained after reaching layer one in body Refinement Realm: his senses had improved a lot, especially his sense of smell. He was shocked when he'd first inhaled the overwhelming fragrance of orchid from Fei'er. It was so pure, but now inhaling the dark smell coming from Li Tang's body, he was disgusted with his own ability to smell. Something was wrong with Li Tang. His blood smelled polluted when compared to Fei'er's or even Li Jia's blood.

And Li Tang's haggard look was evidence that he was tired as hell.

If he'd gained benefits just by reaching layer one of body Refinement Realm, what would he gain when he reached layer two of body Refinement Realm? The jade slip he'd read also mentioned a minor power he would get once he reached body Foundation Realm.

Ragged breath from Li Tang woke him from his ruminations. "Uncle Jia, can we stop for a moment? My internal injuries are flaring up because of your extreme speed. Uncle Jia seems to get more powerful with every passing day."

Li Jia snorted coldly, but he stopped anyway.

"Jia'er, let's take a break." Pushing his palms on his knees, Li Tang dropped his ass on the grass.

"Brother Tang, why do you look tired? Didn't you sleep well with Old Martial City's Fragrance House beauties?" Li Jia asked in a sarcastic tone while putting Wei on the grass.

Li Wei let his body sprawl on the ground. In reality, he was fine. Absolutely fine. But there was no point in showing his improved condition to the Li brothers. It might even become useful once these bastards found the pills.

"Little nephew Wei, how are your injuries?" Li Jia asked as if he cared a lot for Wei.

Wei wanted to smack his face, but he suppressed his rage. If this bastard had cared for Wei, he wouldn't have stomped on his stomach. It almost killed him.

"Uncle, please let this little one rest for half an hour. This little one will be in debt to you."

"Hmm. Make it fast. I don't have too much time on my hands. I have to cultivate too."

"Yes, uncle." Wei spread his divine sense around, noticing every single thing happening in a mile's area. It was a risk, but he had to do it. His divine sense was powerful, and he could spread it around easily, but due to the risk of crumbling his divine sense, he used it sparingly and retracted it quickly.

After a minute, he spread his divine sense again and recalled it back. He repeated this at one-minute intervals until he spotted Fei'er sneakily moving behind them. Every time he used his divine sense, his head hurt like someone hammered it against the ground, but he had to take the risk for Fei'er and himself. There was no other option.

"Fei'er, go around and drop three pills from the ring into the fourth chamber of the Ancient Ruins." He sent a message to the little lass through his divine sense. It was the same hole he had found the storage ring last time. It was a rare treasure in the Mortal Realm. A few months back, while fighting with an enemy, he had slipped into this hole and found a skeleton with this ring. He'd also found a pill and some gold in a pouch attached to the skeleton's waist. When he touched the ring, he'd felt nothing, but it had shone with a strange color, so he'd buried it inside his room, hoping it might sell for some money.

He chuckled. His old self didn't know it was a storage ring and had lost it after running away from the Li clan. He'd worn it on his finger like an idiot, and one expert stole it with force. He'd even bragged about its contents. It had many pills used by humans and beasts. If only he had reached layer one Foundation Refinement Realm, he could have accessed it in his previous life.

Wei sighed in his heart. He'd made many mistakes in his previous life, and he wanted to fix them all. The first thing was to get himself out of this predicament. His plan was simple: With Fei'er's help, he would throw three pills in the same hole. That should satisfy the three brothers. What these bastards did with the pills was up to them.

"Let's go." Li Jia got up and brushed his ass to remove grass pieces stuck to it.

"Uncle Jia, please wait for a few more minutes." He made a puppy face. "My stomach injury is still not good. If it's aggravated, I might die." His voice came out as that of a weak and fragile youth.

"Hmmm." Li Tang grunted. "Kid, make it fast, else don't blame us for dragging you there." His face suddenly turned cautious, and he rose from his place and looked in the direction Fei'er had stood a moment before. "Someone's there."

Wei's heart squeezed in fear. If Li Jia went after Fei'er, she would be in trouble. Deep trouble.

Chapter 12

Escape

Li Wei's lungs constricted when Li Tang got up and looked in the direction Fei'er had vanished. If Li Tang decide to check further, Fei'er would get caught and she would be in trouble.

A resolute look flashed in his eyes, and his back muscle twitched. He circulated Blood Essence Body art to push all his energy to his legs lying on the wet grass. If Li Tang made a move, he would jump up and obstruct him.

Darkness covered everything, and it was impossible to make out anything with bare eyes. Even with Foundation Realm cultivation, Wei doubted Li Tang could sense anything in the dark veil of night.

"I smell something from that direction." Li Tang pointed in the direction where Fei'er had vanished.

Perspiration formed a river on Wei's lower back. The more Li Tang suspected, the more he sweated. He felt a strange nervousness moving through his body for the whole time Li Tang kept suspecting. In fact, Wei had never given a second thought to Li Tang. But his perception was better than Wei had thought.

Fortunately, Li Tang sat down after staring at the bone-biting darkness for a few more breaths. Taking a piece of meat from his bag, he started munching on it. It smelled like Pink Rabbit's meat, something Fei'er had brought for Wei, but she'd dropped it when she spotted him lying in blood. What a waste. When he saw the meat going bad after he opened his eyes, he'd regretted it.

"Elder brother, what was that?" Li Jia's hoarse voice broke the silence.

Wei's shoulder muscle contracted, perspiration forming a thin film over his forehead. Did Li Jia notice something too? But how?

"Nothing. I thought I felt someone, but it must be an animal," Li Tang replied with his eyes closed.

Relaxing his back muscles, Wei wiped his perspiration and stared at the starry sky. Wang Zia loved staring at the sky as she practiced Star Sky Body Cultivation Art.

Suddenly he wanted to slap himself. Why the heck was he thinking about her? She killed him, and he hated her. There was no point in thinking about her.

Sighing in his heart, Wei closed his eyes and recited the next cultivation chant for Blood Essence Body Cultivation Art. After ten minutes, he opened his eyes and coughed before saying they could move.

Twenty minutes later, they all stood in front of the fourth chamber in the Ancient Ruin city. In the dark night, the ruined city looked creepy and grim, but Wei had spent many nights here and knew that, for some unknown reason, no Ferocious Beasts stepped in the city boundaries.

"Three pills. Elder brother, this kid is telling the truth. There are three Body Refirming Pills in this pit." Li Jia jumped out of the hole with dirt covering his face, but his eyes lacked any annoyance. They were beaming with joy.

Good job, Fei'er. Wei sighed in his heart. That little lass had hidden the pills below ground with the withered pouch she had dug from his room. It already looked ancient, so it didn't arouse any suspicion from his uncles.

Li Tang broke into a greedy smile, but it soon turned into a bitter one when he opened the worn gray pouch and dropped three white pills on his palm.

The atmosphere suddenly turned tense, and Wei could smell blood in the air.

"Jia'er. How should we divide these pills?" Li Tang was first one to speak.

Wei snorted inside his mind. This elder uncle was trying to make the younger one sacrifice. Damn sure he expected the younger one to give up on two pills.

"Elder brother, you're already at layer five Foundation Realm, and I'm at layer four. Shouldn't I take two pills, so I can reach layer six along with you? Think about how much power the Li clan will wield in the city if we have three layer-six Foundation Realm martial artists in the clan. With the ancestors standing behind us, we might be able to contend against Du clan."

Once again Wei snorted. This younger one was shameless, talking about going against Du clan. Was that even possible?

"Okay, let's do that," Li Tang said in a casual tone, but something was wrong with his disposition. Wei sensed a killing intent from him. "I don't like it, but I'll sacrifice for our clan." Picking two pills, he extended his left hand for Li Jia to take them.

Wei squinted. The elder uncle wasn't left-handed. Why was he extending his left hand? Something was fishy here, but Li Jia's greedy eyes didn't seem to recognize it, and he stepped forward to grab the pills.

Swoosh!

Blood sprayed out of Li Jia's gut as Li Tang stabbed him with his right hand. It was so fast that even Wei didn't see Li Tang pull out the knife. Only when a tiny amount of fire qi leaked from the dagger did Wei realize Li Tang had used qi to break through Li Jia's defense.

"Elder bro. . ."

Li Tang broke out in a wicked smile as he stabbed his own brother again and again.

Wei couldn't resist shaking his head. Another family had fallen to greed. In his two hundred years of life, he had seen this numerous times, and it always baffled him.

It happened so fast that Li Jia couldn't react at all. All he could do was die with his eyes wide open in shock.

A bad premonition took over Wei's heart as Li Tang tilted his head to look at him. Although he didn't care what these two brothers did, being an eyewitness was troublesome.

"I'm sorry, my dear nephew, but you must die." Li Tang's knife hand slashed down.

The knife descended like lightning, and Li Wei had no chance of avoiding it. In a moment's flash, he remembered how he'd died in his previous life. That time too he was killed by a family member. Yes, he'd considered senior sister Zia family, She was even betrothed to him by the sect leader.

He still remembered the Ice Jade fragrance senior sister Zia used to spray on her clothes.

Yet she'd killed him ruthlessly.

Well, he should just call that bitch by her name, Wang Zia. She didn't deserve to be called his senior sister.

Right now, his own uncle wanted to kill him. That, too, after Wei had done so much for him. Maybe it was good that the Li clan was annihilated after he left in his previous life. If people like these ruled the clan, there was no way the clan would remain righteous.

Suddenly he felt better at his own decision to walk alone on this path. There were no good family ties when people like Li Tang existed in the family. Now, he didn't even feel guilty about making his stepfather a scapegoat for his plan. Everyone deserved their end.

But he still regretted that Chi'er had died, and Fei'er had vanished.

The knife pierced through his chest, just a fraction away from his heart. If he hadn't moved slightly, it would have pierced his heart, killing him in one go.

"Uncle, you . . ." He sprayed a mouthful of blood over Li Tang's face.

Wei sensed a movement not far away. It was Fei'er moving out of her hiding place.

Wei sent a message with his divine sense. "Fei'er don't. I'm all right. Just stay where you are." She seemed restless, and he didn't want her to get into this mess.

Li Tang groaned, wiping his eyes with the back of his hand. "Brat, you ruined this father's face. I'll slice you to pieces."

Ignoring Li Tang, Wei pressed his hand to his wound and stopped the bleeding. This was his chance. When the duo came to his room for asking about the pills, he had foreseen this event. He'd thought both of them would try to kill him; Li Tang killing Li Jia was out of his expectations, but the fewer people to tackle, the better the outcome.

Flipping onto his stomach, he went on all fours and threw himself in the pit where the Li brothers had found the pills. It was an interconnected network of tunnels, and he knew them like the back of his hand. When he'd found the storage ring and pill, he had been stuck in these tunnels for almost a month, and he had made a map for himself. The tunnel opening in the fourth chamber would allow him to step out from the other side of the Ancient Ruins, and that should be enough for him to walk away from the Li family's clutches.

As far as he remembered, the storage ring had a few more pills and enough gold for Fei'er to live a good life. If she was smart, she would cultivate and reach a respectable level using those resources. "Fei'er. Go back to city right away. I have the Blood Nourishing Powder on me, so don't worry about me." He sent a divine transmission message and crawled under the pit. This was his goodbye to Fei'er. If he had to bring her with him, she would face too many troubles. She had a family here in Old Martial City, and she would do well with her own kin.

Pain radiated through his wound when a stone brushed against it. Although he had recovered previously, the new wound left him bleeding once again, but he had no other option. This pit was his only survival option. The pit was long, and it wouldn't let a large-framed guy like Li Tang follow him.

"Little brat, you are courting your death," Li Tang shouted and thrashed something in the pit. "Die, little brat. This pit will serve as your grave."

A bright light shot from behind him and pierced through Wei's chest and crashed with the tunnel mouth ahead, destroying it in one go.

Dust and pebbles flew everywhere, blinding him. The light that passed through his chest had torn apart his muscles and bone, and he was losing blood rapidly.

This was bad. No, this was worse. His escape route was closed off, and he was bleeding like a tap.

Chapter 13

Du clan

Li Ti watched over Li Sua, husband of his only sister, Li Min. Seeing Li Sua, Li Ti felt disgust to his bones. Li Sua was a degenerate bastard who had more concubines than a city lord, and Li Ti hated such people and wished he could refine these degenerates in his alchemy furnace. This degenerate even smelled like shit.

To this day, he regretted letting him marry his sister.

Unfortunately, he had to look over this degenerate and even feed him Blood Nourishing Powder so he wouldn't die. The patriarch, his father should decide his fate. Although they had confirmed that Li Sua didn't steal the pill from the Li clan's treasury, he'd defied elder brother Tang's command, so Li Sua deserved a heavy punishment. If they had gotten that pill, their father could have received a lifeline. In fact, he knew their father needed this pill to break through and deter Du clan's forces.

Anyway, it didn't matter anymore. Once he entered Divine Fragrance Palace as an external disciple in the upcoming disciple selection exam, he would get a

Foundation Refirming Pill for himself, and he would offer it to his father. He could even get his hands on more pills if he spent some money. If he was fortunate, he might even get to learn from an alchemy teacher and concoct a few low-grade pills himself. Father had invested so much money in him, and he wanted to repay his debt by concocting pills so he could overcome his cultivation bottleneck.

While walking through the room, his gaze fell on the trunk hidden below a wooden bed. Out of curiosity, he pulled it out and checked the contents, and he was shocked to his bones.

The wooden trunk was filled with silver coins. How did this degenerate earn so many silver coins? He must have swindled them from the clan, but he'd seen no suspicious entries in the accounting books.

Then how did he have a wooden trunk full of silver coins?

Suddenly, the door opened, and elder brother Tang stormed in with his palm placed on the right side of his chest. Blood dripped from his wounds and mixed with his tattered sky-blue robe, painting it red.

"Elder brother Tang." Li Ti jumped out of his lotus position and helped Tang to sit on a wooden chair. This room only had chairs, so he helped elder brother Tang to sit on one.

"Give me . . ." Blood spurted out of Tang's mouth, and Li Ti grew worried. His elder brother seemed to be in a dire situation, but fortunately Li Ti had a Blood Vitality Pill on him that could save his elder brother.

Pulling out a jade and red pill, he fed it to his elder brother.

In five minutes, Tang's condition improved. His breath settled to a normal rhythm, and his wounds slowly healed. Even his face regained its color.

"Ti'er, thank you for helping me."

Li Ti smiled. "Elder brother is overpraising me. This is my duty. But where is brother Jia and that little rascal Li Wei?"

Li Tang's face turned darker, like something bad had happened. "That kid . . ." Tears dropped from his eyes.

Li Ti's heart pulsed with an unknown pain. Something was definitely off here. "Elder brother, tell me what happened?"

Elder brother Tang wiped his tears and exhaled. "That kid, Li Wei, really lead us to a place where we found few Body Refirming Pills, but a gang of bandits attacked us and Jia'er and that kid . . ." He lowered his face and sobbed hard.

Li Ti dropped on his butt. Elder brother Jia was dead. This would be a major blow to his father. He was already besieged by Du clan. Losing brother Jia would be detrimental to their clan. And that rascal Li Wei had perished too. Father wouldn't be happy about that. Although his father didn't show it, he cared for that little rascal, as he was the only remaining memory of their sister Min'er.

"But I fought and saved one pill for father. Please keep it safe." Elder brother Tang took out a pill and handed it to Li Ti.

Sniffing, Li Ti took the pill and dropped it inside a jade box. Although they'd lost a formidable brother, they'd gained a pill that could help father.

Not everything was lost.

⟫⟫ ⟪⟪

Du Xin scanned the map brought by Tian Yun. The old parchment belonged in Tian clan's treasure vault, but Tian Yun had stolen it and brought it to him.

"Brother Yun, are you sure this is real?" This map pointed to Ancient Ruins near Old Martial City, but that place was forbidden by the ancestors, and no one dared to march in those ruins or the tunnel system that ran everywhere throughout the colossal area. In fact, his father, Du clan's local branch head, Du Lufang, had sent one Foundation Realm cultivator to search the ruins, but he'd never come back. So, the whole local branch of the Du clan in Old Martial City was forbidden from stepping into the Ancient Ruins.

"Brother Xin. You remember Tian clan patriarch, Tian Wu? He suddenly broke through Foundation Realm a few years back. Recently he rose to layer eight Foundation Realm. It was possible because of this map."

Du Xin nodded. It was a surprise for Old Martial City. Tian clan was among the low-level clans in Old Martial City, and they'd suddenly became powerful when their patriarch had broken into Foundation Realm suddenly. Although it didn't affect Du clan, as they had three Foundation Realm cultivators in the local branch, the power dynamics shifted overnight. Suddenly, three clans had Foundation Realm cultivators in Old Martial City: Li clan, Du clan, and Tian clan.

"He broke through with the help of this map. He didn't get the main inheritance, but he obtained one heavenly fruit that allowed him to break through in one go. He once told my father that if he could get the main inheritance, he would have reached Boiling Blood Realm directly.

"Boiling Blood Realm?" Du Xin's heart galloped faster than a horse at full speed. Boiling Blood Realm was a legendary realm, and only sects and great clans of the royal city had Boiling Blood Realm experts living in them. Even the emperor recognized Boiling Blood Realm experts. If Tian clan had raised one Boiling Blood Realm master, they would instantly reach the status of a Tier 2 clan, and they would rule over a region, and Du clan could never compete with them.

"Think about this, brother Xin. You and me. Once we become Boiling Blood Realm experts, we'll reach the clouds, and all the riches of the world will be at our feet."

Du Xin nodded. This was indeed true. He glanced at the map once and vowed in his heart that he would become a Boiling Blood Realm master. No matter what.

>⤳⤳⤳ ⤲⤲⤲

"Young master. Wake up." A soft palm caressed his cheek, and Wei suddenly woke up in a daze and found dirt all over his face. A familiar orchid fragrance mixed with something ancient overwhelmed his senses.

Where was he? With half-open eyes he spotted two sharp blue eyes staring back at him. Darkness had swallowed everything else. Other than Fei'er's warm hand resting on his face, and the warmth that exuded from her body, he couldn't sense anything else.

A throbbing pain emerging from his chest, reminding him of his predicament. That bastard Li Tang had used a Bronze Grade Light Shooting Talisman to blast through his chest and made him fall in the forbidden tunnel.

"Young master, are you okay?"

"F—" He spat a mouthful of weird-tasting soil.

Spreading his divine sense, he checked around as finger-thick darkness restricted his viewing.

"Fei'er, what are you doing here?" Blood jumped to his throat, threatening to come out, but somehow, he suppressed it. His condition wasn't good, and his entire body was in pain. Especially his ass which felt like his father had whipped it for the entire night.

"Young master. Eat this Blood Vitality Pill I found in your ring. This should help you recuperate." She pushed a cold pill between his lips.

Shaking his head, he grabbed the pill and handed it back to Fei'er. "Keep it in the jade box. If I'm not dead, then I'll be okay." He didn't need a pill to recuperate. He could use this predicament to his advantage. Blood Essence Body could be better cultivated when he generated new blood using this cultivation art. If he wasn't injured, it would be quite slow to absorb essence energy into his blood and body.

But falling in forbidden tunnels wasn't a good thing. Spreading his divine sense, he tried to sense their position. There was a tunnel to their right, but even after a mile there was no end. Their left and front was covered in metal walls, while the entrance was a thousand feet above their head.

It was impossible to climb back.

"Young master, what is this place?" Fei'er asked innocently.

"Lass, you shouldn't have come here." He sighed in his heart. He might die here, but he didn't want that little lass to die with him. The Ancient Ruins was a weird place. From the outside, it was a monument left by some dynasty that was plundered again and again. Not a single building stood erect, and the passage of time had destroyed everything.

Well, except for one thing: the water and sewage tunnel system that ran below the city. It remained as good as new. Even the metal walls looked like someone polished them every week. Many people had explored these tunnels and formed a map of this complex maze system. On land, anyone could walk through the ruined buildings facing no danger, but these tunnels were different. Only five percent of the overall maze system could allow one safe passage, while ninety-five percent were forbidden tunnels.

A few months back, his previous self was forced into these tunnels by Du family kids, and they had lost two people before getting out of the tunnels. If someone fell or entered the forbidden tunnels, they didn't come back.

And right now, he was in one of those forbidden tunnels without a way out. At least not with their current cultivation.

"Young master. Let's get out of here. I came here after that villain left this place. He even threw his own friend in another tunnel."

"Li Tang." Wei gritted his teeth. "I'll have my revenge."

"Young master, let's go back."

Wei signed, his shoulders slumping. "We can't. These forbidden tunnels have a weird suction force, and we can't climb up. We can only go down or horizontal."

"Young master, let me try." Fei'er got up and tried to climb back, but she couldn't and flopped down on her tiny tushy. "Young master, how are we going to make out of here?" Her voice quivered.

Wei was about to reply when a soul-stirring roar came out of the other side of the tunnel. Something was coming for them, and that thing was powerful as hell.

They were in danger.

Chapter 14

Beast Subduing Pill

Li Wei shuddered when the beast's roar struck his eardrums, filling his heart with intimidation. Not that he hadn't fought with Ferocious Beasts in his previous life, but he had never fought with them in a situation where he was completely helpless. In his previous life, he always had something to rely on. Array disks, flags, formations, talismans, and whatnot.

But this time he had nowhere to run. The only way forward was where the beast's roar came from, and the tunnel was too cramped for him to get up and fight. Not that he could fight in his current condition.

Hot air blew from the other end of the tunnel before a Two Fang Wolf marched into view. In the dim light Fei'er had set up, he spotted two dark red eyes raging at them. Two white canines protruded from the corner of the beast's mouth. This wolf was famous for its tough hide and sharp white canines that could pierce through even normal metal.

"Young master." Fei'er shifted toward him, her tiny body huddling closer, her orchid fragrance distracting him for a moment.

"Fei'er, get behind me." Wei licked his parched lips. This was a tough situation, but he remained calm. Spreading his divine sense, he judged the cultivation of this beast.

Pain shot through his brain when he used his divine sense, but in a fraction of a moment he scanned the beast's cultivation.

Ferocious Beasts could cultivate. At low levels, they followed the same cultivation realms as humans. This beast was around body Refinement Realm layer five or six. Something he couldn't handle in these conditions. Despite having rich experience in fighting Ferocious Beasts, he had no way to overcome four layers of difference. It was impossible in his injured state.

If he was in peak condition, he might have fared better because of his strong body. But Fei'er . . .

Was he going to die right after being reincarnated?

No, he definitely wouldn't. Using all his brain capacity, he scanned through the obscure techniques he had learned or seen in his previous life. There had to be something he could use to battle across realms. In fact, there were few, but none were useful now. If he had a qi cultivation base, he could use an obscure forbidden technique to boost his powers and break through a realm, but he didn't have qi cultivation. Fei'er might be able to use it, but without having strong experience in cultivation, she couldn't use that technique.

Wait, there were some more pills inside the storage ring he'd given to Fei'er. When the expert showed him its contents in his previous life, he'd mentioned that a few were beast pills. And he'd found this ring inside the tunnels. So, if the tunnels had beasts, the pills might be helpful.

"Fei'er, give me one of each pill from the ring. Quickly!"

Growling, the beast stepped forward. It seemed to analyze its prey before attacking, a natural instinct for predators. It looked thin and hungry, and both of them were enticing food. Especially Wei himself, with so much fat over his body. In his past life, when he'd joined Heavenly Firmament Sect, he lost all the fat, turning into a handsome man. Many junior and senior sisters of the sect chased after him, but he only had one beauty in his mind: Wang Zia, that bitch.

A strong medicinal fragrance wafted in the air as soon as Fei'er pulled a few pills out of the ring. Even the beast sniffed the air and stared at the pills with greedy eyes.

Wei scanned the pills, his jaw almost hitting the ground when he recognized a few of them. The expert that had stolen this ring from him in his previous life must not have known much about the pills, else he wouldn't have told Wei about the ring's contents.

One of the pills was a Bone Barrier Hitting Pill, a precious pill used by qi cultivators to break through to Bone Baptization Realm. It was quite precious in the Mortal World, and only sects had access to this pill.

"Young master, what are those pills?" Fei'er asked.

The man that died must have been a high echelon from a sect. Many of these pills could be only found in sects. Common people wouldn't know about them. But Wei had two hundred years' experience from the future, so he knew these pills. Although he wasn't an alchemist, he'd consumed many of these pills when he joined Heavenly Firmament Sect, so he could easily recognize them.

The wolf growled and leaped forward; its eyes fixed on the pills in Wei's palm.

This was it. One of the pills was a Beast Subduing Pill. It was a common pill used for subduing Ferocious Beasts and killing them. It had a unique scent that beasts found irresistible. Mixed with a strong sleeping herb, this pill could turn the tide of a battle.

Wei threw the Beast Subduing Pill just a few feet away from him. He didn't want to throw it too far away, nor too close. If the beast had to choose between the pill and his bloody body, it might choose him instead, and he didn't want that.

The wolf howled greedily, halting at the pill lying on the metal ground. It reeked of blood and dirt, and Wei wanted to plug his nose. After advancing in body cultivation, his senses had improved a lot, and these overwhelming odors mentally tortured him.

Lifting the pill with its tongue, the beast devoured it in a breath's time. With the pill in its stomach, it turned its red eyes toward Wei. But before it could take a step, it dropped on the ground, unconscious. The pill had worked, and the beast was down.

"Young master, what did that pill . . ."

"Kill it first." Wei hurried her. The pill was good, but it wouldn't put the beast to sleep for eternity. They only had a minute or two before the pill's effect wore off, and they had to kill the beast before that.

Fei'er's petite figure dashed forward, and she attacked the wolf's stomach with her knife.

"Stupid lass, attack the eyes first and pierce its brain." The Two Fang Wolf was known for its tough hide, and with just layer one qi Refinement Realm, Fei'er could cut all year long and wouldn't slice through the beast's hide.

Fei'er giggled sheepishly and then struck with her knife at the beast's eyes. The blade pierced through there easily, and then she stabbed the beast's brain a couple of times, killing it on the spot. "I did it, young master. I killed a Ferocious Beast." She sounded like she'd won a thousand gold prize in a martial competition.

Stupid lass.

"Young master, this beast has solved our problem for food. I found a portable stove in the storage ring you gave me."

"Did you?" Wei's eyes shone with surprise. He didn't remember this. But of course, the expert wouldn't tell him about every insignificant thing he'd found inside the ring. Why would he?

"That's good, but we have to mask the smell of its blood, or more beasts will come our way." He coughed. His blood loss was too much, and he was once again on the verge of fainting. He had to cultivate, else he would need to eat a pill, and he didn't want that. "Fei'er, do you have anything with a strong smell on you?"

"I have another White Cicada Fruit." She pulled the white colored fruit from a tightly wrapped cloth, and suddenly the blood smell and her orchid fragrance vanished in the spicy smell of White Cicada Fruit.

It smelled really nasty.

"Good. Place it at least twenty feet away from us."

Fei'er followed his instructions.

"Fei'er, which qi cultivation method are you following?" he asked. When she said she had cultivated to layer one Refinement Realm, he was shocked. In his previous life, she didn't cultivate.

"I'm cultivating Nine Lotus Fragrance Qi Cultivation Art."

Wei arched his brows. "Do you want to be an alchemist? And where did you get it?" Nine Lotus Fragrance Qi Cultivation Art was a rare qi cultivation art that Divine Fragrance Palace core female disciples practiced. Only girls of wood attribute Spirit Root could practice them, and Divine Fragrance Palace kept it a secret. Had she stolen it? If this news got out, she would be haunted by all the sect elders.

"Alchemist? No, I know nothing about it. I just want to protect young master," she said in a firm voice.

Her resolve touched his heart, making him regret leaving her alone in his last life. By the time he'd returned to Old Martial City, she was gone.

This lass was always dedicated to him, and he'd failed to save her life.

No, that wouldn't happen again. In his current life, he would make sure she lived a comfortable life. Without worrying about anything else.

"Don't worry about me anymore." He smiled. "Your young master has so many methods to protect himself. But how did you get this cultivation art?"

Fei'er's face broke into an innocent smile. "I once helped an injured elder sister, and in return she gave me this qi cultivation art. She was like a fairy. Jade white skin and beautiful peach shaped eyes. She even wore a white dress. She also told me if I could reach Foundation Realm using it, I should seek her out at Divine Fragrance Palace."

So, it was related to Divine Fragrance Palace. "What was the name of that elder sister?"

"Tang Sia," Fei'er replied. "Young master, is this something bad? I practiced it so I can help you."

Wei sighed in his heart. Tang Sia was a beautiful fairy. In fact, she excelled not only in her looks but also her prowess. In the future, she would emerge as the sect leader of Divine Fragrance Palace. Having a relationship with her was a good thing for Fei'er.

"No. It's not bad. I was just enquiring. How many levels does this qi cultivation art have?"

"Just until Foundation Realm."

"Hmm." That made sense. Tang Sia wouldn't hand over the whole qi cultivation art. She must have spotted something good in Fei'er and helped her out of gratitude. "It's good. Let's cultivate, and you should reach as far as possible using the pills."

"Young master, do you have a way to get out of here?" Her blue eyes filled with hope.

Wei shook his head. "I don't. But we have a way to go in." He glanced at the other end of the tunnel. If a Ferocious Beast had come from that way, then they might find their way out.

They might survive after all.

Chapter 15

Blood Essence Body

Li Wei gritted his teeth and pushed the remaining blood toward his Yangming meridian. Sweat formed under his ears as he tried to absorb essence energy through his body, but it wasn't working. The damn essence was refusing to enter his body. This had never happened with him.

Pushing his palms on the cold metal surface, he took a deep breath and tried it again. Maybe he was too used to heat because of his previous body cultivation art, and the cold slipping through his skin restricted his cultivation?

System: Blood percentage critical. Activating hibernation mode.

Surreal music spread inside Li Wei's mind, calming him. First, his sense of touch vanished. He forgot he was sitting on a metal surface inside a tunnel. Then his sense of smell vanished. The spicy smell of the White Cicada Fruit vanished like it'd never existed.

Then the sound of Fei'er fiddling with something vanished.

Then the darkness from his vision vanished, followed by his pain. Memories faded. Self-perseverance faded and then he lost himself to the surreal music.

Almost.

Wei's eyes opened like a predator sensing its prey. The message once again showed up in his mind, and this time he remembered it clearly.

What was this system, and what did this hibernation mean?

He racked his brain, but nothing came to mind. Had something happened when he reincarnated?

For a long time, he tried to remember, but nothing came to mind. Finally, he gave up and spread his divine sense inside his body. He had to take the risk, but he was afraid this risk taking would lead to his divine sense's decimation. Every time he used his divine sense, the pain increased by a margin, and it was becoming unbearable.

This . . . He couldn't believe what he saw inside his body. How could his body regenerate forty-five percent total blood in the blink of a second? And what were these pearl-like blood drops moving through his body?

Using his divine sense, he zoomed on these new type of blood drops. There were many of them, throbbing with life energy. After reaching layer one body Refinement Realm in Blood Essence Body, his blood had transformed from an egg into a dragon's cub. But compared to his normal blood, these blood drops were more like an adult dragon. So much vitality surged through these blood pearls that it could compete with his Heart Blood. No, they could surpass his Heart Blood by a tiny margin.

There were forty-five of them rushing through his body.

This Blood Essence Body Cultivation Art was something else. He would have to study it properly. It was too bad he didn't have the jade slip with him. There were a few parts he didn't read. There was one part that talked about constellations, and he had only superficial knowledge about them. Once he reached Foundation Realm, he should complete Earth Constellation of Blood Essence Body, but what that meant he didn't know.

"Fei'er." He stared at the girl sitting cross-legged in front of him. She was stitching a long gray robe she'd found in the storage ring. Well, he'd asked her to cultivate, but it seemed the little lass wanted to stitch the robe into a smaller version so he could wear it.

Priorities. She had set her priorities wrong.

"Yes, young master."

"How long have you been working on that robe?"

"Around half an hour." She put down the shirt and scratched her head. "Don't you like this style, young master?"

Wei shook his head. When he'd started cultivating, she had just started working on the robe. That meant he had gone into a strange state for half an hour.

What sorcery was this? Had he achieved a Selfless State in his cultivation?

No way. If he'd achieved it at this stage, immortals would die of shame. Even after cultivating constantly for ten years, people didn't get into this state. Then how could he achieve it so quickly?

Then what was this? And how could he explain forty-five percent blood gain in half an hour?

"Young master, what did you do? Your cheeks are red again." Fei'er stared at him in a daze.

Smiling faintly, he closed his eyes again. Before entering the strange state, he'd been trying to absorb heaven and earth's essence into his body, but couldn't. He wanted to try it again.

This world was filled with heaven and earth essence energy for cultivators to absorb and use as a fuel to perform immense feats that seemed impossible. Qi cultivators absorbed it and converted it into qi to store in their dantians, while body cultivators absorbed it into their bodies and stored it in their whole bodies. This also improved their fleshly body by a huge margin. One could become indestructible by following body cultivation path. But that didn't mean qi cultivation was weak. Qi cultivation had its own advantages. Qi cultivators had a myriad of martial skills, while body cultivators could only utilize a few divine arts. Qi cultivators could use their qi to perform auxiliary arts like alchemy, talisman crafting, and artifact crafting while body cultivators could destroy mountains with their punches.

Both had their advantages. In his previous life, Wei had practiced Firmament Fire Body Cultivation Art. That made him harmonious with various worldly fires. While others would die inside a boiling furnace, he could temper himself with the same fire. It even let his normal punch carry the power of fire.

However, Blood Essence Body Cultivation Art, or Blood Essence Body, differed from other body cultivation arts. Cultivating it required one to go through two steps: essence accumulation and blood replenishment.

In the essence accumulation phase, one inhaled the essence of heaven and earth and stored it inside their blood. While attacking, one could expand their blood to increase their attack power or other physical attributes. It acted like qi. One could use it to enforce their punches and kicks. But unlike qi, which was constrained by the limited space of one's dantian, blood essence could be stored endlessly in one's body. The more blood one could store, the more they could burst forth. It might lack the iron-like skin and unbreakable bones, but it made his body unkillable by increasing his healing powers.

Thinking about it, the new type of blood droplets—he'd call them blood pearls—could also be used for the same. Well, he had to test it himself before making any presumptions.

Blood replenishment was the second phase. It replenished the used blood with cultivation, and he was doing the same while cultivating. He'd used this phase after killing the beast. He was in a dire condition because of the blood loss, but now he was half full. But as per the text, this phase was the slowest one. Yet somehow, he had refilled forty percent of his blood in half an hour.

Five percent was his bottom line, he would die if he went below that, and now he had forty-five total.

Anyway, he had to replenish his remaining blood, so closing his eyes, he started cultivating again.

With a deep breath, his body absorbed essence energy from his surroundings and mixed it with his existing blood. The same blood then went through his Yangming meridian, replicating and then spreading throughout his whole body. As the blood filled his meridians and muscles, his lost energy returned.

One after another, he went through the cycles of cultivation and lost himself in a tranquil state. It wasn't the same as the selfless state he'd miraculously experienced before, but it was like a fraction of it. After moving his blood 100 times through his Yangming meridian, he spotted the birth of a blood pearl. A shiny drop of vitality emerged in his body and then moved through all meridians.

"Young master. Are you hungry?" A soft voice pulled him out of his cultivation trance. Opening his eyes, he glared at Fei'er who had been busy stitching the gray robe for him. But upon seeing her innocent expression, his anger vanished.

"No. I'm not hungry yet." His growling stomach betrayed him, and Fei'er broke into a beautiful giggle.

"I'll cook then."

"You should stitch one for yourself too." He glanced at her slightly torn gray gown. It showed her fair white shin a little.

She hurriedly hid her skin with her hand. "Young master, you shouldn't look at a girl's skin like this."

Chuckling, he jumped up and tousled her hair. She was still a kid in his eyes, and she acted like a kid too. "Let's cook some meat and then cultivate again."

"I can't." She shook her head. "Elder sister Sia said I can only cultivate in the morning dew while sitting under the most luscious tree present around my house."

Wei smirked. The lass didn't know how many pills there were in the ring, and out of those, one was exactly useful for her. The Essence Gathering Pill.

Chapter 16

Rapid Breakthrough

Flames leaped at the meat stabbed onto the metal skewer, spreading an intoxicating aroma around the small space Li Wei and Fei'er had made their temporary resting space. The textured aroma of fresh meat brought up a few memories of a year he'd spent in a dangerous forest, hunting and cultivating. At that time, he'd started from scratch and learned to roast by himself. If not for cultivating, he might have turned back into the Fatty Wei his friends called him in childhood. Well, he was fat right now, and he wasn't ashamed of it. In fact, he liked his chubby body.

Wei rotated the bloody shirt he used to hold metal skewer they'd found inside the ring. Fei'er had finished stitching the gray robe for him, so he'd readily changed into it.

Thinking about the ring, the man who'd had it must have been a traveler. The ring contained everything one would need for an adventurous stay in a forest: pills, extra clothes, a portable stove, wood, swords, deboning knives, gold, spices, and whatnot. Of course, the pills were the most precious things among them. The man must have been extremely rich, as he had stored ten Foundation Refirming Pills and six Essence Gathering Pills. When Wei was in Heavenly Firmament Sect, he'd received one—yes, a single Foundation Refirming Pill—in five years. That sect was quite cheap to start with. But he couldn't blame them for it. For starters, he'd only had a Bronze Grade Spirit Root.

No one wasted their resources on Bronze Grade Spirit Root. If he hadn't had metal qi used for weapon refinement, no one would have let him step foot in the sect. The pills were costly too. Only Divine Fragrance Palace, the heavyset sect in alchemy, could give them to their disciples as a yearly quota. When he'd learned about the riches of Divine Fragrance Palace, he'd wanted to quit artifact refinement and join it to learn alchemy, but too bad. Once one joined a sect, no other sect would accept them.

Anyway, ultimately, he'd moved away from refinement and walked the path of arrays.

Tender smoke rose from the meat, pulling him out of his flashback. Slowly, he rotated skewer to let the other side enjoy the same treatment of fire.

"Ten more minutes." He whispered at Fei'er who had been turning the robe into a smaller gown for herself.

She smiled at him and got back to her stitching. For a moment, he stared at her fingers effortlessly moving the needle around the soft cloth. It was almost like a painting.

Shaking his head, he concentrated back on the roasting. One half was done, and it already exuded a nice aroma. He licked his lips, remembering the taste. This was their sixth meal after getting stuck here, and the meat from the beast's body was almost gone. If they wanted to survive, they must enter deeper in the tunnel.

"Fei'er, next time you skin a Ferocious Beast with thick blood, remember to collect its blood in a pot. It can be used for array carving."

Fei'er nodded. She had skinned the wolf since he was injured, but she'd let the blood go to waste. It was thick enough to carve some temporary arrays.

Heat coming from the stove penetrated into the meat piece, turning it brown. It even slipped into his skin, making him feel warm. It felt awesome to sit next to a fire, and thanks to the White Cicada Fruit, they didn't have to worry about the roasted smell escaping into the tunnel.

While the meat got roasted over the fire, he extended his divine sense into his body. After a whole day of cultivation, he had nearly replenished his initial blood loss. Right now, he had eighty blood pearls sitting inside his Yangming meridian. After producing the fifteenth drop, they'd suddenly moved to the Yangming meridian and stayed there. After their movement, his cultivation speed increased slightly. He had a gut feeling that once he accumulated one hundred drops, something good would happen.

Good, what? He didn't know yet. But his strength should reach one hundred pounds of power. That was a given.

Fei'er had left him in the dust when it came to cultivation. That lass ate one Essence Gathering Pill and broke through two layers directly and reached layer three qi Refinement Realm. She wanted to eat another pill, but fearing cultivation deviation, he stopped her. This girl was crazy. If this continued, she would reach layer nine before he reached layer four or five in body Refinement Realm. That was just inconceivable. Her Spirit Root must have been at least Gold Grade, because the qi cultivation art was okayish in his eyes. Now he wished he could impart a better qi cultivation art to her, but he was helpless. He remembered many qi cultivation arts, but he had no way to teach them. Until he formed a soul space for himself, he wouldn't be able to impart information using his divine sense to others.

He sighed in his heart. There was no guarantee that his divine sense would survive until he reached that illusionary realm.

Fei'er had progressed well, but she didn't know a single martial skill. All she knew was how to debone a beast with her knife. Nothing else. Well, he knew a few low-level martial skills, but he didn't have qi to practice them. And for divine arts, he would have to wait until he reached Refinement Realm in his Blood Essence Body.

If they were going to embark down the tunnels ahead, they had to learn some fighting skills.

Wait, there was a high-grade sword martial skill he knew. One Sword Strike, a Gold Grade martial skill he had learned in his previous life. Although it was a high-grade martial skill, it was impossible to master it, so Heavenly Firmament Sect let every disciple learn it after joining. Although it required qi to master, the first level didn't require one to use their qi. The first level only comprised basic attack patterns to hone one's sword basics.

If it didn't involve using qi, he could even teach it to Fei'er.

"Fei'er."

She lifted her head.

"Let's practice sword martial skill after we eat."

Stopping her needle, she nodded her head firmly. "Yes, I'll learn it quickly and protect you from the beasts."

Wei didn't know if he should laugh or cry. This lass didn't know the heavens and earth if she thought she would kill the wolves by learning a basic sword skill. But he liked her determination. Very much.

Chapter 17

One Sword Strike

A light film of perspiration formed on Li Wei's forehead when he swung his sword for the tenth time through the air. It took everything from his arm, and he almost lost control on the last strike. But this was expected. The swords he'd found in the ring were heavy swords made up from low-tier Silver Grade material. But the craftmanship wasn't good enough to make that sword a true Silver Grade martial artifact.

"Puff." Exhaling, he tried to calm his burning body. His gray robe was drenched in sweat, and he had already practiced this move for at least a hundred times. Although his body was exhausted, his mind wasn't. After all, he was practicing the same move after almost two hundred years.

"Young master, you looked like a general when you swung your sword continuously." Fei'er stood close to him and reached with a handkerchief to wipe the sweat from his forehead. She was wearing the makeshift gray gown she had made from the traveler's extra clothes. After making her gown, there was so much cloth left from the original robe she made small handkerchiefs out of it, and she was using one to wipe his sweat. Looking at her gray gown and his gray robe and the gray handkerchief in her hand, he was suddenly sick of gray. They both looked like a band of gray, and their oversized clothes looked quite ugly.

"Did you even look at the sword? You have to practice these moves," he asked in a despair-filled voice. A salty taste spread over his tongue as he licked his lips.

"Yes, but you were so mesmerizing that I couldn't take my eyes off you."

"You lass . . ." Reaching forward, he flicked her forehead. What was wrong with her? For the last two hours, he'd been trying to show her the basic movement of the One Strike Sword, but she kept murmuring about how good he looked when he swung the sword. Out of the ten basic moves he performed, she didn't even look at one. And that damn sword martial skill required him to complete ten moves on everything he practiced. If one practiced the move, they couldn't stop it in one go, they had to swing it ten times. It was a martial skill that required comprehension to master it, and first level comprised of ten moves. When one could superimpose these ten moves, he would master the early completion. So, one had to practice ten moves when one lift his sword.

Anything less was considered a taboo and an insult to the martial skill.

That was how it was. In the many years he'd lived in Heavenly Firmament Sect, many people had practiced this skill half-heartedly, but they all lost their motivation in the end and deviated from cultivation. They never succeeded in their endeavor of cultivation. After reincarnation, he understood why the martial skill required one to practice ten moves every time. It built up the cultivator's martial will. Martial will was something every cultivator needed on the arduous path of cultivation. Cultivation wasn't easy, and no one said it would be. It allowed one to live eternally, but no one looked at the sweat and blood one donated to the soil while traversing the path of cultivation. If one couldn't even stick to a principle while practicing a sword martial skill, what destiny they had to walk on the path of cultivation?

His resolve became firm after realizing this now. If he wanted to achieve early completion of One Sword Strike level one, he had to push forward with his martial will.

A martial skill quality was defined by grades, and each martial skill had levels. Some had only one level, while some had three levels or five levels. One Sword Strike had three levels, and each level was further divided into completion levels. They were early completion, middle completion, late completion, and then peak completion.

One didn't need to achieve peak completion to learn the next level, but late completion was mandatory.

One Sword Strike had three levels. The first level focused on the basic sword movement. The second level focused on qi enablement, and the third level could allow one to become a killing machine that could destroy a mountain with one sword strike. Of course, reaching third level was almost impossible, and other than a couple of elders in the Heavenly Firmament Sect, no one had even touched the level three threshold. But then many disciples discarded this simple skill after obtaining better and easier skills. So, it was given. Even he had discarded it after being stuck at middle completion of level one for years.

No more. In this life, he wouldn't discard this skill and deviate from his martial will.

"Young master, I can't even lift that sword, then how can I practice it?"

Wei shook his head. This lass was too weak, and she also practiced wood qi, so she wouldn't hold a tyrannical amount of strength. "Once you reach Foundation Realm, you'll gain some strength to use this sword."

"Then how can you swing it so fast and accurate." She batted her eyelashes. "It's like you've practiced this move thousands of times."

He patted her head. Of course, he had practiced this tens of thousands of times when he'd joined Heavenly

Firmament Sect. With his metal qi, he was chosen as an apprentice to a refiner, but before he could even touch the hammer, he was asked to practice One Sword Strike level one ten thousand times to build his arm strength. At that time, he had almost reached peak completion in the first level of One Sword Strike. Maybe this time he would pass the threshold of peak completion. Although he didn't carry the muscle memory, his mind still remembered the exact feeling. So, practicing it to perfection shouldn't be an issue in this life.

"It's not as hard as you think," he said. "The trick is going with the flow. Lose it when you think you grasped it." Raising his sword, he swiped it again at an angle. When his sword moved, he felt like his soul connected with that move, and it flew like an air current through the air. The next thing he knew, he had completed the move. Pulling his sword back, he struck again, and then again. It was a menial activity, but he had to do it hundreds of times to reach the early completion. Right now, he needed thirty breaths completing ten moves. Once he could do it in ten breaths' time, he would achieve the early completion. To master level one, one had to complete all ten moves in ten breaths' time. It was taxing on the body, but once mastered, one could even jump a level to fight with Refinement Realm cultivators.

After all, Refinement Realm and Foundation Realm only helped one to get acquainted with their qi. It only cleansed one's body to a certain degree, and only a meager amount of qi would be stored in their dantian. Only after entering Bone Baptization Realm could one be called a real cultivator, as qi would permeate their bones and change the fundamental properties of one's body. It exponentially increased one's battle strength, and they could use a bit of their qi with the help of martial artifacts.

Mortal stage of cultivation was divided into six stages, namely, Refinement, Foundation, Bone Baptization, Marrow Cleansing, Boiling Blood, and finally Heart Blood Realm. Qi and body cultivation realms shared same name, but they had different ways to achieve these realms. Body cultivation, in particular, differed with every new cultivation art.

Anyway, it was a long road ahead.

After his perspiration turned into a small stream, he stopped and sat down.

"Young master, this is the first time I've seen you so focused and tenaciously practicing. Why didn't you ever practice like this in Li clan compound? You always got beaten blue by old master," Fei'er asked with a sullen face. She was a lass who never took a step back while complaining about his father. Her loyalty toward Wei was unending.

Reaching with his hand, he tousled her hair.

"Don't mess my hair." Her beautiful big blue eyes blinked rapidly. "Answer my question."

"Would you believe me if I said I can cultivate?"

Her brows turned into a straight line. "But your dantian . . ." She cupped her mouth and looked away. He didn't like to talk about cultivation, and she knew that.

"I'm not practicing qi cultivation, but body cultivation. You'd better not tell anyone about this, lass."

She nodded. "Which layer have you reached? Is that how you gained the endurance to swing that sword hundreds of times? You must be at layer six or seven." She sighed. "I can't even lift that sword." She purred. "Stupid me."

"No." He chuckled after hearing her naïve questions. "I've only reached layer one in Refinement Realm. It's nothing impressive. You're way faster than me."

"Then why can't I lift the sword back after swinging it?"

Well, that was strange. Although body cultivation and qi cultivation used different paths of cultivation, there wasn't much power difference between them. Of course, body cultivators had stronger bodies, but qi cultivators had qi that refilled faster and was easier to cultivate.

So, if she was two layers above him in cultivation, why couldn't she lift the sword back up?

Unknowingly, he started comparing his current condition with his previous life experience. When he'd started practicing this sword martial skill, he had already reached qi Refinement Realm.

Yet he'd faced many difficulties while practicing this martial skill. Swinging it ten times was hard, because one had to let go of the sword to complete the movement. When one released control, the sword would move along with gravity. Gaining control back at the last moment and pulling it up had required too much power. When he'd started practicing, he was like Fei'er, unable to gain control back at the last moment. It took him months to reach the point where he could practice for hundreds of times. It required him to build up strength in his shoulders and arms. That's why his refinement teacher made him practice this move, because artificing was a game of arm strength, and he had to swing his hammer for hundreds or thousand times in a sitting.

Then how did it become easy in this life? It had been only two hours, and he could swing the sword for one hundred times already. It couldn't be just the memories of his previous life, right?

Could it be his Blood Essence Body?

Carefully, he practiced the same move again and observed his blood.

Damn, this was awesome. His body was expending a little blood and then providing him a boost to continue without fatigue. The little blood his body expended was replenished in the next few seconds.

Suddenly his heart filled with excitement. This Blood Essence Body was something awesome.

Chapter 18

Three-Fold Strength Defense Array

Li Wei walked cautiously through the metal tunnel leading to a vague place. Despite the possibility of losing memories, he intermittently expanded his divine sense toward the end but found nothing.

Fei'er followed him with silent steps. Thanks to their gray clothes, they blended with their surroundings and didn't stick out like his stomach flab. And with the White Cicada Fruit in Fei'er's hand, their bodily scents were masked neatly.

Two more days had passed since he'd started practicing One Sword Strike. Although he hadn't reached early completion yet, he'd gotten his ten moves down to seventeen breaths. It satisfied him, as he'd had to practice for six months to achieve a similar phase in his previous life.

They halted abruptly.

Something screeched, like a claw of a beast scraping against a metal wall, to their left. It was so intense that it sent shivers down his thighs.

The thing let out a low, powerful growl, and it didn't sound like a Two Fang Wolf. It sounded more like a hungry bear beast's growl. It actually made his heart beat faster. It wasn't something he could take on at this stage. He didn't even think about probing with his divine sense. If that thing caught his scent, they might end up dying prematurely.

Fei'er huddled closer and grabbed his arm, her palm quivering a little.

Placing his finger on his lips, he asked her to remain quiet and slowly walk forward. Although he portrayed himself to be calm, he was shocked to his core. What kind of beast could make his heart shudder even after reincarnation?

Damn! If it wasn't for their food source drying up, he wouldn't have ventured from their hiding place before reaching level five in Refinement Realm in Blood Essence Body.

However, he wasn't sure if he could do that in the next few days, even if he had enough food. For the last two days, he'd been stuck at ninety-nine blood pearls, and he knew his level up depended on those blood pearls. It was inconceivable. Even after spending 200 years cultivating brutally, he was stuck at a bottleneck. This was idiotically stupid.

After ten more minutes of walking, they stopped at a fork. One tunnel led to the left and one to their right. This decision was quite simple. No matter what, they couldn't head left.

Right was the only choice. Yet he spread his divine sense and quickly retracted it after finding nothing in a mile's radius. But that tunnel to came to a dead end inside a room.

A room.

How could there be a room in the sewage system? And why wasn't there another tunnel connected to this room? If this was a dead end, they had to go left, and that might lead to quicker death.

Wei frowned as he scanned the room. It was impeccably clean. Not a single speck of dust covered any surface, nor did the room smell like anything. When he lit a candle, he found the walls shone with a metallic luster like they were polished recently.

"Young master, what should we do?" Fei'er whispered.

"Let's check this room carefully. I doubt it's a dead end." At least he hoped for it not to be a dead end. Tracing his palm over the walls, he moved around the room, checking every inch of the wall and ground. Seeing him doing that, Fei'er followed suit and started checking the other side of the room.

"Young master," she called to him after a few minutes. "I think there's a door here. Come here."

Halting his search, he took out his gray handkerchief and placed it on the ground to remember his last position. Then he marched to Fei'er's side. To his surprise, the little lass had really found a small hatch present in the wall. After moving his candle around the hatch, he confirmed it was a door. But there was no handle, and it was tightly closed. He couldn't even use his fingers to move it aside. It was that close.

No, if there was a door, there had to be a way to open it. There should be some mechanism. So, he started carefully observing the door in the dim candlelight.

His heart forgot to beat for a moment. How could it be? Why was there an array marked on the sewage system wall?

It was a Two— No. He traced his finger over the array diagram carvings. It was a Three-Fold Strength Defense Array.

Inconceivable. This was the Mortal Realm. How could it be?

It was simply . . .

"Young master, why are you murmuring to yourself while standing in front of a blank wall?" Fei'er leaned closer and peered at the wall. "Oh, there is a diagram. Do you know this diagram, young master?"

Wei shook his head in shock. "No, I haven't seen the complete diagram before." It was the truth. Once he had seen some traces of this diagram in one of the inheritance jade slips, but that was it.

This array was beyond the Mortal Realm's capabilities.

The world they lived in was divided in two realms, the mortal realm and the martial realm. The first few stages of cultivation were called the Mortal Realm, and after breaking through the Xiantian realm, one could step into the Martial Realm.

It was easier said than done. In his previous life, after spending so many dog years working in Mortal Realm, he'd made it to the Martial Realm. He had seen its vastness. The Mortal Realm was like a grain of salt in a huge desert when compared with the Martial Realm. But once someone stepped into the Martial Realm, it was impossible to come back to the Mortal Realm. How did this array appear in the State of Zin? Even though it wasn't a heaven-defying object or something, it was a Soul Array, and on top of that its array diagram was lost in the passage of time. Soul Arrays were difficult to attune and carve, so how could a mere city located in the corner of the world have an array like this?

Unfathomable.

Arrays followed the generic system of grading used in the cultivation world. Starting from Bronze, Silver, Gold, etc. But people differentiated them using the energy source used to sustain them. In the Foundation Scripture of the Array Masters, it was said that any energy could be used as the array source, but humankind only used a few types. The basic was qi and essence energy that qi and body cultivators cultivated. But there was another energy only very high-level Array Masters could use, and that was soul energy. Wei's divine sense was a kind of soul energy manipulation, but as his body wasn't strong, he couldn't regenerate it right away, and he was constantly on the verge of losing it because of his low cultivation level.

Arrays used Qi Stones to power arrays. There were Essence Stones available, but they were too rare, so everyone used Qi Stones as a power source. But Soul Arrays used Soul Stones, and right now he was seeing one of those strange arrays.

With trembling hands, he tapped at the corner of the array repeatedly. He had studied One-Fold and Two-Fold Strength Defense Arrays, and he hoped that the method to unlock the power source would work on this too.

He failed his first two attempts, but the third attempt worked like a charm. A purple fluctuation emerged from the center and spread outward when he tapped on the tenth power point.

The center piece changed, and a half-broken purple stone came out of the center. As soon as it came out, the room filled with dream-like purple light.

Damn, it was a Soul Stone. In his previous life, he had only seen this thing in an auction where he couldn't even open his mouth to speak a single word. Now he saw it from inches away.

"Wow, what a brilliant stone." Fei'er reached for it. "I can create an earring with it."

Wei quivered and slapped her hand hard. If the stupid lass accidently touched it before de-activating the array, she would lose her soul instantly. "Stay away. Not every shiny object is a good thing."

Arrays had powerful mechanisms embedded in them. Even though one could activate the power source of low-grade arrays by knowing the proper power points, if one dared to touch the power source, it would explode. High-grade arrays didn't even allow one to view the power source. They had a different mechanism altogether.

"Ouch, it hurts, young master." Fei'er stomped her foot and stepped away.

Wei heaved a sigh of relaxation and wiped his sweat away. The lass had almost died a moment before. If he hadn't studied that ancient book for fun, he wouldn't know about this type of array, and he might have died too.

But who the fuck put such a formidable array in a sewage system? Unless something precious lay beyond this door, no one would put a Soul Array, right?

He grew excited suddenly, and he touched other points of the array. Although this array was beyond his capabilities, it was severely damaged, and for an Array Master like him, it was a child's play.

"Young master . . ." Fei'er quivered and huddled close to him.

"Fei'er, stay away from this thing. It's dangerous," he shouted.

"Young master, there's . . ."

Annoyed, he turned toward her, but his gaze jumped to the ten Two Fang Wolves standing at the tunnel entrance.

Shit!

Chapter 19

Inconceivable Strength

Li Ti moved through the forest allocated to the Li clan near Old Martial City. Since Li Sua was in the dungeon, he had to look after the business and day-to-day activities of the branch. Although he'd found no fraud in the accounting books maintained by this branch of the clan, he couldn't find the reason for Li Sua's apparent wealth either.

There had to be something he had missed, but he couldn't find it even after searching the Li clan compound and accounting books ten times. He'd even checked all their servants' houses, and there was nothing suspicious.

Then where did Li Sua get the money in the chest from? If he didn't know better, he might have thought Li Sua had bought that Foundation Refirming Pill, but that wasn't possible. The legit kid of Li clan, Li Wei, had found it in a hole in the Ancient Ruins; Tang had confirmed it with his own eyes.

Then where did this money come from? While walking through the small encampment established by the wood cutters, he found an enclosed area.

When he asked around, he found Li Sua had enclosed this area, and everyone was forbidden to enter. They claimed there was a strange Ferocious Beast living there, and Li Sua had told them to not enter if they didn't want to die.

Out of curiosity, he walked inside the enclosed area. Ferocious Beasts were dangerous, but with his cultivation he could at least save his life and run away.

However, after walking for five minutes he didn't find any Ferocious Beasts in the area, nor there were any tracks that supported Li Sua's story.

When he was about to turn back, he spotted another small enclosed area. And after entering it, he found the answer to his question. His heart raced faster and faster as he stared at the small Earthly Fruit Tree growing in the middle of the forest. Earthly Fruit Trees produced a rare herb that could fetch a lot of money at market.

With a thumping heart, he turned back and dashed to the Li clan compound. This had to be reported to his father, and this tree had to be protected. This city might become the next headquarters of the Li clan in the future. That tree was much too important for their clan's development.

It had to be protected at any cost.

꙾꙾꙾ ꙾꙾꙾

Ten pairs of vengeful red eyes stared at Ki Fei, and her heart almost gave up. A shiver passed through her tailbone, and she lost strength in her legs and flopped down. That beast also had ten pairs of eyes lined on its neck, and it always said it wanted to devour her like it had devoured her parents.

Her soul wanted to jump out of her body and run away when the beast licked its fangs. For fifteen years, she'd faced this nightmare, and many times she'd wanted to give up on her life so the beast would stop hunting her, but then the young master had come in her life, and the beast had vanished.

But it was back.

This time even her young master couldn't save her.

"Fei'er, give me the beast pills," her young master said, but she was out of her wits. She shrank back until her back touched the metal wall. The beast was here to eat her, and she was going to die.

"No, I don't want to die," she cried, and then everything went black.

⇥⇥⟩ ⟨⇤⇤

Li Wei frowned. No, his heart almost jumped out of his ribcage when the little lass dropped on the ground, and then she'd passed out after blabbering some nonsense. What was wrong with her?

Fear jumped to his throat. How could she throw a tantrum at this moment and pass out? Without the Beast Subduing Pills, he couldn't face all of these beasts together. Damn, if only he could access the storage ring himself! But he lacked qi cultivation, so he couldn't.

Squatting, he slapped her soft cheeks. "Fei'er, stupid lass, get up."

But she didn't react.

Damn this girl.

All ten beasts stepped forward in unison, their canines out and thick white saliva dripping from their fangs. Under purple light from the array, they looked like ugly monsters. It irked him to the bone. Their message was clear. These bastard beasts wanted to shred him into pieces with their sharp canines.

Dream on.

With no other option, he drew the sword from the back of his gray robe and stepped forward. Thank god, he hadn't put the sword in the storage ring or he would've had to fight with his fists. That would be suicidal.

"Come and become our food!" Shouting, he activated One Sword Strike and hit the nearest beast with a rapid motion. Like a knife cutting tofu, his sword pierced through the beast's hide, drawing a line of blood along its path.

Blood. Wei's eyes glimmered when he spotted the blood. It acted as a stimulus, and he attacked the beasts in a frenzy.

Three strikes in, he'd nearly cut one beast down. This strength almost exceeded that of a layer two qi Refinement Realm cultivator. All these wolves had strength equivalent to a layer three qi Refinement Realm cultivator, and normally only a layer two qi Refinement Realm cultivator could hurt them, but he'd done it with his layer one body cultivation.

This was inconceivable and thrilling.

However, before he could enjoy his little discovery, two beasts charged at him from other sides. They were coordinating their attacks.

Wei spun on his toe and avoided the attack. While he swung around, his sword cut through a beast's body horizontally. When the sword tip met the body of the beast, sparks flew and the rebound force jumped through his sword into his right arm, numbing it for a breath's time.

Why did he fail?

Once again, he activated One Sword Strike and chopped at the same beast. This time his sword tip cut through its neck with ease.

It was the martial skill. The martial skill only worked when he attacked overhand. Although he hadn't put a single drop of qi inside the blade, the martial skill had been perfected to exert all of his might in that attack, and that didn't happen when he swung his sword horizontally. Basically, he lacked the strength to cut through these beasts with lateral attacks.

That made sense.

A beast leaped at him out of nowhere, and its fangs pierced his left shoulder.

Wei stabbed his sword into the beast's eye and pushed it away. The beast howled in pain and retreated, but in the momentary gap another beast sank its fangs into his right side.

"Damn you bastards." Pain shot into his brain, and he punched the beast with his left hand to push it away. His punch worked somehow, and the beast retreated, but it retreated with a big chunk of oblique muscle in its jaws. Torrents of pain shot through his whole body, and blood sprayed from the wound. The whole room swirled around him for a moment, and a small pool of blood accumulated around his legs. That bastard beast had taken a big chunk out of him, and he was losing blood like a tap left open.

This was bad. With this injury, how could he swing his sword with all his might? If only he had those Beasts Subduing Pills, he could win this easily and see what was behind the defense array.

Shaking his head, he pushed that stray thought away. Now wasn't the time. Although his body couldn't take this pain, his mind could. In his previous life, he had spent days inside a boiling furnace, and this was nothing compared to that torture.

He could do this. No, he had to do this. He couldn't die just after getting reincarnated. If he did, that would be the biggest joke of both of his lives.

Gritting his teeth, he slashed his sword at the next beast coming to take a bite out of him.

No, he would not die here. He had to save Fei'er too. So, for that, he had to continue on.

Chapter 20

Blood Pearl

Pain shot across Li Wei's whole body when he tried to move his right arm. The pungent taste of blood filled his mouth. It was impossible to move even an inch. Without his consent, the cold metal sword in his hand tilted down like it weighed a thousand pounds. It took everything he had to hold it tight.

He licked his dry lips. His chest heaved like he'd run a thousand miles and couldn't control his breath anymore. The battle had taken a bad turn.

But he would not give up. In the corner of his eye, he spotted a beast marching toward Fei'er, so he dashed madly toward her. "Die, you bastard." Cursing, he kicked with all his might. If he failed, Fei'er would die, and he couldn't let that happen. In his whole life, only that lass had cared for him. He couldn't lose her.

At least not in this life.

His right leg ignited with a might unknown to him, and his foot shot forward with crazy fast speed. So fast that he nearly lost balance from his other leg. If it wasn't for his divine sense being strong and sensing his body's condition, he might have fallen flat on his back.

When his leg closed on the beast, something ignited inside it, and its speed increased to an unfathomable level, almost blurring and reappearing an inch away from the beast's stomach.

The beast sensed something was wrong, and it tried to stop its advance, but it was already in motion so it had to take on Wei's kick head on.

Just before his kick thrashed in the beast's stomach, Wei felt an unfathomable power exploding in his right leg, and his leg grew hotter and hotter with every fraction of a second.

His leg hit the beast's stomach like an elephant ramming into a wooden tree. The beast's body caved in. It was sent flying at the opposite wall, and when it crashed with a bam, it dropped in a pool of blood and meat.

The beast didn't even have time to howl or cry. It was dead before it hit the metal wall.

What the hell was that?

The rebound force from the kick shot inside his leg and nearly paralyzed it, but he didn't care anymore.

Wei gasped in shock. How could his leg explode with this power and kill a layer four Refinement Realm beast with a single kick?

But he had no time to dwell on it, as the other beasts would not wait for him to recover. They had already leaped at him.

Planting his still-sane left leg, he attacked with One Strike Sword and cleaved another beast's head.

Another shock spread through his mind. Even after losing a piece of his right oblique, he could wave his sword like it didn't matter.

One Sword Strike. The sword descended like an avalanche and sliced through another beast's head.

How was this possible? After losing a fist-sized piece from his body, he still had the same momentum to fight. It was like that part went numb after the beast's bite tore it off him.

While attacking another beast, he cast a quick glance at the wound. A fist-sized piece of flesh was still missing from his body, but the wound had stopped bleeding, and he felt his blood avoiding that part while moving through his meridians.

Was this even possible?

Taking another risk, he sent his divine sense into his body and almost lost his balance. This was the epitome of receiving one shock after another. Even after losing so much blood that it pooled on the metal floor, his blood percentage still neared ninety eight percent.

But then he spotted a change, and his eyes lit up with understanding.

His ninety-nine blood pearls had reduced to eighty-one. That had to be the reason he still had ninety eight percent blood in his body. There was no other explanation. The blood pearls could be used to increase his strength and replenish his blood in dire needs.

Yes, it had to be that.

Wow! If more people knew a cultivation art like this existed, immortals would fight over it. No matter what, he could let no one find out about this, and he had to get into that secret realm in this life too. Just to prevent anyone from finding out this cultivation art.

Two beasts leaped from either side of him, but with his newfound power, he roared like a beast and thrashed them with his sword.

The battle continued.

The madman that didn't care about his injuries and the seven crazy beasts that needed to kill that madman fought like wild animals, stabbing, slicing, and biting each other. But the casualties only occurred on the beasts' side, while the man became more enraged with every new wound on his body. It was like with every drop of blood he spilled, he gained new strength.

A strength that could transcend the heaven and earth.

Ki Fei regained consciousness in the middle of battle and immediately wished she hadn't.

Her young master stood a few feet away from her in tattered clothes. His untied black hair rested on his long black, and his right shoulder was missing a big chunk of meat. Blood streamed from his shoulder and traveled down his arm, finally dripping from the tip of the sword he held in his right hand.

He looked like a god of war.

His demeanor frightened her.

"Young master." She wanted to cry, but she couldn't. Despite being naïve, she knew he fought with all his might and disturbing him would only break his concentration. The way he stood, he seemed to be in control, but anxiety filled her heart. In the last ten days, her young master had bled constantly. It was like the curse of a blood god haunted him. The more he bled, the more the blood god felt satisfied.

But why? Why was he facing such hardship? Why couldn't he rest a little and let go of his worries? One after another, desperate situations fell upon him, and he had to face them without being able to cultivate properly.

Maybe it was because she wasn't strong enough to help him. If she could wield a sword and fight alongside him, he might not suffer this much.

Her mind settled, she rose from her place and pulled a sword out from the storage ring. She was going to give all she had in this fight. If she died, then so be it, but she would help her young master.

"Stupid lass, if you are awake, throw some Beast Subduing Pills, would you?" the young master panted and struck with his sword, finishing off a half-dead wolf beast.

"Aiyaa." She wanted to smack her face. How could she forget that? Suddenly she realized the young master suffered because of her, and guilt struck her heart.

But that beast . . .

Suddenly hundreds of red eyes appeared in the doorframe, staring at her, threatening her soul. Fear crawled up her spine, and she lost her will and dropped to the ground. Unconscious.

She'd once again failed to help her young master. Maybe she should just die instead.

Chapter 21

Desperate Struggle

Drip. Drip.

Blood dripped from Li Wei's sord, adding to the blood pool formed under his feet. It was his own blood, mixed with the beasts' blood, and it gave him goosebumps. He'd done his fair share of killing in his previous life, but it was all done under unavoidable situations. He'd never enjoyed killing to steal resources or to enact revenge. When he'd had to kill, he'd done it cleanly. He could say he wasn't fond of blood in his previous life.

But this life was different. Standing in tattered clothes with a warm heart and cold eyes, he felt different. Something he'd never felt before. Seeing all this blood on the ground didn't disgust him, nor did it make his heart quiver like before. It actually sent a thrill down his core, and he seemed to like it.

Maybe the cultivation art had a true meaning.

Blood above all!

Licking his lips, he scanned the four remaining beasts growling low. His heart urged him to jump in between them and make spurt blood from their bodies.

Unfortunately, he had to suppress this killing instinct and think about his blood pearl consumption. He was dripping blood, and replenishing it at a greater rate, but he had also used seventy blood pearls killing six beasts. It was a waste of his resources.

One of the beasts moved, and when he glared at the bastard, it stepped back like it feared him. His heart beat faster than a flying sword traveling at the speed of sound. He bet his enemies faced a similar situation. Although they had a number advantage, he'd proved himself to be their nemesis.

So far.

But before he could relax and recuperate, he had to kill them. Swiftly. If he couldn't finish this fight quickly, he might die here. He had already consumed seventy blood pearls, and every full strike consumed ten blood pearls. If he survived this, he might need to learn a method to reduce the consumption or utilize it through a few medium-strength strikes instead of one full-blown attack.

Because of all the blood seeping from his wounded shoulder, his sword hilt had turned slippery, but he held on to it. His brain was working on overdrive to calculate the best way to deal with the four remaining beasts.

The beasts growled, their red eyes looking behind him, and he realized Fei'er had regained consciousness.

There was a rustle behind him, and he knew she had gotten up. His bloody lips curled in a faint smile. This should cut him some slack. "Stupid lass, if you are awake, throw some Beast Subduing Pills, would you?"

Suddenly his heart thumped with an unknown danger, and his gaze jumped to the door illuminated in purple.

"Fuck, no." Dozens—no, hundreds of eyes stared at them from the connected tunnel. A huge number of Two Fang Wolves had come to hunt them. They must have been attracted to the blood smell permeating the room.

Damn, he should have placed the White Cicada Fruit outside of the room to avoid this trouble.

All his viciousness and strength slipped out of his body, and his legs turned weak.

Yes, he was afraid. There was no way he could survive this. If only he had hundreds of Beast Subduing Pills, he might have a chance to escape.

Yes, he needed to throw all the pills at the beast horde and then make a beeline through the array behind them. The array was a defense array, so he would have to break or deactivate it to open the door. Only that way could he save their beaten asses.

However, when he looked over his shoulder, he found Fei'er lying unconscious again.

"Damn, this stupid lass." It was like she was hell-bent on killing him today.

What should he do? The future looked bleak, and he wasn't ready to die just after reincarnating in a new start.

Did he have to die today? Did he have to lose his only chance of embarking on a different path than before?

Desperation surged through his heart, but he saw no option. His previous enemies had spotted their backup, and they seemed to sneer at him.

Was this his end?

No.

This wasn't.

A light flashed in his mind. There was still a way out. But it was dangerous, and it might destroy his divine sense, but that could save them both.

The Soul Stone. It was a half-used Soul Stone, but it possessed the unending might needed to destroy all these beasts in front of him. But the moment he pulled it out of the array diagram, it would strike his soul and destroy it. If he wanted to deactivate the array, he would need a few breaths, and he didn't have that much time.

There was only one way. He had to form a protective cocoon of his divine sense when he pulled out the Soul Stone and then throw the stone at the beast pack. But that might just destroy his fragile divine sense, making him lose all the experience of his previous life.

He might even damage his soul and lose all his memories.

But there was no other option.

Gritting his teeth, he turned and dashed toward the door.

The beasts howled and charged. He could hear their footsteps coming closer to him with every passing moment. He only had a few breaths before he would be drowned in the beast tide.

Stopping right in front of the array, his fingers dashed around the array diagram, tapping on a few power points, and then suddenly the Soul Stone lost its luster a bit.

This was it.

This was the moment before array could be deactivated.

This was the step that could destroy the whole array.

A formless energy wrapped around his right arm, and he clawed at the Soul Stone, using all his might. Fortunately, the array had lost its luster because of remaining active for so long. It had drained a lot of power from the Soul Stone, so it was easier to pull it out.

Suddenly, a purple stone fell in his hand and a purple light surrounded him. It pierced through the protective barrier he had formed with his divine sense.

His divine sense failed at that crucial moment, and the soul energy that should have wiped out the beast tide actually shot for his soul.

This was it. He had failed to protect himself and Fei'er once again.

This was the end.

Chapter 22

Soul Stone

Bone-cutting cold entered Li Wei's skin when the purple light from the Soul Stone penetrated through his divine sense cocoon—cold like someone had put ten-thousand-year-old ice below his skin.

In a split second his arm froze, including the vigorous blood he was proud of. It was so cold that he feared his mind would freeze too. The tyrannical energy coming from the Soul Stone wasn't something a mere layer one Refinement Realm body cultivator could withstand.

This was the end.

The complete end.

There was nothing after this end.

And yet his mind was clear as crystal water from Heaven's Spring, a treasure found in the Martial Realm.

The purple light passed through his arm and into his brain, freezing every drop of blood along the way. It was shooting for his soul, and despite his low cultivation, he spotted his tiny soul for the first time since reincarnating. It wavered like a boat in a huge sea storm.

When the purple light reached his tiny soul, it broke into pieces.

He wanted to shout as unimaginable pain swept across his being. People said the tearing of one's soul was the worst pain imaginable, but he'd never thought about it. Today he felt it. Felt it with all his might. It was the most excruciating pain he'd felt in his two lifetimes. Even after spending ten days in a thousand-degree furnace, he hadn't felt this much pain.

It was inhuman torture. Every piece of his soul stung like ten thousand ants bit it from all sides and his soul had split into thousands of tiny pieces.

Yet he wasn't dead.

But why?

After all this happened, he wondered for many days on this question. This was impossible. When a cultivator's soul broke apart, there was no tomorrow. Heck, there was no next moment. It was final destruction. Even if his body survived, he would live as a corpse. The most precious thing he would lose would be the belonging of self, his mind. And yet Wei could observe everything from a corner of his mind, like someone else's soul was being destroyed.

System: Power source found. Activating Absorption Mode.

Once again, the mysterious system popped into his vision, and then something happened that made his mind quiver.

His tiny soul pieces gathered together at a rapid pace. Even the divine sense he'd brought from his previous life was sucked into the soul pieces.

But there was something else coming with his divine sense. The Soul Stone had entered his body and moved toward his soul pieces.

What the heck was happening, and why was he still alive? Not that he regretted it, but this was all inconceivable.

Wei didn't understand anything. It was like some deity had been playing a game with his soul, and he was left outside to watch the game.

System: Activating Merging Mode.

His divine sense and the Soul Stone smashed into the blob of his soul pieces and everything swirled around each other. The bean-sized Soul Stone suddenly cracked into thousands of pieces and joined the fun his divine sense and soul pieces were having in the whirlpool. It painted everything dark purple, and then it started changing. His soul pieces absorbed his divine sense and the Soul Stone powder, merging to form a bigger piece.

The process went on for an unknown time that felt like months until it finally converged in a big fist-sized soul.

A soul without a soul space. How was that even possible? If someone had told him this was possible, he would have laughed out loud, but it was happening in his own body. He couldn't deny it.

This was just impossible. Every person had a soul, but it remained hidden in one's body until they formed a soul space. It was a qualitative change in cultivation, and it required a person to undergo metamorphosis. And before forming a soul space, one's soul would be bean sized.

But he had formed a fist-sized soul and that too without a soul space. Then he felt a new entity emerging out of his soul.

His divine sense. And it wasn't something he'd brought from his previous life, but his own divine sense formed from his soul.

What the heck?

A bout of pain shot across his brain, and his memories and experiences merged with his soul. They flooded his soul like a river meeting the sea, but his soul wasn't a sea. It was just a stream, and the river was about to overrun it.

It was too much for his tiny soul. Although he now had divine sense merged with his soul, he didn't have enough space for all those memories and experience. His existing soul could store his memories, and his divine sense could carry his previous life experience, but after merging, his soul had increased in size while his divine sense had shrunk by a huge margin. It was like an infant when compared to his previous adult divine sense. Both of them combined couldn't handle his 200 years of memories and experience, and it was growing exponentially in value.

The memories and experience kept rushing in, and if this continued, his soul would explode, and there would be no coming back.

It would bloat, expand, and then boom.

If he'd had a corporeal body, he would have been sweating like an animal. He'd had a fortuitous encounter and gave birth to a strong soul with divine sense, but he was going to lose it in the end.

System: Storage function unlocked.

System: Absorbing large memories and experience.

System: Initiating index creation.

What the heck was this "system" thing?

He had no clear answer, but after whatever storage function was activated, his soul calmed down. Memories and experiences stormed inside, but it didn't bloat and explode like he expected.

Suddenly everything calmed down, and he found himself in control of his body. He stood in front of the now lifeless array diagram while the beasts charged him.

What the heck? It felt like he had spent months inside his mind, but it took only a fraction of a second outside.

Bending down, he scooped up Fei'er's fragile body and tapped on the array diagram, opening the door for himself.

But before he could move through the door, a beast leaped in the air and latched onto his left shoulder. His hand went numb, and he accidentally dropped Fei'er.

Fear gripped his heart. He was just a moment away from going through the door, and the bastard beast had ruined it.

Now he had two options: jump through the door along with the beast and kill it, but that meant giving up on Fei'er, or pick Fei'er back up and then most probably die under the beast tide.

No way. He couldn't leave Fei'er behind. Nor he could die here after his soul had formed a divine sense for itself. It was a miracle, and it would be foolish to give up on the opportunities life provided him.

So, he chose a third option.

Turning back, he burned his remaining thirty blood pearls and struck with one last One Sword Strike. Power surged around his Yangming meridian and tore apart small blood vessels connecting to it. Piercing pain flooded his body, but he felt the emergence of power greater than he could imagine.

A volcano exploded in his body, sending waves of power through his muscles to his sword—the sword that had already reached a crazy momentum with his final strike. It cut through the air and struck the ground next to him.

The tip of the blade cut through the metal ground and sent tremors through the floor like an earthquake. It rushed toward the beast tide.

The hundreds of beasts sensed something, and they all halted and turned back to leave.

But how could a sword strike activated with thirty blood pearls be easy to dodge?

Before the first line of beasts could step out of the door, the quake had hit them hard.

It was a clusterfuck.

Hundreds of beasts howled in pain and dropped on the ground one after another. Their inner organs churned through the vibrating wave, and they lost all their prowess. Wei could see this clearly because there were two beasts that he had wounded, and he saw their viscera churning inside and then turning into a jelly.

It might have killed all the beasts, but he didn't linger to verify. Instead, he collected all his strength, mixed it with his willpower, and lifted Fei'er to jump through the door. He had suffered heavily after using thirty blood pearls, and he knew he wouldn't last long.

The last thing he heard was the metal door slamming shut, and he lost consciousness with a smile on his face.

Chapter 23

Golden worm

Something crawled over her face, jolting Ki Fei out of her half-unconscious state. After struggling to open her weighted eyes, she spotted a six-inch golden worm crawling over her arm. It looked like a silkworm, but it didn't at the same time. Silkworms didn't have a golden color.

Then she suddenly realized it was a worm crawling over her arm. And she hated worms and insects. Its tiny legs crawled over her soft skin, sending chills across her core. It felt so weird and disgusting that she wanted to throw up her last meal, but she was too frightened to even do that.

Worms and insects were the most frightening things in this world for her. No, ghosts would be first.

"Young master, save me!" Shouting, she waved her arm like her life depended on it, and the worm dropped onto the young master's blood-soaked body.

"Young master," she said again, but the tone had changed from fear to desperation. He lay in the pool of blood, and his chest wasn't moving even an inch.

Grabbing his arm, she checked his pulse, but she didn't find it.

Fear gathered under her heart, forming a lump, and it was worse than the worm crawling over her skin. It was a cold fear, a fear of losing her young master. No, this couldn't be happening. She didn't know when, but she'd become dependent on this young master from her childhood. He was like the last flickering candle in a dark storm, and she couldn't lose him. She would die without him. That scary beast would devour her.

"Are you afraid of death?" Someone spoke, and she almost jumped away from the young master. It wasn't his voice, and that meant someone else was here too.

But where was she? Her gaze traced her surroundings. It was a strange rectangular room with an invisible fourth wall. Golden and black silk threads covered the other side of the room, hiding it from her.

"I asked you a question, lass." That voice spoke once again, and it came out shrill, like someone was talking for the first time after a long, long time. A man in her neighborhood had lost his voice for a decade, and when he'd got it back, he'd sounded like this.

"Who, are you?" She picked up the sword lying next to her. "Don't you dare come near me, else I'll cut you into pieces . . ." She hesitated. "I'm a super cultivator, and I'll cut you into pieces just with a thought."

A low chuckle echoed in her ears, and her fear heightened. Who was it? Was it a ghost?

No way. There was golden light everywhere, so how could a ghost come here? The young master once said ghosts fear light, so she always burned a candle in her small room every night.

"I don't care if you are super cultivator or a naïve lass who can't even pee straight."

What? Her head spun at the verbal attack. What did—whatever it was—mean by she couldn't pee straight? She could very well pee straight. Straighter than an arrow.

Could she?

"Answer my question. Are you afraid of death?"

Afraid of death? What a weird question. Everyone was afraid of death. Didn't this stupid thing understand that? Wait, maybe this thing could help.

"Do you have a pill to save my young master?" Her gaze dropped to the lifeless body of her young master. He was missing big chunks of his body, and she wasn't sure if anyone could save him from this condition. Looking at him again, the lump in heart expanded. Any more and it would stretch to the limits of her heart.

"Are you afraid of death?" The same question came again, but it seemed to be a different voice. This voice had a bit of smoothness in it.

"Yes, I'm afraid of death." Ki Fei bit her lip. "But I'm more afraid of my young master's death. Can you save him?"

"A brat with a strange smell. Why are you afraid of his death? He is beyond help."

"Then I'm not afraid of my death," Ki Fei answered. If the young master wouldn't live, her life had no value. It was he who had taken care of her in her direst hour. He'd sold his precious amulet from his mother so he could treat her wounds. Her life was his lease.

"Biyu, you take her. She is suited for your yin power. I'll eat this lad's body. He has so much blood vitality." This time the voice came out of the golden worm lying on the young master's body. It then slipped into one of the wounds and vanished inside the young master's body.

"Hey you . . ." She was going to do something when a black thing shot from behind the golden threads and drilled into her skull right between her brows.

Pain fiercer than anything she had ever experienced shot from her forehead. That black thing pierced her skull like it was tofu. Rolling her eyes up, she could see the black thing was a worm like the golden one.

She tried to move her hands, but they didn't move. She had lost control of her body.

Desperation filled her heart. Was she going to see her young master die like this?

"No!" a shout came from the young master's body, and the golden worm shot out of the wound. It trembled like it was afraid of something.

The black dot that was drilling into her brain shot out too and landed next to the golden worm. It looked exactly like the golden worm, other than its pitch-black color.

"Niyu, what happened? Why did you jump out?" the black one asked.

"This lad can't even pee, and he has a Blood Essence Body. When I tried to devour his heart, it sucked half of my blood instead. Let's get away from his body and just devour the girl instead."

It was black worm's turn to shudder, and it leaped away from the young master's body, but it was too late. A thread of blood shot from the young master's body and wrapped around the two worms, sucking them dry. In less than a breath's time, their shiny bodies turned into bloodless corpses.

Ki Fei couldn't relate these things to anything she had seen in her life. This was out of her league. Two worms that talked like humans, and they wanted to devour her and the young master but were devoured by the young master's blood instead?

What was happening?

Ignoring all those stray thoughts, she bent forward and checked the young master's pulse again. Somehow, it had returned. It wasn't as vigorous as previously, but a slow pulse was better than no pulse.

The lump in her chest loosened, and she picked up those tiny worm corpses and put them inside her ring. They looked exquisite. Maybe she could use them to make some accessory.

But if a higher-level cultivator knew what she was thinking, they would have killed her ten times at least.

Chapter 24

Strange Power – Dantian repaired?

Li Wei's body hurt like someone had put him through a grindstone, crushing him for hours until every bone in his body cracked or turned to dust. It was raw pain. Pain that reached his very soul.

But then the pain vanished suddenly, like it'd never occurred.

Was he dreaming?

When he opened his eyes, he found two big blue eyes staring at him from above, pain evident in them. The pain radiated from her eyes into his heart.

"Young master, are you feeling okay?" Fei'er asked, sadness leaking through her voice. Her small body in her big gray gown quivered as she spoke.

His face twisted in pain, and her beautiful eyes watered.

"I—" His parched lips failed to separate; it was like being thirsty for thousands of years. "Wa—"

Fei'er fetched a leather skin filled with water. They had found it inside the storage ring, and it had remained surprisingly fresh even after—who knows how long the owner of the ring had been dead.

Pushing the mouth of the skin in between his lips, she released some water.

Cold, soul-filling water entered his throat. It felt so good that he closed his eyes, moaning inside his heart. Water had never felt this good before. It was like a soothing music to his pained soul.

Well, where was he?

Opening his eyes, he sent out his divine sense. He didn't need to worry about destroying it anymore.

His divine sense stretched out. They were inside a small room, and there was something blocking his divine sense at the other end of the room. The remainder of the room was filled with sharp golden and black threads. They were so sharp that they even cut his divine sense when it passed through. If it wasn't for the rebirth of his soul and divine sense, he would be in big trouble.

Huge trouble.

Wait, he'd been badly injured before they fell into this room. why didn't he feel any pain? He spread his divine sense inside his body.

"Damn, what—" He coughed when the water entered his breathing pipe. Shit, he was still drinking water, and he'd tried to talk. What an embarrassment!

"Young master, what are you doing?" Fei'er complained and pulled the water skin away.

"I'm—" What was wrong with him? He must have seen things. How could he . . .

His divine sense spread through his body once again and counted the blood pearls inside his Yangming meridian. There were four hundred and fifty of them.

He had broken into layer four of Refinement Realm in body cultivation. All his injuries had been healed, and he felt like a newborn baby.

Inconceivable, or a miracle? Using the last of his blood pearls had helped him break through three small stages of a realm? Was it even humanly possible?

"Young master, are you feeling weird anywhere?" Fei'er asked.

"No. I'm absolutely fine." Moving his hand, he checked his muscle reaction, and it was absolutely fantastic. It had never felt like this before.

"Thank the heavens. You've lost so much of weight in the last four days that I was worried sick about you."

"Four days?" He sat up and found himself in a gray robe. "Did you dress me?" When he fought the beasts, his clothes had taken a beating.

She nodded with an innocent look.

Red rushed to his face. Had she seen him naked? What a stupid question. If she'd changed his clothes, she'd seen him naked. She didn't have a magical art to change men's clothes.

"Wait, why did you ask me if I feel weird? What happened in the last four days?" His blush retreated as fast as it came. He'd been out for four days, and he'd broken through to new levels. That shouldn't be a normal thing, right?

"Because you devoured two worms when you were dying, and then you improved a lot."

He arched his brows and blinked a few times. "Come again."

"There were two worms, golden and black. They tried to eat us, but your blood moved out of your body and sucked them in. Only their carcasses remained behind." She waved her hand, and two lifeless worm bodies appeared on her palm.

He furrowed his brow. Those worms looked like someone had sucked their blood dry.

Did he do it?

"Did I drink their blood?" he asked, ashamed. When he'd practiced Blood Essence Body, he'd decided not to use anyone else's blood, but it seemed he'd failed in his choice at the first difficult step.

Maybe he should stop cultivating this bloody art altogether.

"No. But they tried to devour you. The golden one entered your body, and the black one pierced inside my forehead." She pointed at a black mark on her forehead. It looked like a tiny black dot, but when he looked closer, he realized it was a hole made by something quite sharp.

"So, I was unconscious at that time . . ." He rubbed his forehead. What kind of cultivation art was this that could devour other things when unconscious? It seemed vicious.

He should probably scrap it completely. But then how could he walk on a different path this life? Blood Essence Body was a critical piece in a puzzle he wanted to solve in this new life, and giving up on it meant he had no advantages.

But he couldn't become a bloodthirsty killer. He couldn't suck others' blood.

A headache hit his brain, and it drained his mental capacity instantly.

"Fei'er." He opened his eyes. "Am I a disgusting person? I sucked someone else's blood. Does that make me a bad person?"

She shook her head like her life dependent on it. "No, young master. You're a good man. Actually, you are the best. Those two filthy things wanted to kill us, and you killed them. How can you be bad?" Her gaze jumped to a pile of bloody clothes lying on the ground. "Then you fought with your life on the line with those wolf beasts." Tears rolled down her pretty cheeks. "I was so stupid back then. I fainted and almost got you killed. It's me who is disgusting. How can you call yourself disgusting?"

He wiped those water pearls away with his thumb. When she cried, his heart thumped like never before. Once again, he regretted leaving her behind and not coming back in time. He had left this pure-hearted lass alone in this brutal world. That thing was disgusting. Not checking back on her after getting strong was disgusting. Leaving her to die was disgusting.

But not in this life. He wouldn't repeat that mistake again. So, he couldn't just let go of this cultivation art yet. Not until he reached his goal to become a lazy immortal. And to become a lazy immortal, he needed people he cared about, and Fei'er was one of them.

So, he would live on and protect people like her even if he had to die.

Yes. To become a lazy immortal was his goal, and he needed Fei'er for that.

System: New organization detected.

Cell structure undergoing mutation.

Activating Scanning Mode.

Cell structure mutation finished.

Repairing ethereal organ, Dantian.

Repairing ethereal organ, Spirit Root.

Chapter 25

Five Elemental Way Qi Cultivation Art

Black and golden threads weaved around each other like two snakes making love. They were inseparable and quite sharp. When he sent his divine sense out last night, it was cut in half when it tried to move past these threads. That roused his interest, because only a few materials could do this. The divine sense was a non-physical entity, and not many things could block it. Normal stone or wooden walls, or even extravaganza things made up with Essence Stone or Qi Stones, couldn't block it; yes, there were people in this world that made huge palaces out of Qi Stones, and he had met one in his last life.

When he moved his face closer, an exquisite fragrance bombarded his senses. It wasn't detectable at a distance; he could smell it only after moving within a few inches' distance of the threads. They smelled like . . .

Flipping Cleaver Bee honey. Yes, they smelled like those special bees. It was a delicious honey produced in the

Martial World that cost a ridiculous amount. Although he'd earned a lot of money in his previous life, he'd only tasted it twice.

Wow! If he could eat this honey every day, wouldn't it be heaven's blessing on him?

Just the thought made his mouth water, and he wanted to lick these threads. If not for his fear, he might have tried licking them. For a fatso like him, food mattered most.

Damn, he had lost a lot of weight in the four days he was unconscious. The fat around his stomach had almost halved. If he was going to put the weight back on, he had to eat more, and to eat more, he had to cut through these threads.

He finally decided to try an external weapon. "Fei'er, do we have a spare knife?" Somehow, he had to get past these threads, else they might die of starvation. The little lass had nearly eaten a whole beast in the four days he was unconscious, and that was the last of the meat they had. Looking at her small and fragile figure, he wondered where all that food went.

Anyway, since they had only enough meat left for a few meals, they had to get out of here. One option was to get back to the previous room and kill some beasts. With his current strength, he could do that, but the door was gone. After they'd passed through the door, it vanished from this side. It might be hidden by another array, but he couldn't find one anywhere in the accessible area.

So, his only option was to go to the other side of the room hidden behind these threads.

"I've got one." Fei'er handed him a knife. Lately, she smelled like a banquet of orchid flowers. The lass had eaten two Essence Gathering Pills and broke through to layer six Refinement Realm in the four days he was passed out. She'd wanted to be strong and help him.

Well, it wasn't to his liking. He would have preferred she stabilize her cultivation first and then advance, but what could he do with a done deed?

Grabbing the cold black knife's hilt, he carefully tried to cut the nearest thread. The result didn't surprise him, though. Instead of the thread, the tip of the blade got cut in half. The golden thread was as tenacious as a Silver Grade artifact.

Should he try with his finger? Well, at layer four in the Refinement Realm of body cultivation, his body should be on par with a normal metal, but it wouldn't cut a Silver Grade artifact. So, he decided not to go through with that stupid option.

Rubbing his forehead, he tried to think of a solution. Wait, hadn't he sucked two worms dry that looked like silkworms? Even their golden and black colors matched with the thread colors. If those worms had created these threads, their body should be able to cut through them. They might have hidden something precious behind the jungle of threads.

Maybe a heavenly treasure.

At the thought of a treasure, his body boiled in excitement. It had to be a treasure, otherwise his divine sense wouldn't be blocked. From his previous life experience, he knew where quite a few treasures were scattered across the Mortal and Martial realms, but they would make him sweat for them. But here he had already sweated for this treasure, so no way he would go without getting it.

"Fei'er give me those two worms."

She nodded and handed him the two small worm bodies. It seemed like she wasn't afraid of them after their death. If these were alive, she would have jumped here and there. Once, a worm had entered his room when she was prepping food for him, and she'd made so much of a drama out of it that people thought he was doing something unscrupulous to her, and a few people had come running to save her.

A cold sweat broke out over his back. Damn, that was close. That day he'd almost gotten beaten up for no reason.

Fei'er dropped the soft warm bodies on his palm. He was about to pick up one with his other hand when something stirred inside his soul. From the depths of his soul, a call came, and the bodies vanished into his arm.

What the heck?

System: New organization detected.

Activating Scanning Mode.

Cell structure mutation finished.

Cell structure is repairing ethereal organ, Dantian.

Frowning, he sent his divine sense inside his dantian.

Seeing the scene inside, he nearly lost his wits. What was happening with him? The worms were rotating inside his dantian, and it was healing faster than his divine sense could scan. Previously, the weird system had said something about healing his dantian, but nothing had happened even after a whole night. So, he'd thought the process was slow, or it was a weird system that came up with his reincarnated soul.

But things had taken a U-turn. Somehow his dantian was being healed after those worms entered it and started revolving around each other mysteriously.

System: Information interface detected.

Activating information transfer.

Receiving Five Elemental Way Qi Cultivation Art.

Chapter 26

Divine Refinement City

A stream of information flew in Li Wei's mind. Some was forceful and mysterious, while some was simple and yet profound. Some information roused his mind, and some scared the shit out of his soul.

A gentle wind flew out of an invisible opening that circulated air inside this seemingly airtight room, blowing across his face. Like a mother's warm hand, it caressed his cheeks and woke him up in a refreshing mood. Piercing light reflected over the golden and black threads into his eyes, but it didn't matter to him. In fact, it felt more like an enlightenment penetrating his mind. With more light, things became clear in his mind. It reminded him of the Heavenly Lake of Enlightenment in Firmament Sect's secret grounds in the Martial Realm. Its sweet and fragrant water had a power to enhance one's comprehension speed.

The cultivation art he'd received was called Five Elemental Way Qi Cultivation Art.

A thin film of perspiration formed around his whole body when the information stopped pouring into his mind. By the time he digested the information, he was sitting on the metal ground, grasping for breath. If he thought Blood Essence Body Cultivation Art was a top class one, then this qi cultivation art was the father of the top class. If there was a grade above the heavens, this cultivation art would fit into that.

World begins with chaos.

Chaos brought yin and yang.

Yin and yang gave birth to five elements.

Five elements developed life.

Walk on the Five Elemental Way to return to Chaos and rule this universe.

And the strangest part, he qualified to cultivate it because of his attributeless qi.

"Young master, are you all right? Did you hurt yourself?" Fei'er sat beside him and rubbed his back lightly. With her other hand, she pulled the water skin out and held it in front of him.

"I'm—" No, he wasn't all right. This qi cultivation art was something different. It allowed him to cultivate five elemental qi.

That was impossible. In the whole Mortal or Martial Realms, no one could do that. Not even the once-in-a-million prodigy had that ability.

In this world, a person was born with an attributed Spirit Root. The attribute fell in one of the five elements:

Fire, Water, Earth, Wood, Metal. Or it could be Yin or Yang. Sometimes, it could be a rare element like Thunder or Wind. He'd even seen a young man joining Heavenly Firmament Sect with a Light attributed Spirit Root. Even elders from the parent Firmament Sect came to watch him a couple of times. Of course, he'd quickly advanced into the Martial Realm and joined as an inner disciple of Firmament Sect, while Wei had to struggle as an outer disciple for decades when he joined.

A Light elemental Spirit Root was once in a millennium.

Then there were a few like him with an attributeless Spirit Root. His Spirit Root didn't have any attribute, so he was treated as trash in the cultivation world. He'd had no future in the path of qi cultivation. Of course, one could practice with attributeless qi, but it would be super hard and fail against any other elemental qi on the same level. Practicing it took four times the effort than any elemental qi. It was harder than not getting a beating from his stepfather.

If he hadn't had an Earth Grade Physical Root, no one would have cared about him. But attributeless qi cultivators had one advantage: they could use external means to convert their qi into one of the attributes. Wang Zia had carved a Metal Qi Transformation Array in his body so he could practice basic metal qi cultivation art and enter the Heavenly Firmament Sect. But it was a forced method, and he could never reach a higher level of cultivation with a borrowed knife like an array. So, in his previous life, his main source of advancement was his body cultivation art.

But everything had an exception. Although the Metal Qi Transformation Array carved in his dantian had a lower efficiency and could only transform forty percent of attributeless or white qi into metal qi, there was another high-level array, Metal Qi Conversion Array, that could convert sixty percent of pure qi into metal qi. In the later years of his cultivation, he had carved Metal Qi Conversion Array into his dantian, increasing his cultivation speed.

Then he could use pills and treasures to advance his cultivation, even with a borrowed method. To solve all his issues, he was planning to become an alchemist in this life. He had set his eyes on the Advanced Wood Derivation Array that would convert eighty percent of white qi into wood qi and planned to use pills to aid his cultivation alongside.

He was so close to attuning that array in his last life before he died. If he had attuned it, he would have become an inner sect elder in Firmament Sect eventually.

In the end, he'd died miserably. Who knows if Wang Zia kept his corpse intact or mutilated it?

Anyway. He wouldn't have to carve his dantian with a painful method and risk damaging it all together this time.

With Five Elemental Way, he would have access to all five elementals from the start, and he could use his cultivation art to convert one hundred percent of attributeless qi into any elemental qi.

It was like a tailor-made cultivation art for him.

"Young master, why are you sweating, and where did the worms go?" Fei'er wiped his sweat with a gray handkerchief.

"Nothing, really nothing," He said nothing. Not that he didn't trust her, but something like this should never be told even to one's wife. Fei'er was just a friend. "I'm trying to find a solution to this thread." He delved deeper into the information that had come with the cultivation art.

Apparently, this cultivation art was rewarded for completing the first trial in Divine Refinement City, and only given to young geniuses in the city. This was their first Inheritance Chamber that could be reached after completing the first challenge.

The challenge was to make a way through the golden and black threads and reach the Divine Yang Worm and Divine Yin Worm. They were guardians of this place, and they rewarded the geniuses who made it through with a Divine Yin or Divine Yang power to cultivate this Five Elemental Way Qi Cultivation Art. This was just the first challenge, and every prodigy would go through another challenge after reaching a higher cultivation realm.

But somehow, he had found a way to the target location of the challenge and devoured the Divine Yang Worm and Divine Yin Worm.

But how did he do it? Was it because of the Blood Essence Body?

It had to be it. There was no other way around this. At least he didn't know any skill in his previous life that could devour divine beasts in his dantian. But could he really cultivate Five Elemental Way Qi Cultivation Art? And also, he didn't have the Divine Yin and Divine Yang power to start on the cultivation.

With that thought, he poured his divine sense into his dantian, and he was once again shocked to his core.

His dantian was almost repaired, and the worm bodies were emitting strange golden and dark power around them.

Was this Divine Yin and Divine Yang power?

Then he frowned. A lot.

Chapter 27

Dilemma

Li Wei's frown deepened as he read through the other details of the challenge and reward system. When he read through everything, he looked up and gazed at the golden and black threads forming a strange structure in front of him. It formed a maze for the disciples from the other side, but from this side, he could appreciate their intrinsic details. Especially the exquisite fragrance they emanated. After the worms entered his dantian, he'd felt a strange connection with those threads. As long as he touched them, he bet they would move on their own.

Could he taste them now?

Licking his parched lips, he stared at the threads for a moment before he heard a rustle.

Fei'er sat close to him, working on the huge gray robes packed inside the storage ring. Her metallic needle moved effortlessly between her fingers and the cloth, altering them constantly. There were fifty martial robes, and she seemed to change them into his and her size in one go.

Her gaze jumped up, staring back at him. She had a loyal look in her eyes that always amused him. That lass had always stuck to him as long as he'd known her, and she had shown him dedication everyone else had failed to show. Although he was a Li clan member, servants treated him unfairly, and his stepbrothers and sisters treated him like a trash. But no matter what, this lass treated him like he was a treasure in her eyes.

Well, it didn't feel bad to be appreciated by someone.

But today he felt sad. In his previous life, he couldn't pay back her gratitude. But seeing her like this, full of hope, he vowed in his heart. He would take care of her in this life.

"Young master, what are we going to do next? We only have enough food left for a few meals."

Wei sighed. That "we" had a meaning attached to it. Earlier, he'd wanted to give this lass the storage ring and let her live a happy life. But now he couldn't do that. Being an orphan, she had no one to take care of her. Now he planned to help her break into the Refinement Realm and join Divine Fragrance Hall. That would be best for her. "We'll get out of here soon." He shifted his lotus position a little.

"Then why were you frowning? I thought you faced some issue again."

"No issue, it's just that . . ." He gulped his words down. There was no issue but the Five Elemental Way Qi Cultivation Art he'd received was only for the first six realms in cultivation. Once he reached the peak of the Heart Blood Realm, he would have to come back and search for another challenge room.

Finding a challenge room was another issue. The token should help him identify the challenge room, but he had no map of this tunnel system, and he didn't even know if other challenge rooms had survived the destruction of Divine Refinement City. The city itself was in ruins, and this room remaining intact was a miracle in itself.

"Just what, young master?" The girl's brow furrowed. "Is your body unwell somewhere?" She reached with her hands to touch his body.

Red flooded his face. This lass had changed his clothes, and she must have seen everything. Although he'd lived two hundred years in his previous life, he was a virgin and had done nothing that a man and a woman did. "No. Let's go." He rose to his feet. It was decided. He would first get out of here and make a probing round of the other trial rooms. If those trial rooms were intact, he would cultivate this awesome art. Otherwise, he would have to find something else. Now that his dantian was almost cured, he should aim for an effortless top-tier cultivation art for attributeless qi.

"But the threads? They can cut a metal knife. How can we get out then?" Fei'er got up too.

"Let's eat first. Don't we have some meat left?" He glanced at the hacked wolf's body. Fei'er had done a good job of skinning the wolf.

"Yes, Fei'er is hungry too." She rubbed her stomach while pouting.

Wei couldn't hold his laugh inside. Her action was carefree and innocent. It reminded him of his reincarnation.

Yes, he had reincarnated, and he didn't have to worry too much about the things that haunted him in the past. This life he wanted to live freely and become a lazy immortal, and to become one he had to gain sufficient powers.

Smiling, he sat with his back resting on the cold metal. Fire danced in front of his eyes, leaping at the piece of meat Fei'er held with a metal rod and the gray patch of cloth she had torn from the big martial robe left in the storage ring.

The aroma of roasting meat assaulted his senses and calmed him down. While waiting for meat, he suddenly realized there was some blood lying in a small pot near the wolf's body.

"Fei'er did you collect the blood?"

Fei'er nodded without looking away from the meat. She concentrated fully on her job and didn't care what went on beside it.

"You said you can't lift the heavy sword, right?" he asked, an idea popping in his mind.

"Yes, that's too heavy for Fei'er."

"Then let me make it light for you." With a smirk, he pulled the blood closer and tore some of the skin off the dead wolf.

Chapter 28

Strength Array

Pinching the piece of wolf fur in between his index finger and thumb, Li Wei wrapped it around a small wooden stick and then tied it with the stitching thread Fei'er carried with her.

"Brush done," he said with a proud smile appearing on his face. Well, he had refined a few low-level weapons, but he had never created a brush. It smelled like rotten eggs and threatened to burn his senses, but he still liked it.

He dipped a small wooden stick in the thick beast blood and then smelled it.

"Yikes, young master, what are you doing?" Fei'er screamed from behind the stove.

"Just smelling it to see how much essence energy it has." Although it looked thick, the essence energy inside was slowly waning. So, he had to hurry up and carve arrays before the essence energy dried out and he lost the chance.

"Young master, let me stitch a good brush for you. We have a lot of clothes remaining," Fei'er said, blinking her carefree eyes.

Wei rolled his eyes. Not again. "No, this one is fine," he said, tapping the makeshift brush on the metal ground, scattering dust caught in the fur. Unfortunately, he couldn't get it clear as a fresh brush made up from Ten Tail Horse's tail, but it was okay-ish for the crude job he planned to do on the Bronze Grade swords.

Being an Array Master meant he had to dip his foot in Artificing as well. Knowing the ins and outs of the materials was an essential skill every array cultivator had to learn. Having good quality materials didn't equal a quality end product. In fact, eight out of ten martial artifacts failed to achieve the same quality as the source materials. This sword was the same thing. It was made of Cold Thunder Iron and mixed with a Hardened Fiery Gold to give it weight and strength, but in the end, it only produced a high-tier Bronze Grade sword.

Anyway, he didn't need to worry about such trivial matters. With the low-level Ferocious Beast blood, he couldn't carve a temporary array on a Silver Grade martial artifact. It would definitely fail. So, this was a good fit for the temporary Strength Lightness Array and Strength Expanding Array he planned to carve on two Bronze Grade swords.

But when he tried to remember the array diagrams, he felt blank, like those diagrams had vanished from his memory.

System: Accessing dormant memory block. Search query: Strength Lightness Array and Strength Expanding Array.

Boom!

Information exploded in his mind like a textbook page separating and appearing in front of him at the same time. When it appeared in his mind, it sank into his memories, giving him a complete memory of both arrays.

His mind went blank. For a moment, dizziness filled his consciousness, and then it vanished like it never occurred.

What the heck just happened?

For a moment, Wei didn't know what to think about this experience. Was this the storage function he'd awakened after merging with the Soul Stone?

At least it seemed like one.

Glancing at the arrays, he thought about array types and practice and the same system didn't get invoked. Did that mean only array diagrams and corresponding memories were stored in the so-called storage function?

He didn't know the answer, nor had the system responded to any of his thoughts. It only acted when he was in danger, or something unusual happened.

Anyway, he had beast blood, a martial artifact, and an array diagram. So, he started carving Strength Lightness Array at first.

Emotions flooded his mind when he placed his makeshift brush on the sword blade. Today he could do it on a whim, but when he'd first started, he'd struggled a lot. When he'd joined Heavenly Firmament Sect, he was forced to be a refiner at the start. After spending years doing menial jobs in the Hall of Refinement, he'd stumbled on a jade slip belonging to an Array Master. It wasn't an inheritance, but it contained multiple array diagrams. When he showed it to the sect, they'd made a deal with him, allowing him to join the Hall of Arrays, and in return he submitted that jade slip to the sect.

That's how his journey on the path of array had started.

He sighed in his heart. His previous life was full of struggle and pain, and that's why he had to make this life a comfortable one and live like a lazy immortal.

Anyway, if the chance came, he should get that jade slip for himself. Although he planned to walk on the path of alchemy, he should get all the advantages he could get early on.

Getting back to the Strength Lightness Array, it was a two layered array. Lightness From Strength Array made the outer layer, and a standard Qi Absorption Circle Array made the inner layer. When it was carved, the inner array would absorb qi from the cultivator to trigger the array system, and then the outer array would make the heavy artifact lighter and disperse the heaviness into added strength. This was a low-tier Silver Grade array used by many heavy weapon cultivators. It had a fairly simple process.

But he'd overlooked one thing. He was an Array Master in his previous life, so it was easy to craft for him. It might not be the case for others.

Dipping his makeshift brush in the beast's blood, he started drawing the array diagram. Unlike qi cultivators, Ferocious Beasts stored essence energy inside their blood, hence their blood was used in carving arrays. When thick beast blood was used, it could penetrate low level artifacts without damaging them. That's how a carving was made. When a cultivator poured their qi or used an external power source to pour qi, these carvings would be activated and start functioning.

However, beast blood could only carve temporary arrays. It would vanish with wear and tear, and if one wanted to carve a permanent array, then they would need to find someone who could carve using their metal qi. In fact, anyone could use a converter talisman to change their own qi into metal qi, but it failed to match the quality and efficiency of a metal qi array cultivator. Only a metal qi array cultivator could carve a high-level array and bring the true might of the array carver to bear.

Slowly and methodically, he carved the inner array on the sword. Lack of practice almost made him miss a line a couple of times, but with his divine sense guiding him, he didn't fail. When he'd practiced this array in his previous life, he had failed hundreds of times without the guidance of a divine sense. He'd sucked at it first, but he was known for his perseverance, and he finally succeeded.

Those were good days. He'd had many friends back then.

"Done." When the last paint stroke appeared on the sword, it shone with a bright blue color and then the red blood vanished inside the sword, replaced by a thin red line that could only be seen when one looked carefully.

A small dainty hand reached forward and wiped sweat from his brow. Of course, it was Fei'er.

"Thanks." Smiling, he dipped his makeshift brush in the beast blood and started carving the outer array, Lightness From Strength Array. He had to be a little more careful about this one because he had to match the source points for the whole array to work. Two Layered Arrays worked by connecting two arrays with a particular set of source points.

Every array had source points. Like an interface, they acted as connecting points between two arrays. They could also be used to for safe passage in the case of large array formations, or they could be used to deactivate an array given one was familiar with the array. Arrays also had power points, and these points acted as gateway to heaven and earth's essence energy, or any external source like a cultivator's qi or a Qi Stone.

Before drawing the outer array, he had to analyze and match the source points with the inner array. Matching only two would make this whole array functional, but that would be a low-quality version. He didn't do low quality, so he had to match five points perfectly. Without divine sense, this task was very difficult, so only high-level array cultivators worked on Layered Arrays of any type. Two Layered Arrays were still simple, but for Three or Four Layered things turned complicated. Even with divine sense, people tended to fail. Only after reaching Array Master Realm could one carve a Four Layered Array.

Anyway, that was in the future. Currently, carving a Two Layered Array was as simple as eating meat for Wei.

The sword in his hand shuddered when he put down the last paint stroke, and he held his breath. Now was the time when he would know if he succeeded.

Or not.

Chapter 29

Danger

Thirty minutes letter, Li Wei finished the outer layer of the Strength Lightness Array by matching the five source points between the inner and outer layer arrays. Dazzling blue light swept across the whole room when the last source point matched, and the sword hummed lightly as the red carvings penetrated the steel, leaving behind only a faint mark of an array.

Unlike the sword, which seemed to come to life, Wei wore a strained expression. Now he remembered how taxing it was to carve a simple array in the initial days of array carving. Placing both hands on the metal floor, he moved into a lotus position and closed his eyes. Although he carried the experience of an Array Master, it didn't mean he could start carving high-tier arrays right away. Experience was one thing, but muscle memory and mental fortitude was another. As he lacked practice with this body, he'd had to rely heavily on his divine sense, and it drove his mental fortitude nuts.

"Young master, are you finished? Come and eat," Fei'er said in a soft voice as she flipped the meat on the metal skewer.

Wei studied his first creation of this life and sighed regretfully in his heart. Too bad he couldn't test it, as he had yet to cultivate any qi.

But Fei'er had wood qi. She could test the might of this weapon. "Fei'er. Come here and push some qi inside this sword."

She stared at him with dumb eyes while flipping the meat.

"What? Come on!" He threw his hands in the air. "You cultivate, so this should be easy to you."

"Young master, I know nothing other than the cultivation technique. Big sister told me nothing but that."

Wei wanted to smack Tang Sia's forehead. Why did she only impart a half-baked cultivation art?

"Leave it. I'll impart a new cultivation art to you. You can practice it once you reach Foundation Realm," Wei said dejectedly.

"Can I change it at Foundation Realm?"

"Yes, you can. But only when you breakthrough to Foundation Realm and before you cultivate layer one Foundation Realm. In Refinement Realm, you only cultivate pure qi, so you can't change it until you reach

Foundation Realm. After that, your qi will be converted into wood qi. Once that happens, changing a cultivation technique is impossible, unless you want to start from scratch."

A smile as innocent as a five-year-old's popped on her face. "As you wish, young master. I'll practice this new cultivation art."

Putting the sword down, he moved closer to the stove and started eating slowly. Eating roasted meat and enjoying a calm chat with Fei'er. What else could replenish his mental energy faster? Half an hour later, his mental fortitude had recovered, so he started carving the first array on the second sword. He would have liked to wait a bit longer, but the beast blood would lose its potency soon, and he had to finish before it did.

Strength Expanding Array. It was a low-tier Silver Grade array carved using two layers: Qi Absorption Circle Array and Strength Enhancing Array. He could have used a Power Enhancement Array instead of the Strength Enhancing Array to increase his battle powers by a couple layers, but he didn't. This sword was heavy as a boulder, and it would serve another purpose for him. Generally, qi cultivators liked lightweight swords because they lacked physical strength to handle heavy swords—like Fei'er who couldn't even swing it properly. But he wasn't a pure qi cultivator. With his Earth Grade Physical Root, he would have a better path with body cultivation, so he had to choose a heavy sword. Once he could imbue some qi into the sword, it would do wonders, as this array would increase its physical strength by a great margin.

And what qi cultivators despised was a weapon that could hit hard. They could protect their bodies by imbuing them with qi, but in front of absolute strength it was meaningless.

"Young master, why are you smiling like a depraved person? Are you thinking about some maiden?" Fei'er asked while chewing on a meat piece. Contradictory to her thin figure, she was a glutton.

He rolled his eyes. In fact, he had smug thoughts, but not about a girl. "Fei'er, be a good girl and don't disturb me while I'm carving arrays."

She giggled and went back to her stitching.

Half an hour later, a bright blue light shone through the room again, and the second sword hummed while red lines spread through its surface. But Wei wasn't in any condition to check on it. Instead, he closed his eyes and lay on his back, resting his mind to replenish his mental fortitude.

Array carving was a tough job.

Half a day later, he opened his eyes and spotted Fei'er sitting next to him, staring at him with worried eyes.

"Don't worry, I was just exhausted. Let's go. We have to get out of here." Now that the arrays were carved, he had nothing left to do here. It was time to leave. But before that, he had to collect something from the room. Heading toward the back area of the metal room, he searched for a hole inside it. It had been mentioned in the information he'd received from the worms. It had mentioned something about a metal token as a reward for the challenger.

A bright gold and black metal token fell into his hand when he pushed his hand inside that opening. It was a square token with a Qi Transformation Array carved on it. Along with it, a stack of approximately one hundred fruits came out. They were all Yin Yang Fruits, bean-sized with half gold and half black. They exuded a rotten and a sweet smell at the same time. He had seen this fruit in his previous life, and it was quite costly.

Wow! He was super rich now. Even selling ten fruits could bring him riches equal to the Li clan's yearly profit.

Awesome!

Divine Refinement City was surely a super city. Although Qi Transformation Array wasn't something top class, it required a lot of special ingredients to carve on an artifact, and that artifact also had to be top class. Until he reached his previous success in array carving, this would definitely help him with lower-level cultivation. While cultivating, it would gather essence energy and convert it into pure qi to help his cultivation. It was a priceless Gold Grade artifact and no one in the Mortal Realm would know anything about it. Even in the Martial Realm, only personal disciples of sect masters would have something extravagant like this.

"What a shiny thing, young master. Can you give it to me? I want to make some ornament out of it."

Wei wanted to smack that lass's head. Did she even know what those sect disciples would do to her if they know what she had in mind? It was a Silver Grade artifact, not a shiny fake stone people used for making trinkets.

"Wait until I find something better for you." Her words reminded him of a stone mine that would be found in a few years. It had a Golden Emerald buried inside it. The gem didn't have any special properties and only helped one in slowly healing their meridians, but it was stunningly beautiful, and princesses and noble ladies of the Mortal Realm went mad for it. It sold for quite a lot at auction and even attracted attention from female sect disciples as well. After all, what girl didn't like to own a shiny beautiful stone?

Maybe he should take a trip there and mine that stone before anyone else. It wasn't a dangerous place either.

"Let me clear these threads for us." Saying this, he extended his hands and touched the threads.

Zap! Zap! Zap! Threads shot into his fingers.

Chapter 30

Yin Yang Threads

Li Wei felt like thousands of blades pierced his skin when he touched the black and golden threads. They invaded his body from all over, and he couldn't do anything. Before touching these threads, he was confident he could move them away, but his confidence shattered like a glass falling on a paved surface.

He flopped on the hard surface and grabbed his head.

It was something outside his expectations, and painful. Consider someone putting a thread through your finger and taking it out of your leg, and that was happening in every inch of his body. Those threads were running amok inside him. And the irony, there were no wounds, not a single drop of blood outside of his body.

"Ahhhhhhh." Crying, he rolled on the ground, ignoring the cold metal tearing his robe. The first golden thread that had entered his body shot into his right hand and vanished. Then the first black thread vanished inside his left hand, and like this every other thread started vanishing inside his hands.

"No!" With every thread shooting for his hands, his insides tore apart, and it felt like someone crushed his body, revived him, and then crushed him again.

It was inhuman, and he couldn't stop it.

"T-h-" His tongue twisted inside his mouth. He was losing consciousness, and the pain was crushing his soul. Even when his soul had broken into pieces, he didn't feel this much pain. It was a hundred times worse than when he'd refined his own body in a thousand-degree lit furnace.

"Young master!" Someone dropped next to him and shook his body, but he had no strength to answer.

The pain was overwhelming him, and he knew he was going to die.

However, he couldn't even die. The pain just kept increasing, and he was going mad. In just few breaths, it became unbearable to the extent that he wanted to cut his hands off rather than endure it another moment.

He slapped his hands on the ground, trying to do something about the pain, but he could do nothing. It kept coming to him, wave after wave.

No, he couldn't take it anymore, else he would go mad.

Somehow, he raised his wobbling body and steadied his legs firmly on the metal ground.

Fei'er reached forward to help him, but he pushed her away and ran toward the metal wall and slammed his head on it with all his might.

However, it didn't comfort him. Instead, the pain increased and overwhelmed the pain from his crash. He wanted to bleed and fall unconscious, but the pain didn't let him. It was tearing him from the inside, but he had no way to stop it.

Why couldn't someone just cut his hands off instead?

"F-e-r . . ." He wanted to tell her to cut off his hands, but he couldn't even speak a word.

Minutes passed, maybe hours, but the pain didn't stop. He rolled on the ground endlessly, and when he couldn't he just lay there with white pupils, unable to mutter a single word, his chest heaving in an erratic motion.

But he didn't die.

Then it abruptly stopped. It finally stopped after the last black thread entered his left hand.

There was no more pain.

As if it was an illusion, he couldn't sense those threads inside his body at all.

But how could it be?

Heaving heavily, he spread his divine sense down his arms and checked their condition. But there was no change. They were the same as before.

Did they enter his dantian?

Sending his divine sense out again, he checked on his dantian, but he found nothing. Those worm-bodies lay there motionless, and there was no trace of those threads.

Then where the heck did those threads go?

He got up and looked around and found Fei'er curled in a fetus position, crying silently.

"Fei'er." He touched her head and shook her a little.

"Young master." Crying loud, she dived into his arms. Her tiny hands wrapped around his back, and she wet his chest with tears.

An indispensable feeling covered his heart. He rubbed the stupid lass's back lightly, but he had a tear in his eyes.

"Fei'er don't cry. I'm all right."

But her sobs deepened, and she cried like someone had died in her close family.

He didn't know what to do with this emotional lass, so he just patted her back.

After ten minutes, she pulled away and glared at him. "Did you play a prank on me?" Young master had vanished from her greeting, and that meant she was pissed off. Badly. "Why were you shouting like someone was cutting you apart while your body was unharmed?"

What could he say to her? His gaze dropped to his arms, but there was nothing about them. Their internal structure had shredded apart, but everything had healed like nothing had happened at all.

System: Information interface detected.

Downloading Yin Yang Hand Divine Art.

A divine art?

Chapter 31

Yin Yang Hand Divine Art

Yin Yang Hand Divine Art

Li Wei glanced at the words appearing in his mind. What kind of divine art was this?

When he muttered in his mind, a stream of information flew at him, the details of the cultivation method of Yin Yang Hand Divine Art.

For a moment, he didn't understand where it came from. Then he realized it must have come from the mysterious "system." When he'd gotten Five Elemental Way Qi Cultivation Art, it had displayed same words about information interface. This should be something related to the cultivation art.

He had to read more on this. "Fei'er. Give me some time to adjust to my condition. Then we will go."

She nodded.

Closing his eyes, he sat on the metallic floor inside the now empty room and focused on the information. Before he closed his eyes, he spotted Fei'er pulling out her needle and gray robes.

Damn the lass.

Ignoring her, he focused on the information coming to his mind.

Lightning bolts shot across his mind when he read the next few lines.

This was a divine art, and not a martial skill. But why was there a divine art in the Inheritance Chamber of Divine Thunder City? It should give out martial skills.

A divine art was like a martial skill, but there weren't many in the world. While one could learn hundreds of martial skills, one might only find one or two divine arts in their whole life. It also had impossible thresholds when compared to martial skills. Martial skills had low starting thresholds. Like his One Sword Strike. It could be learned from Refinement Realm, but all the divine arts he had seen required one to reach higher cultivation realms. The minimum he had seen was Houtian Realm. Fortunately, the Blood Essence Body jade slip had its own divine arts mentioned, and they were innate arts that he would learn when he reached a new realm and completed a constellation. That was one of the main reasons he'd practiced this cultivation art in this life.

This divine art was an outer art that he could practice after meeting its requirements.

A thin film of perspiration formed over his neck when he remembered how much he'd had to suffer to obtain a fire type divine art in his previous life. It had high requirements. To initiate the divine art, he'd had to peel his own skin back and stuff his muscles with fire type material. It was another painful period of his life. If it wasn't for Wang Zia, he wouldn't have gone through that torture.

Would he suffer something similar if he wanted to practice this?

No way. He would rather choose not to learn this if he had to go through the same torture once again. He had already suffered enough torture when the Soul Stone fused with his soul, and then when the golden and black threads entered his hands.

It was more than enough. Martial skills were easier and powerful.

Yet he glanced at the requirements to cultivate this divine art.

The first requirement was Yin Yang Hands. That was expected. Thinking about it, it had to do something with the yin yang worms in his dantian and the yin yang threads he'd absorbed.

It had to be the reason.

Reading further, he determined he had met this requirement by absorbing the yin yang threads. After absorbing golden threads in his right hand, it had had become a Yang Hand, and after absorbing black threads in his left hand, it had become a Yin Hand.

So, this was it.

There was a second requirement: Houtian Realm. Once he reached Houtian Realm in his body cultivation, he would be able to cultivate the first stage of Yin Yang Divine Hands. Until then, he could only use its power using external sources.

"Shit! What is this thing?" He couldn't resist shouting when he read its usage.

"Young master, what happened? Are you in pain?" Fei'er dropped her shiny silver needle and bent forward to grab his arm.

He shook his head. "No. I'm just surprised. You continue." And he closed his eyes once again.

This was epic. No, this was a cheat divine art. How could such a divine art exist in this world?

Ying Yang Hands allowed him to control the vitality of living things. His Yang Hand acted as the giver, and the Yin Hand acted as a taker. The information said the gods of life and death combined their power to create this divine art, and once someone mastered it to the highest stage, stage seven, one could become a life and death god themself.

Damn. God of death and life. Would he become immortal then?

His face fell when he read the next line. It was like getting a plate of heavenly food in a restaurant, but then the waiter came to take it away, saying it was a mistake.

He couldn't use this power on himself. Even using it on other humans required him to reach a higher stage. The first stage would only allow him to use it on small plants and animals.

This was way long. For current him, Houtian Realm was like a distant dream. Even with his previous life's knowledge, it would take years to reach that realm.

But there were things that could allow him to use this divine art in a limited capacity, and it required external things to activate it. Something that had both yin and yang in harmony. Something like the hundred Yin Yang Fruits he'd gotten from the secret cache of the worms.

But where should he try it?

"Young master. Are you done? I'm feeling hungry. Let's go. The passage is open." Fei'er tugged his gray sleeve, and he came out of his ruminations.

"Yes, let's head out." They needed to get out of this ruined city and find food if they wanted to live. Analysis and rumination could wait.

Glancing around, he made sure he'd left nothing behind and then walked forward. Now that the threads were gone, the room looked quite plain. It smelled like nothing, nor had it a speck of dust.

But in passing, he spotted some carvings on the side walls. When he looked carefully, they looked like array diagrams. When he compared them to the array diagrams in the Inheritance of Array Master book, they didn't match.

Maybe these diagrams were advanced diagrams. Well, the Inheritance of Array Master was supposed to have three volumes, but two were missing. These diagrams might have some similarities to them.

With that thought, he focused on the first diagram.

He went over to the first diagram on the righthand wall, trying to discern its meaning, but even after spending half an hour studying it, he found nothing that resembled his previous knowledge.

Maybe he was wasting his time.

He sighed in his heart. "Let's go."

System: Scanning complete. Saving new diagrams in database.

Chapter 32

What!

What!

Wei frowned and stopped, his heart beating erratically. The strange system had popped up again in his vision, and it had said something about the diagram.

Opening his eyes, he traced the strange diagram on the metal wall with a fingertip. The metal felt warm around the diagram, and that meant it had some profound meaning. He was just too low level to understand anything.

But what could be so profound that even he, an Array Master, couldn't understand?

Goosebumps spread over his arms when he thought of various possibilities.

"Young master, are we going or not? If you are going to stay, I'll complete the next robe," she hissed.

Black lines popped on Wei's forehead. More because of this little lass than the strange system saying it had done something impossible.

Unable to restrain himself, he flicked her small forehead with his middle finger. Suddenly, he realized she looked fairer than before. It must have been because of the cultivation improvement.

"Ouch, young master." She rubbed her forehead and stepped away from him. "You're bullying me now."

"It will take us some time." He glanced at the diagrams. There were ten, five on each side of the metallic wall. If it took half an hour for each diagram, then they would be here for at least five hours. "Finish your work."

But before he started with anything, he wanted to look at the diagram the system had stored somewhere. Because it was impossible to copy these diagrams. If one wanted to copy them on paper, one had to first understand and comprehend them. Without comprehension, the diagrams wouldn't get copied. That's why the Inheritance of Array Master book was open to all who had basic knowledge of arrays. In fact, many people had tried to copy array diagrams from the book and take them away, but they'd failed to draw a single line on paper. His master used to call it Comprehension Lock. One had to learn and comprehend the essence of the diagram before copying it.

That's why he doubted the system's ability to copy the diagram. But if it had, then that would be awesome. It might bring unending benefits in the future. Once, in his previous life, he'd met a Tea Master by accident. He was his senior brother Jiang Jia's master. They'd hit off, and the Tea Master had told him about how he came to learn the Art of Tea Making. In his childhood, he'd roamed an ancient tomb outside of Fragrance Herb City and he'd stumbled upon a jade slip that had taught him tea making. At the time, he didn't know what it meant, but when he grew up and saw a Three Leaf Tea Plant for the first time, he'd regained the knowledge to become a Tea Master. In a mere five years, he'd risen to fame as a Tea Master. Even high-level cultivators had to show him respect if they wanted to taste heavenly tea from his abode.

Sipping that tea, Wei wished he'd also gained some knowledge about tea making and wine making. That would have been a perfect for a lazy lifestyle. In fact, if he learned it in this life, it would fit perfectly with his plan of being a lazy immortal. Now that he thought about it, he knew when and where the man would meet with the beggar. Maybe he could take that jade slip for himself.

Well, he wouldn't steal the jade slip, just learn things from it and leave it there for that Tea Master to find it in the future.

He tapped on the metal wall with his fingers, absorbing the little heat coming out of the metal.

Yes, that sounded like a good plan. After getting out of here, he would find that jade slip.

So, if the system had stored this strange diagram somewhere, he might find it useful in the future.

Before that thought vanished from his mind, a diagram popped up in his mind. And damn, that diagram looked legit. Seriously legit. He could feel the warmth coming out of it, and when he concentrated, he could deduce the essence of the diagram slightly. It gave him the same feeling he got from the Inheritance of Array Masters.

Dizziness overcame him. This was impossible. How could the system copy the essence of the diagram? It must have been some trick, so he compared the two diagrams.

Holy heavens. It was exactly the same diagram. This meant he could access the Inheritance of Array Masters and store it in the system. That would save him a lot of time, because everyone had to earn slots to read the Inheritance of Array Masters. If he added up the total hours, he'd spent reading the Inheritance of Array Masters in his previous life, it would've come close to two hundred hours.

And what was two hundred hours in two hundred years of life?

Nothing more than a fart.

With this system, he could store all the big books on the materials and herbs he had seen in the sect libraries. Wouldn't that be awesome? That would save so much time for him in future.

In fact, he would be treated as a prodigy in the sect if he could remember everything he read. Of course, once his divine sense improved, he wouldn't need to remember it as it would store everything he read once. But that would be only possible once he reached a higher level of cultivation. Even though he had a divine soul right now, it was quite small for remembering things in one go.

"Young master. I have a question. Did you store the golden and black threads in your body? Is your cultivation art related to those things?" Fei'er asked when he moved to the second strange diagram.

"Kind of." He moved to the second diagram.

System: Scanning initiated. Remaining time: Thirty minutes.

This was good. He just had to spend some time around the diagrams, and they would be stored in his system.

A smile played on his lips unknowingly. This was a great advantage. He didn't feel weird about having a strange system with him anymore.

"What do you mean, kind of? Are you a worm now? Can you shoot those threads from your fingers, like a spider man?"

His brow furrowed. "No. I can't shoot the threads from my fingers." He couldn't understand what this little lass wanted from him.

"So, those threads are useless for you. Can you give them to me? I can use them to stitch your robe." She sounded dreamy. "A gray robe with golden threads. You'll look super handsome, young master. Please give me those threads." She clapped like a little girl getting a sweet.

Wei sweated all over. This lass was crazy. She wanted threads that could cut one's divine sense to stich his robe. If she could do that, he would be cut into pieces instantly.

Goodness, this lass always came up with weird thoughts. Those threads were heavenly material, and even if he could shoot them from his fingers, he wouldn't give them to her for knitting. That would be such a big waste.

"Fei'er. Shut up and do your work. You are forbidden to speak of the golden threads to anyone. Otherwise, I'll spank your ass red."

Suddenly he heard someone's voice coming from the other side of the metal door, and he shushed Fei'er. There was trouble outside.

Chapter 33

Supreme Inheritance

"Brother Yun, what is this place?" Du Xin asked, observing the dark metal corridor they had stepped into. In the dim light of the candle he held, the corridor looked gloomy and dangerous. The odd smell coming from the corridor made his skin crawl with fear.

Heck, it had been a dangerous journey just to get here. After five intense battles with Three Eyed Bear packs and ten hours in the metal tunnels, they'd finally arrived here. But it had cost them a lot. His five guards were dead.

Tian Yun nodded his small head. "We've reached our destination, brother Xin. This is marked as the Supreme Inheritance Ground on the sacred map. We have finally made through the perils and reached our treasure," he exclaimed loudly, his small chest heaving rapidly.

Du Xin relaxed a little and carefully observed their surroundings. It was a simple metal corridor, and it didn't look like anything special. But Tian Yun had shown him the map, a map to a secret place in the Ancient Ruins outside of Old Martial City. This seemed to be the same place.

But why did it feel so empty?

"Here is the door, brother Xin. See, there's a notch for an array source." Tian Yun tapped on an intricate diagram marked on a metal door that one could easily miss if not looking carefully. If they didn't have the map, they might have passed by this area and never found this place.

Du Xin traced his fingers over the hair-thin line that marked the door.

"Once we get through this door, we will get the supreme inheritance, and we will reach Houtian Realm directly." He laughed. "Brother Yun, we will be unstoppable after that, and Li Chi will beg to warm your bed."

Du Xin's body quivered in excitement. Houtian Realm. What a beautiful world. There was a heaven beyond heaven, and once he became a Houtian Realm cultivator, how would Li clan reject his proposal to marry Li Chi? In fact, even becoming his maid would be her good fortune.

No. He should marry a princess of the State of Zin. Marrying a princess was better than marrying a low-level clan's daughter. And that girl wasn't even a real Li clan member. A bastard named Sua had sold himself to the Li clan by marrying their patriarch's daughter, and so he became a Li clan member, but Li Chi was his third concubine's offspring. So, she was a low-level girl after all.

Should he even take her as a maid, or just fuck her once and then throw her out?

"Brother Xin. Take out the low-quality Qi Stones you brought with you. We need them to activate the array to open the door," Tian Yun said.

Du Xin frowned. "Brother Yun, do we really need a low-quality Qi Stone to activate the array?" Tian Yun was his best friend, and he had stolen a sacred document from his clan's treasury. That document had a map to this secret space, but it also mentioned the need of a low-quality Qi Stone for activating the final array, and Tian Yun lacked it, so he'd asked for Du Xin's help. But now that they were here, he hesitated. A low-quality Qi Stone was a precious thing even for Du clan, and Du Xin had only received it after begging to his master Du Su from the main branch. His master doted on him very much, so he'd given him a low-quality Qi Stone.

And now Tian Yun was asking for it to activate an array that might not work at all.

"Brother Xin, this is from a sacred document. How can it be false? Once we obtain the inheritance, we'll be rolling in Qi Stones? Even the emperor will have to show you respect after you reach Marrow Cleansing Realm. Why are you worrying about one low-quality Qi Stone?"

Du Xin felt tickles all over his body with the image of the emperor bowing to him. Marrow Cleansing Realm was a major milestone in the cultivator's life, and he would live a most leisurely life in the State of Zin.

"But . . ."

"Brother Xin, we have already sacrificed so much. Let's not dilly dally anymore and receive the inheritance." Tian Yun's voice turned threatening, and Du Xin felt fear touching his mind. Tian Yun was a layer four Refinement Realm cultivator, and he could easily squash Du Xin to death.

"Brother Yun is wise, so I will hand over the low-quality Qi Stone to you." He pulled the stone from his pouch and handed it to Tian Yun with a hesitant heart.

⟫⟫⟫ ⟪⟪⟪

Li Wei pressed his ear to the cold metal wall, listening in on the conversation on the other side. Surprisingly, once he placed his ear against the wall, he could hear even their ragged breaths from this side. They were exhausted, and their vitality was not in an optimal shape.

"Du and Tian clan," he muttered, brushing his nose. The metal wall smelled too fresh for his liking. In his initial years in Heavenly Firmament Sect, he'd worked with metal day and night, and he'd developed nausea around it. One of his teachers, an apprentice refiner, had told him that refinement wasn't his path, so he'd stepped on the path of arrays, never to look back.

Fei'er too stepped closer and put her ear to the wall, but by her annoyed look, she didn't seem to hear anything substantial.

This was the effect of body cultivation.

"I hear someone outside. What are they doing here?" she asked, sounding a little afraid.

He smirked. "They are here to die." His fingers traced over his sword hilt, rousing his battle intent.

"They deserve to die," Fei'er clenched her fingers and replied bashfully.

Du and Tian clans were Li clan's arch enemies in every city they operated in. Du clan had even destroyed Li clan in his previous life, so he wouldn't go easy on them. Especially after finding out that Du clan abducted his cousin sister, Li Chi. For Chi'er, he'd vowed in his heart to destroy them from the Mortal Realm. Although he'd destroyed them in his previous life, doing it again would soothe his heart.

Quickly, he slipped his divine sense through the metal door and gauged their cultivation level. They were Qi Refinement Realm layer three and layer four.

He could easily take them with his body Refinement Realm cultivation.

"It sounds like Du Xin. That lecher is pestering elder sister Chi constantly," Fei'er whispered, her face turning red.

Although he didn't know who exactly had abducted Chi'er in his previous life, he'd had a gut feeling it had something to do with this bastard Du Xin. Although he didn't have any particular attachment to the Li clan, and he hated that bastard Li Tang for trying to kill him, he would still take revenge for Chi'er. It was Du clan that had started trouble for Chi'er, so he could save her from some trouble before he left the clan behind. Even if he couldn't save the whole Li clan, he would try his best to save Chi'er.

Yes, he should do that.

When he heard Du Xin and Tian Yun's plan, he smirked. They didn't know they were walking into a trap. Sure, this room held an inheritance, but how could a human gain an inheritance of divine beasts? And that too by going through yin yang threads that could cut even one's divine sense into pieces.

Was it a joke for them?

With the Qi Stone they possessed, he could even set up an Essence Gathering Array to help Fei'er's cultivation. For himself, he could use the metallic token he'd gotten from the Inheritance Chamber, as it had a Qi Conversion Array already embedded in it.

So, he had to open the door from the inside before those stupid people used the low-quality Qi Stone. The door was locked by a simple Bronze Grade Two Stage Lock Array from inside. For him, it was easier than taking a breath.

Tapping on the source points, he activated the key, and the metal door slid open without making any noise, like it was oiled regularly.

The door opening was so sudden for the tall youth standing on the other side that he stumbled forward, still clutching the Qi Stone in his right hand.

It was Tian Yun, a local tyrant of Old Martial City. Wei knew him very well, because he was one of the people that had forced him and his friends to hide in the Ancient Ruins a few months back. Wei had lost a couple of good friends trying to find a way out.

They shared a deep enmity, and that bastard deserved to die.

Without giving Tian Yun any chance, Wei snatched the Qi Stone from his hand and threw it toward Fei'er. "Keep it safe."

Tian Yun frowned while trying to firm his feet on the ground. "Li Wei, you are courting your death." He flapped his hands in the air, but he couldn't regain his balance.

Wei sneered and attacked with a straight punch on Tian Yun's nose.

Tian Yun tried to jerk his head aside, but Wei's attack was too fast for him. While falling forward, it was impossible for him to move his face away. Even a Foundation Realm cultivator couldn't do it, and he was only in the Refinement Realm's early layers.

What could he do?

Wei felt something squishy connect with his knuckles, and then something warm gushed along the gaps between his knuckles, and he heard a deadly scream coming out of Tian Yun's mouth.

"Li Wei, you are courting your death! White Tiger Metal Palm!" Du Xin attacked with a palm, and before Wei could react, Fei'er had leaped in between him and the attack.

Shit! His heart nearly jumped out of his rib cage when he spotted Du Xin's palm reaching Fei'er.

Chapter 34

Fei'er in Danger

Li Wei's heart jumped into his throat when Du Xin attacked Fei'er with a metal palm attack. His palm turned metallic gray, and it shot toward Fei'er, and Wei wasn't in position to stop it before it hit Fei. Du Xin had acted sneakily while Wei turned Tian Yun's face into a pulp.

That was a mistake. He shouldn't have lowered his guard. If Du Xin injured Fei'er, Wei would regret it for a long, long time.

Pushing his leather shoes on the metal ground, he leaped toward Fei'er, intending to push her away. But he quickly realized he couldn't reach her before the palm attack landed. He lacked cultivation to increase his speed, nor had he any martial skill that would allow him to travel faster.

Damn. Lack of cultivation haunted him like a nightmare.

"Explode." He shouted inside his mind, burning twenty blood pearls. There was no other option but to burn his blood pearls. If not, Fei'er might lose her life today. That palm attack was aimed at her throat, and although she was higher in cultivation, she lacked a defensive martial skill.

Once this was over, he should teach her an arsenal of skills to protect herself.

Power burst through his body, tearing the small blood vessels around his Yangming meridian. It rushed through his meridians and provided his legs a large boost that was unrivaled.

Like an arrow, his body shot forward and his punch hit Du Xin, who had dared to lay hands on Fei'er. Du Xin's chest caved in, but Wei had been too late by a fraction of a moment. Although his punch connected before Du Xin's, his palm attack still landed on Fei'er's shoulder.

Fei'er's face went pale, and she screamed in agony. Her fragile body wobbled backward, and she dropped on her back, powerless. Maybe dead.

Blood rushed to Wei's eyes. "You bastard!" he shouted and burned twenty more blood pearls.

Power rampaged through his body, destroying everything in its path. Blood vessels bled and ruptured under pressure, but it gave him an unending supply of power to trample an elephant.

Du Xin's face turned grim, and he spurted blood from his mouth. "Li Wei. If you kill me, my master will find you and kill you. Let me go, and we will treat this like it never happened."

Wei chuckled. "Even if your master comes today, he can't save you from me."

Du Xin spat another mouthful of blood, his face turning deathly pale. Turning backward, he tried to run out of the metal door, but how could Wei let him live? With the new power surge, he punched Du Xin's back, targeting the same spot he had hit from the front. His punch pierced through Du Xin's back and crushed his ribs like an elephant crushing a human head below its feet. It was as easy as that.

Before he died, Du Xin looked over his shoulder. He wanted to say something, but he couldn't. His life was over.

"You— What did you do?" Tian Yun shouted in fear.

"Now it's your turn." Wei glared at Tien Yun. That bastard was responsible for this mess too. He'd brought Du Xin here, and that's why Fei'er was in danger. He deserved to die.

But before that, he had to take care of Fei'er.

Squatting, he checked her pulse. Thanks to the heavens, her pulse was fine. Her face was pale, and her right shoulder was a bloody mess. Thank goodness she had lost consciousness, or she would be in a lot of pain. But she was bleeding, and if he didn't treat her quickly, she might die or suffer an immense injury that may take a lot of time to heal. From his own pouch, he withdrew some Blood Nourishing Powder and fed it to Fei'er with water. As she alone had access to the storage ring, he kept a pouch with himself in case of troubles. That was becoming useful in this situation. Maybe he should keep a pill or two with him as well.

Maybe he should cultivate qi and keep the storage ring with him.

When her breath stabilized a little, he got up and stared at Tian Yun. With a pulped nose, he looked like a bloody ghost. He quivered when Wei stared at him.

"Li Wei, let me go, and we will close this matter. You don't know who you are messing with." He spat blood when he talked. "Just let me go, and I'll ask my father to send you some compensation. Let's be sworn brothers and finish this, okay?" He panicked as Wei stepped forward.

Wei halted. Pain pulsed through his heart. Burning blood pearls gave him immense power for a short time, but afterward the power tormented his body from the inside. If he didn't sit down and recuperate, it might damage his body beyond repair. Right now, he was standing up with willpower, and he could feel the power vanishing from his body.

However, if he dropped right now, he would hand over his and Fei'er's lives to this bastard Tian Yun, and that he wouldn't let happen.

"Explode." Ten more blood pearls exploded in his body, and he shot forward like a cheetah. Ten was his limit. Any more, and he risked permanent damage to his body. His sword passed through Tian Yun's throat, showering Wei in blood.

Wei chuckled. A mad chuckle. In his previous life, he'd always remained on the soft side. But no more. So, he swung his sword and sliced Tian Yun's and Du Xin's heads from their bodies.

Enemies could come back from death, but enemies with missing heads wouldn't.

Bending down, he checked both of their pockets and found a Lesser Healing Pill and a low-quality Qi Stone along with an old parchment.

His eyes were blurring, and he could feel his blood vessels rupturing throughout his body. The power surge he'd borrowed from his blood pearls was wreaking havoc inside his body, and he had to sit down and cultivate Blood Essence Body to heal himself.

If not, he might lose his consciousness and suffer worse than just a few injuries.

But before that, he had to make sure Fei'er would survive. Opening her soft lips again, he stuffed the Lesser Healing Pill in her mouth and helped her gulp it down. It was a common low-tier Bronze Grade pill found in the Mortal Realm, and it was so-so in quality.

But it was all he had.

After making sure her breathing had stabilized, he sat next to her in the lotus position and started cultivating Blood Essence Body. His blood was in turmoil, and he wasn't sure if he could make it out of this with his cultivation intact.

Chapter 35

Back to Old Martial City

Li Wei walked down the forest road, carrying Fei'er over his shoulder. Her fragile figure shook when he jumped over a tiny crevice.

"I'm sorry. I'll be careful next time." He patted the tiny head resting over his shoulder.

Stopping a bit, he wiped sweat from his forehead with a gray handkerchief. This time he didn't feel disdain when he looked at the cloth. Instead, guilt surged through his mind. Because of him, Fei'er had been poisoned. That metal palm attack contained a profound poison, and it had already affected Fei'er. If he had kept an eye on Du Xin, he couldn't have attacked her.

"Just hang on for one more day, and we will find something to treat you." He said with determination. No matter what, he would find a solution for Fei'er's problem. For the last two days, he'd carried her over his shoulder, and even with his cultivation it was growing difficult. At his current pace, he would at least need two more days to reach Old Martial City. If he didn't take a break every half an hour, he might get there a couple hours earlier, but time was of the essence. He had to find a cure for the Nerve Blocking Metal Poison Du Xin had used. It was a peculiar poison, and that bastard had coated his palm before attacking Fei'er. It had penetrated through her blood and sealed her dantian so she couldn't gain an ounce of qi to heal herself. It was also corroding her body from the inside, and if not given an antidote soon, she would die.

If it wasn't for the Blood Nourishing Powder and Lesser Healing Pill, he'd given her, she might have already died. If he could access the storage ring, he had a Blood Revitalizing Pill in there that he could use, but he couldn't access it. He could have stayed back and cultivated to the first layer of qi Body Refinement Realm to access the storage ring, but staying might have caused more trouble for both of them. For starters, he didn't know if any strong cultivators had followed the Du and Tian clan youngsters. If there were any, that would have meant death for both of them.

He had to be fast, or the poison might leave her crippled or dead.

That thought almost made his soul jump out of his body. If she died, he would regret it the rest of his life. The same regret he'd suffered in his previous life.

No, he couldn't let her die. He had to find an antidote to save her from this poison, and that meant reaching out to Old Martial City's Du clan. If they had this poison, they should have the antidote. He hadn't wanted to return to Old Martial City right away, but now he had to go back and find a solution, so he'd rushed out of the Inheritance Chamber and took a path leading to the city. Too bad, the path he'd chosen had let him out on the other side of the Ancient Ruins, so he'd had to take a long detour to get back on the correct path.

Out of the whole ordeal, only one good thing had happened. He'd broken into the fourth layer of body Refinement Realm because of his consumption of blood pearls. Currently, he had three hundred and ten blood pearls. Considering the brutal method of burning his blood pearls had worked twice, it was tempting to use it again and again, but he knew that would have a detrimental effect on his cultivation. This insane method of powering up had left a few wounds inside his body that were taking days to heal, and he couldn't try this power up again before healing them all.

Maybe he shouldn't try it again at all.

His ears caught the sound of horses rushing toward him, so he left the path and headed deeper into the forest. After running for ten minutes, he lay Fei'er down in a comfortable position and climbed the tallest tree he found to check on the people going toward Old Martial City. Only a few people used horses, as they were expensive to maintain, so he was curious about the rich people traveling toward the city.

First, he spotted a cloud of dust, and then strong auras invaded his divine sense's range. There were a lot of peak Refinement Realm people, and five people who had even reached Foundation Realm. Although they were nothing compared to old him, who had far surpassed these ants, this group was quite strong for Old Martial City. Seeing their dark blue clothes, his forehead broke in black lines. They were Li clan people, and the person leading them was his maternal grandfather, Li Shua.

Why was he coming to Old Martial City? Did something happen while Wei was gone? Beside Li Shua, Li Ti rode on a brown horse, and they all seemed to be in a hurry.

Suddenly, all of them stopped and turned their attention toward the tree Wei sat on.

Did they notice him? That couldn't be possible. He was almost a hundred yards away. It was impossible for them to notice him without divine sense, and the strongest warrior was only in Foundation Realm. Then how could they notice him without divine sense?

Li Ti pointed at the tree Wei sat on, and they changed direction, spurring their horses to a gallop.

Wei knew he couldn't run away from them. Horses were always faster than mortal men.

A strange, itchy feeling crawled under Wei's skin. How the heck had these people found him?

But whatever, he had to greet them. Running away with Fei'er on his back was impossible. Even if he could run away, if they were coming for him, they would find his tracks after all.

As he dropped from branch to branch, his forehead itched in pain. He had a bad feeling about this. He couldn't guess the outcome of this event, as it hadn't happened in his previous life. In fact, so far only five percent of the events he'd experienced in his previous life had come to pass. So, he couldn't even take advantage of his future knowledge.

By the time he dropped on the ground, the Li clan men had reached the tree. They stopped, seeing him standing next to a girl.

Li Shua frowned, seeing him there, and there was hostility in his deep black eyes.

This would not go smoothly.

Chapter 36

Lesser Isolation Array

Li Tang gloated when he peeked at the transparent jade bottle lying in the cloth pouch attached to his dark blue robe's waist. It held two Foundation Refirming Pills, and those were his path to greatness. Once he digested them, no one could stop him. The injuries he'd suffered from necrosis should get cleared out as well.

That was it. His path to living. If he didn't have these two pills, he might only survive for a year or two, but now he would live on until his grandchildren died of old age.

Thanks to his brother and that brat's sacrifice, he had gotten his fortuitous encounter.

He sighed in his heart. If he could get the third pill from the pit and the one from their treasury vault, that would be perfect. He could start taking them right away.

But no worries. They would come to him soon. The old haggler wouldn't be eating the pill he gave to Li Ti. That stupid father of his would save it in the treasury for some future extraordinary descendant. That old man was frustratingly difficult. Li Tang had begged him for that pill for months, but he never took it out. That old man was hateful.

Li Tang chuckled with lots of evil intentions.

Soon. Soon enough he would break into layer seven of Foundation Realm, and then he would take both the pills by force, and then nothing could stop him from reaching layer nine of Foundation Realm. After that, who would dare to stop him?

Du clan?

Those nasty bastards only had one person in layer seven of Foundation Realm. What could a layer seven do faced with layer nine him?

Nothing. Once he got his hand on those two pills, he would make Du clan roll out of all the cities Li clan controlled. Especially Old Martial City, as they had found a rare plant in the forest. With more money, he would get more pills and soon enter Blood Baptizing Realm.

Then he could take over the entire city.

That sounded like a plan.

He was pulled out of his thought process when the clan door opened, so he zipped his pouch carefully. Despite putting the two pills he had in a jade glass bottle, he couldn't take the risk showing the bottle to his father or brother. That would bring him unending trouble.

"Elder brother Tang, look who I found. Our clan's benefactor, Li Wei. That kid didn't die, brother." Li Ti smiled as he entered the main hall, and a youth in gray clothes walked behind him. The youth had his eyes fixed on Li Tang, and he could feel the cold intent emitting from the eyes.

Li Tang felt his blood boiling and heart squeezing. How could this pest be alive after the talisman he'd used to kill him? Something was off about him. And how did he meet their father? Did he tell Li Shua about Li Jia's death?

Cold sweat broke out under his skin. If his father found out about him killing his younger brother, he would kill Li Tang. His father loved Li Jia a lot and had his hopes fixed on him.

"Grandfather, I survived thanks to uncle Tang who fought with the fierce beast and let me escape. If it wasn't for him, I'd have died long ago," Li Wei answered in a calm tone, but Li Tang saw the cold light flashing through Li Wei's eyes.

Fuck this motherfucker. This kid had to die as soon as possible. Otherwise, how would he, Li Tang, reach the supreme existence?

※※※ ※※※

By the time Li Wei settled in his old room, two maidservants had carried the unconscious Fei'er to his room and placed her on the new soft bed lying in the corner. His shabby room looked odd with a luxury like that in it. But it was for Fei'er. He didn't care for such things. Two hundred years of cultivation had taught him endurance, and he would endure until he reached immortality.

Immortality. What a beautiful word. Once he reached that unfathomable cultivation level, he would roam around the world, tasting the best wine out there and making heavenly teas for his friends and family. What could be better than that?

Sitting on the rough ground next to Fei'er, he lifted her soft wrist and checked her pulse. It was as stable as clear water, so there was no danger for now. At least his grandfather had fulfilled his promise, and she'd had a comfortable ride back home. At his request, he'd let Fei'er ride in his daughter-in-law's carriage and come back comfortably.

That was nearly a wild ride. Wei wiped sweat from his forehead. When he'd met with his grandfather and a bunch of Li clan's elders, he was shocked to his core. They'd never treated him well before, but surprisingly his grandfather had behaved courteously this time. He'd even asked Wei if he was doing okay.

Apparently, Li Ti, his other uncle, had said a few good words about him, and he'd become a benefactor to the clan for showing them the location of the pill. His grandfather had even offered him a horse and gave him ten gold to buy medicine for Fei'er.

What changed Li Shua's attitude so much? Could it be the Body Refirming Pill? It couldn't only be that. There had to be another reason. However, he couldn't figure it out on their return journey, as his grandfather was busy talking secretly with other elders. He couldn't even find out the reason behind the Li clan sending a huge force to Old Martial City. But he learned a small piece of the story. That lunatic Li Tang had made up a story and handed only one Body Refirming Pill to Li Ti. He'd even told everyone that Li Jia and Li Wei had sacrificed their lives to let him run away. He'd described both of them as heroes ready to die for the greatness of the clan, and he became a hero in everyone's eyes.

Well, he didn't talk against their claims. He already knew Li Tang would have made up a story, and if he went against it, no one would support him.

And why would they support a young man with no future in cultivation and doubt a strong cultivator in Foundation Realm?

So, he went with the same story. At least it would make his life comfortable for a few days.

Anyway, this was a better outcome. If he'd returned to the city alone, he wouldn't have gone back to the Li clan compound. That would have been dangerous for him and Fei'er. He would have had to take refuge somewhere and then sneakily attack someone from Du clan to get the antidote. But now he didn't have to worry about Li Tang finding him out.

The enemy's den was safest place in times of turmoil.

Now he needed to get back to work. There were some things he'd gotten from Du Xin and Tian Yun but hadn't had time to inspect, so he wanted to check them out. But doing that in a room with the door open was like inviting more troubles. With his grandfather and his uncles roaming around, he didn't dare be careless.

So, he had to use an array to hide himself in broad daylight. With the low-quality Qi Stone, he could draw and run a Lesser Isolation Array around his room. It was a good low-tier Bronze Grade array that could keep things isolated from others. And unless someone with Marrow Cleansing Realm came checking, no one could peek in his room.

"Yes, this sounds good," he muttered and thought about the array diagram. It was an easy diagram and took little time to draw. And with the low-quality Qi Stone, he could run it for years.

Of course, he didn't need that much time, and once he reached qi Foundation Realm, he wouldn't need Qi Stones to charge such low-grade arrays.

Leaving his shabby room, he plucked a small stick from the Azure Dragon Tree. He should start collecting the leaves from this tree once he could activate a storage ring.

Once he reached the Martial Realm, these leaves would fetch him a great deal of money.

But when he walked back in, he realized an issue with his plan. Being an Array Master, he hadn't needed to carve these low-level arrays for many years, so he forgot he needed Ferocious Beast blood to draw the array diagram. Ferocious Beast blood contained life essence, and it would keep the array stable. If he used normal ink, the array would crumble like a thousand-year-old bone.

How could he forget a small thing like this! In the Ancient Ruins, he had killed so many Ferocious Beasts and drew their blood. He could have collected pots after pot of pure blood.

Was he going to fail with such a low-level mistake? Wasn't it a blow to his status as an Array Master in his previous life?

Chapter 37

Green Fang Dagger

Wu Xiodia trudged through the line of Bronze Grade artifacts lying around the table. Flicking his green martial robe's sleeves, he pushed a few aristocrats requested artifacts away. He disdained them. There were brought by an aristocrat in the nearby cities for enhancements, but he had no willpower to work on any of them. Not that his old bones lacked power to carve arrays, but he lacked the mood to work on simple arrays anymore. All these weapons and armor were made from mid-tier Bronze Grade materials. Something he looked down upon. Low-level cultivators treated them as godly weapons, but to him they were equal to dog's shit.

The best weapon was Ice Panther Sabre. That was a godly weapon suitable for a peak-tier Bone Baptization Realm cultivator.

Sighing in his heart, he selected a sword. It was made of Shocking Iron, and the hilt was made of Toughened Steel. A good weapon for Foundation Realm cultivators. Once he carved Power Enhancement Array on this weapon, it could even upgrade the wearer's power by one or two layers while fighting. But it was just a mid-tier Bronze Grade artifact. It wouldn't help him touch the boundary that he remembered from when he crafted Ice Panther Sabre.

"Fucking useless." He threw the weapon back on the pile of weapons lying in the corner. These things were useless. They couldn't hold the array he was trying to craft. They crumbled under the tyrannical strength of the Fierce Beast blood he used. They were useless. With only a few years of his life remaining, he had no hope to reach the next stage in the path of arrays.

If only he had something that matched the quality of the Ice Panther Saber. With that, he could craft another legendary weapon and advance to Array Apprentice realm.

But it seemed like a dream. He feared he would be stuck in Array Carver realm. Array Apprentice, Array Adapt, Array Expert, and Array Master were like an illusion painted by immortals. An illusion that would never come to truth.

His eyes shone with vigor when he thought about the handsome icy blue saber. He'd crafted the best array years back. That was an Array Adapt work. When he'd touched that weapon, it spoke with him like his own child. It was the first Silver Grade weapon he'd received for crafting, and the master cultivator had trusted him to craft a Double

Amplification Array. A Silver Grade array for a Silver Grade weapon. That time, he'd spent weeks just to prepare special blood, practice, and practice more. Finally, when he'd crafted the array on the weapon over the course of twenty hours, he'd felt his mind touching the boundary of the next stage in the path of array.

However, that moment had vanished as soon as it came. Then came the emptiness. Emptiness that occupied his life thereafter. If he didn't get another equivalent material to craft arrays, he might just die of old age with no achievement in the path of arrays.

For a stray cultivator like him, this might be the ceiling he could reach. Unlike array cultivators from sects, he had limited resources and knowledge. All the arrays he obtained were from fortunate encounters and took his own blood and sweat.

If he couldn't reach the next stage, he would probably die with an empty heart.

That was his biggest regret.

"Master Wu, Du clan's young lord Du Fang is waiting for your audience." Wu Xiodia's apprentice, Kun Fu, walked into his crafting room with his head bent down. He seemed afraid, and he should be. Wu Xiodia's temper was well known among his apprentices, and no one dared to disturb him.

Yet this bastard dared to disturb him.

"What, is he more important than the city lord?" Wu Xiodia spurted his anger out. This apprentice had become a pretentious fool, and he should teach him a lesson soon.

"Master Wu, please forgive this impudent apprentice for speaking pretentiously, but young lord Du Fang has brought a high-tier Bronze Grade dagger with him."

"A high-tier Bronze Grade equipment?" Wu Xiodia's face lit up with a gleam, and he quickly flicked his sleeves to step out of the room. Maybe his chance of re-touching that boundary had come. Even it wasn't a low-tier Silver Grade weapon, it was still something he could try the Fierce Beast blood he'd obtained recently out on.

A young man with a short beard and a long nose sat on the couch in the outer hall, wearing a humble expression on his face. He got up as soon as Wu Xiodia entered the room. "Master Wu, please accept this junior's humble greetings."

Wu Xiodia observed the young man's face. Du Fang's demeanor had undergone a large transformation since the last time he'd seen him. His arrogance and vigorous look had gone, replaced by a haggard, weak look.

He must work so hard that he forgot to take proper lunches. But he liked this young junior. He seemed well educated. All the other young lords he'd met previously had an arrogant demeanor that he hated the most.

"Young lord Fang, what do you need from me?" Although he used the words young lord, there was no respect in Wu Xiodia's words. Why would he respect a junior who came to beg for a carving?

"Master Wu. I've recently traveled through an ancient site near Du Long City and obtained this Green Fang Dagger by accident. This is made up of a quality material, and fortunately it doesn't have any array carving on it. I want to ask Master Wu's help to carve a Power Enhancement Array on this dagger, so it can accompany me in the upcoming Du Long City martial tournament."

Wu Xiodia stared at the shiny green dagger in his palm and felt a tyrannical aura coming out of it. Excellent. Its body was made from Poison-Soaked Steel, and the hilt from Green Fang Cobra's fangs. These were both high-tier Bronze Grade refining materials only found in Du Long City. This was it. He could feel the dagger pulsing in his palm. This dagger should hold on to the tyrannical blood he had obtained.

"Junior Fang, this is an excellent dagger, but carving a Power Enhancement Array would be an insult to the weapon."

"Master Wu, what are you suggesting?"

"There is an array that can increase your power twofold, but just . . ." Pausing, he judged Du Fang's reaction. As expected, his face fell and then rose. Young people these days. They didn't understand the meaning behind words easily.

Du Fang shifted his balance to his other leg when he couldn't seem to take the silence anymore. "Master Wu, please enlighten this junior."

"Do you remember the Ice Panther Sabre I carved years back?"

Du Fang's face shifted from worry to delight, like he'd obtained his ancestor's blessing in one go. "Yes. My father always tells me about it. The magnificence of Master Wu's work shone through the world that night."

Wu Xiodia snorted in his heart. This junior was trying to butter him up now. "I can carve the same array, Double Amplification Array, on this weapon."

Du Fang's eyes gleamed like a thousand candles lit up in the darkest night. "Master Wu, thanks. I can't even think of repaying this debt, but this junior will be in your debt forever."

Wu Xiodia sneered when he spotted Du Fang's gleaming eyes. "Don't celebrate just now. There is a fifty percent chance that the weapon will be destroyed."

Wu Fang's face darkened. His longing gaze jumped to the dagger, but then he nodded. "Please, Master Wu. There is no one other than you who can do this."

"Are you sure?" Wu Xiodia got up and tapped his leather shoes.

"Don't even try that if you don't want to die." A smug sound echoed in the chamber, and Wu Xiodia glared at the source. Who dared to refute his claim?

Chapter 38

Schemes of Du Clan?

When the two people entered the outer room of the shop, Li Wei was talking with the attendant on the front side. It was dark outside, so he could easily see those two entering the guest hall connected to the shop front, and with his strong divine sense he could even hear their chatter.

At first, he'd ignored the duo, but when they talked about a dagger and array crafting, his attention drifted toward their conversation, but not to the level where he focused exclusively on them. How could a mere Array Carver in small Old Martial City attract his attention? In his previous life, he didn't even talk with low-level characters like these. He didn't have any airs when it came to martial arts, but on the path of arrays, who could dare to stand in front of him in both the Mortal and Martial realms? After he reached Array Master level, even Firmament Sect's Master had to show respect to him. That was the main reason he'd betrothed Wang Zia to him.

That bitch. His nostrils flared when he thought about that woman. Until now, he couldn't guess why she'd killed him. His prospects were much better than hers, and yet he'd died at hands.

Rage surged through his blood, but he suppressed it down. Currently, he was nothing in front of her. If he remembered correctly, in a couple of months she would reach Houtian Realm and travel through the Mortal World to gain experience. That's when they first met.

He was lost in thought when a tyrannical aura stirred his divine sense. When he focused, he spotted the dagger in the young man's hand emitting a strange green light. The smell of death protruded from that dagger and targeted his vitality, but it was quickly suppressed by his own vitality.

That was a cursed item. The green light it emitted looked exactly like Blood Sucking Poison. It was a forbidden poison in the Martial Realm, and no one dared to use it. If exposed to air, it would suck life and qi from the surroundings, quickly turning a hundred-foot area into a forbidden lifeless zone.

However, how could that young man hold the dagger in his hands for so long? If it was Blood Sucking Poison, it should have sucked him dry in a breath's time.

Curiously, he observed the duo carefully. The duo stood next to each other. One was old, like old bones excavated from a graveyard and given a green robe to wear. The other was young and haggard like someone had put him through years of manual labor and then gave him a nice gray robe with golden linings to wear. They discussed carving an array on the cursed item, and when the old man talked about carving a Double Amplification Array on that item, Wei couldn't control his astonishment and unintentionally spoke aloud.

"Don't even try that if you don't want to die."

The old and young man turned their fierce attention toward him.

"Insolent brat, are you trying to cause trouble in my shop?" the old man asked in a hoarse voice, his body quivering in anger.

With one look, Wei knew the man was on his death bed, but his eyes had a strange gleam. A glimmer of longing for something, and he was holding on to his life for that one longing.

"Li Wei, are you trying to go against Master Wu's words? Are you afraid of living?" Du Fang asked.

"Are you trying to curse the old man by bringing a cursed item in his shop?" Wei asked calmly.

"Young man, don't cause trouble. That's Du Fang, Du Lufang's third son," the shop attendant whispered hurriedly next to him. "If I, were you, I'd apologize and get the fuck out of here," he added.

"Li Wei, are you trying to slander the Du clan? If you don't kneel and beg, then don't blame me for being merciless." Du Fang raised his dagger in the air, ready to strike anytime.

Wei sneered. With his layer three qi Refinement Realm cultivation, Du Fang was trying to threaten him. With his current condition, Wei doubted if Du Fang could even display fifty percent of his abilities.

"Brat, if you don't explain, then I'll give you a good thrashing for the whole night." Wu Xiodia growled.

Wei arched his brows. What did he mean by thrashing for the whole night? Did this old man have that kind of habit?

His body suddenly shivered in fear. Although the old man had one foot in the grave, he still had third layer qi Foundation Realm cultivation and could trample on Wei easily.

"Du Fang, aren't you feeling weak since you found that weapon?" Wei's gaze dropped on the green dagger in Du Fang's hand. It emitted a strange green light, and if he wasn't wrong, it was a Green Scorpion's Middle Bone dipped in Blood Sucking Poison for days. A strange refining material in low-tier Silver Grade. It was a valuable material, but at the same time dipping it in Blood Sucking Poison had made it into a cursed item.

Du Fang's face turned grim, and he blinked his eyes rapidly. "Who said that? That's a lie. I'm perfectly fine."

He tried to show his vigor by taking an offensive stance, but his body quivered like a butterfly stuck in crazy winds.

⟫⟫⟫ ⟪⟪⟪

Du Fang's body wobbled when he tried to gather his metallic qi in his palm. He couldn't control it and coughed hard, spitting out a mouthful of dark blood. That bastard Li Wei was indeed right. Since Du Fang had found this weapon, he was suffering from all manner of illness. One day he would feel sick to his stomach, the next day his body would turn soft like cotton. On top of that, whenever he touched the dagger, he felt like his life energy was getting sucked into it.

Yet he couldn't let go of it. It was a powerful dagger. Once, he fought with it, and he'd easily defeated a layer six Refinement Realm opponent. How could he throw away such a divine weapon?

So, he planned to get a power array marked on it and double its power. Then he could easily contend with his elder brother in the upcoming clan's martial arts competition and win the first place to obtain a Body Healing Pill. With that pill, he could overcome all the illnesses he'd recently suffered.

But getting Master Wu to craft an array was next to impossible, and he had only come with a tiny hope. Fortunately, Master Wu had agreed. He'd even agreed to craft the legendary array he'd crafted on Ice Panther Sabre.

If he got his hands on a powerful weapon like Ice Panther Sabre, he would be invincible in the young generation of Old Martial City. Hell, he would even surpass all young generations of Du clan.

Then this trash came out and started talking nonsense.

"You are talking nonsense." He coughed more. "This dagger is a divine weapon. How can trash like you know its importance?" Blood leaked from the corner of his mouth. "In fact, you are trash who can't even cultivate, and yet you dare to come and make trouble in Master Wu's shop. Are you tired of living? Then let me send you to the seventh hell." Brandishing his dagger, he dashed at Li Wei standing outside of the shop. With his cultivation level and the power of the dagger, he would instantly kill that trash.

But when he reached Li Wei, something unexpected occurred. Li Wei vanished from his path at the last moment, and the dagger moved through empty air.

What? He couldn't believe his eyes for a moment, but Li Wei had moved a foot away and sent a kick at him.

No, it must have been his sickness that made him miss his strike. Yes, it had to be his own illness, otherwise how could a mortal with no qi move out of his attack range? That was ridiculous.

Li Wei's kick closed on him, but Du Fang didn't resist it at all. What could a mortal's kick do to him? Scratch his balls?

When blood spurted out of his mouth, Du Fang realized Li Wei's kick packed a punch that he couldn't dare to take with all his defenses activated, and he had taken it unprepared.

Too hateful. That man was too hateful. He'd acted as a pig to eat a tiger.

However, Du Fang couldn't say anything, as he lost his consciousness before hitting the ground.

Chapter 39

Dao of Arrays

Wu Xiodia watched the two brats fighting with disdain. How dare they fight in his guest hall? They were insolent, and he itched to teach them a lesson. Although he fought little, he was still in Foundation Realm, so hitting their bottoms wouldn't take much effort.

"My carpet!" he cried when the Du brat spat blood all over his green carpet. It smelled like death, and his heart tightened. Why did his blood smell like death? That meant this Li brat was right about the green dagger being a deadly item.

The next moment his doubt turned into confirmation. When the Du brat used his dagger, his face turned pale, and the dagger sucked a red aura from his body.

This was bad. If he had touched it, he might have lost his life already. How could that slip past his decade of experience of carving arrays on the weapons. The weapon had an evil aura that tapped into Du Fang's heart and drew a power beyond what that brat could handle. In Wu Xiodia's current condition, he could only hold on for a few more years, and if that dagger had sucked his life out, he might have died by now.

His body convulsed at the thought. If that had happened, his dao of arrays would be wasted before he could take the next step.

The battle didn't last long before the Du brat sprawled on the ground, spitting up blood.

But how did the Li brat move so fast? This brat didn't have an ounce of qi inside his body, and yet he'd moved like a cat and avoided every strike from the crazed Du brat. He'd even thrown a kick that had matched the layer four Refinement Realm cultivator's power level.

No, his old eyes weren't betraying him. That Li brat had strange physical strength.

He gasped; air caught in his throat. Could it be that legendary . . .?

No, that was impossible. How could a long-lost cultivation method make its way back to the Mortal Realm? But he couldn't explain the Li brat's strange physical powers another way. Unless, maybe, he'd eaten some spiritual fruit that had increased his strength to this level.

That sounded like a plausible explanation.

The Li brat bent down and picked up the green dagger and placed it in his pocket. "I don't think you want this dagger anymore, do you?" he asked plainly. There was no respect in his eyes, and that shocked Wu Xiodia.

"And what about my carpet?" The carpet meant nothing to him, and he felt gratitude toward this brat, but he couldn't just show it on his face. If the brat had behaved nicely, he might have given him some weapon on a whim, but who'd told him to be haughty?

"Just use a cleaning array. Why are you trying to put an air?"

"A cleaning array?" Wu Xiodia quivered in anger. "Brat, do I look like an Array Carver to you? I'm an Array Apprentice. Do you get it? Array Apprentice." He lied, but what would a brat who was still wet behind ears know? "Do you even know what arrays are?" He tried to curse further, but he couldn't find more words. This was a sore spot in his heart, and he could never overcome it.

"You call this an array?" The Li brat picked up an armguard lying on the counter and snorted. "Array master? My foot. You can't even complete the third circle of Qi Enhancement Array properly, and you call yourself an array master." He flipped the armguard away like it was nothing in his eyes. "This single mistake has weakened your array by fifty-six percent. You can't even compare to the fart of a real array master." Shaking his head in disdain, he walked out of the shop.

"You, you . . ." Wu Xiodia was about to leap at the brat and thrash him when he realized something. Something important.

How did the Li brat know he'd made a mistake in the third circle of Qi Enhancement Array with a mere glance? Had his attendant told him that?

Impossible. His attendant wasn't even allowed to lift a brush yet. How could he talk about that array? Only an array cultivator who could draw Silver Grade arrays was capable of detecting his mistake.

Then how could a sixteen- or seventeen-year-old brat detect that?

Qi Enhancement Array was a high-tier Bronze Grade array, and it had annoyed him for decades. No matter what he did, he couldn't complete the third power circle. Even after crafting a Silver Grade array on the Ice Panther Sabre, he'd failed to complete a single Qi Enhancement Array. Sometimes he wondered if it was a bane on his path of arrays and stopped him from advancing further.

Then how did this brat know about it?

Was he lying? Just showing up?

"You! Li brat, wait. Come back and tell me, how did you know about the third power circle?"

"You are doing it with wrongly arm. Draw from the opposite side and draw it as two half circles. You should finish this easily." The Li brat shouted before vanishing into the crowded street.

A light shone in Wu Xiodia's dark eyes. Was he doing it all along wrong?

Why didn't he think of this before? He was left-handed, so if he used the same direction as right-handers, he would definitely fail. It was fine for normal circles, but when he had to draw the complex third circle while maintaining the qi supply in first two circles it became impossible.

He'd also said to draw two half circles.

"Wait!" he shouted, wanting to stop that Li brat and ask him more about this. How did this brat know he was a left-handed array master? No one knew that. Even when he fought, he used his right hand to hold his weapons, yet that brat had guessed it through his array carvings.

When he turned to leave, he found a diagram carved on an old parchment and his body quivered. He had seen this diagram once but could not comprehend it. It was a Silver Grade array, Two Sword Formation Array.

Heavens, who was this kid? He could even leave a Silver Grade Array behind like it was nothing.

Who was this kid? "Kun Fu."

"Yes master." His attendant rushed over and lowered his head in respect.

"Find that expert guy's whereabouts, and don't disturb me for two days. I can't be disturbed even if city lord comes." He sneered. Although he suspected how the brat knew about his issues, he had given Wu Xiodia a hope of overcoming them, and as a cultivator of arrays, he was dying to try the new method and see if it worked.

That was his dao of arrays.

Chapter 40

Treasure Map

Pinching his nose with his left hand, Li Wei dipped a small wooden stick in the thick black blood he had bought from Wu Xiodia's shop. It stank like a dead rotten animal, but he couldn't do anything about it. It was White Wolf's blood after all. It was a Ferocious Beast in the fifth layer of Refinement Realm, and its blood was used as common ink for carving arrays by Array Apprentices. It wasn't the best, but it was okay.

The small stick turned a little black after a few seconds, and he pulled it out. The Azure Dragon Tree had an elastic property and didn't absorb too much blood, so it worked well for him. Although a normal Array Apprentice would use a special brush made of the hair of a Ferocious Beast, he, an Array Master, didn't need that. The brush was mainly used to control the blood flow. Why would he need that when he had divine sense and decades of practice? After a certain stage, no array cultivator used brushes. Instead, they used their qi and divine sense to carve arrays.

But he was far away from that stage.

After dipping the stick five times and letting it absorb enough blood, he started carving a small source circle at the center of the room. He was carving Lesser Isolation Array, a Bronze Grade array used for concealment and detection of threats. It was the best array for his current situation. First, he wanted to check the box he'd found on Tian Yun's body, and then he had to mix a medicine to suppress the poison in Fei'er's body. All those ingredients were quite rare and expensive. If someone from the Li clan saw him using them, they might raise some suspicions. Thanks to Du Xin and Tian Yun, he had gathered a hundred gold coins, and that let him buy the beast blood and the Poison Repelling Powder's ingredients. His grandfather had only given him ten gold, not enough to buy what he'd needed.

Greed could be a bad thing, and he didn't want to be in the spotlight right now.

As time passed, his hand sped up, drawing circle after circle and then a few symbols in the center. After five minutes, he stopped and wiped sweat from his forehead. It wasn't normally difficult, but with his current condition it was hard. If he hadn't reached layer five body Refinement Realm and obtained stable divine sense, he might not have tried it. While drawing an array, every stroke had to be perfect, and any wrong stroke could ruin it completely. On top of that, he hadn't carved this array in decades, and he was doing it from memory.

Finally, he completed it and it looked perfect, only limited by the quality of blood. If Wu Xiodia saw this, he would be in shock for sure.

Cleaning his forehead, he stepped out of the room and inhaled a deep fresh breath. Stretching his hands, he checked to see if anyone was around using his divine sense. There was no one in a five-hundred-foot radius, so he pulled the low-quality Qi Stone from his pouch and tapped it in the middle of the array source. Dim white light entered the source point and spread across the connecting lines, and then the entire array lit up, and suddenly everything around the shabby room become tranquil.

If anyone saw from outside, they wouldn't find anything changed. They would only see a small girl sleeping inside and a young man sitting in a corner with his eyes closed. There was another function to the array: detection. Although the concealment worked in a ten-foot radius, it would alert the array carver if anyone entered within a two-hundred-foot radius of the array source. It was quite good for recuperation in the forest and other dangerous places.

"Now even a Bone Baptizing Realm cultivator can't barge in," he whispered and checked the energy barrier with his divine sense.

There should be no Bone Baptizing Realm cultivator inside this small city. Even the city lord, the strongest person in the city, would be in the early layers of Bone Baptization Realm, and only a peak Bone Baptization Realm cultivator could see through this array. Only in big cities, like Fragrance Herb City, would he find peak Bone Baptization Realm cultivators, so he didn't need to worry much.

Sitting next to Fei'er's bed, he pulled two pouches from under the cloth wrapped around his stomach. Soon, he should get access to the storage ring. Carrying things wrapped around his stomach didn't feel nice.

"Let's check what rotten things these bastards carried with them." He wasn't optimistic about the kinds of things two Refinement Realm kids carried with them. In his previous life, he had seen cultivators carrying heavenly pills, artifacts, and whatnot. They had rings full of things. Compared to them, what would the two kids carry?

Other than gold, there were two boxes, two books, and an object wrapped in a purple cloth. He already had gold, so he wanted to find the map Du Xin had spoken of.

First, he checked the two books. They were Tiger Metal Palm and Three Metal Qi Art books. The Du clan practiced those, and they were of no use to him. If he wanted to practice metal qi like his previous life, he had much better qi arts in his memories. Throwing them aside, he opened the first box.

Cold wind slapped his face when he opened the box, and it was so strong that he had to close that box.

"What is this thing?" he pushed his disheveled hair down and tied it with a cloth band. That was a strong wind.

Cautiously, he opened the box once again, and as expected a strong wind assaulted his face from inside. But he endured a little and scanned the strange bubble inside the box. It floated inside the box like it had its own conscious, and when Wei tried to probe it, it blocked his divine sense.

That was strange. After thinking for a moment, he threw it aside. He had more important things to do. Then he peeled back the purple cloth, and his jaw dropped to the ground. Qi Initiation Fruit. This was the perfect thing for him right now.

Qi Initiation Fruit was a rare fruit used by qi cultivators to initiate cultivation. When one ate a small piece of this fruit, the pure qi from it invaded the body and nurtured it throughout, making it ready for cultivation. There was another method for initiation. One could ask an elder cultivator to send their qi into a kid's body, doing same as Qi Initiation Fruit, but it left some impurities behind in the kid's body, possibly even hampering the kid's cultivation later in life.

But using Qi Initiation Fruit had no side effects. It was the purest of nature's qi, and it was gentle and delicate. It was the perfect fruit to get one on the path of cultivation, and now it was going to help him to do so.

Wei chuckled. His dantian was completely repaired, and it was time to cultivate, but he lacked a method to do that. It was easier when he'd cultivated the first layer of Blood Essence Body. All he had to do was bleed, bleed until fifty-one percent blood loss, and he could have stepped in the first layer. Of course, he'd gone beyond that and reached ninety-one percent blood loss. That was a wild method he had never thought of using.

Anyway, with this fruit his initiation in qi cultivation would be like drinking wine on a calm evening while hearing surreal music. It would be that easy and awesome.

But he had to find a good cultivation art first. If it wasn't for Fei'er's issue, he would have checked other Inheritance Chambers before leaving the tunnels.

Getting back to work, he opened the second box, and his mind went numb in shock.

Holy heavens. It was a treasure map.

Chapter 41

Murder

Li Wei squinted hard, his heart beating faster than an Iron Marrow Horse. His shabby room swirled in front of his eyes when he glanced at the language of the map.

This was a legit treasure map marked in the language of the Ancient Gods. That meant it was quite old.

Pulling it open, he checked the elasticity of the paper and determined he couldn't tear it. It was strong and flexible at the same time. It even exuded a pungent smell. The same smell that his master's books had exuded.

To confirm it, he put it over a fire torch. Even fire couldn't burn it. It just washed over it like water moving over a flat marble surface.

Holy heavens. It was millions of years old. It had to be. No one in the Mortal Realm would know about this language. Only a few knew about this language in the Martial Realm. If it wasn't for his previous master finding a sacred book on arrays and dedicating his whole life to studying this language, Wei wouldn't have learned it.

Millions of years before, gods ruled these lands, but then they'd vanished, leaving no trace other than a few ancient sites and books scattered here. Otherwise, no proof exited of their existence.

Closing his eyes, he took a deep breath. This was huge. If any big shot from the Martial Realm knew that there was a treasure map present in the Mortal Realm, a blood bath would happen. They would hunt Wei until the end of his life.

This was a good thing and a bad thing at the same time. No one could know about it. But how did this map end up in the mortal world?

This was inconceivable.

With quivering fingers, Wei opened the map again and scanned it. It displayed a complex structure of tunnels, tunnels that looked familiar. They were the same tunnels he had traversed beneath the Ancient Ruins. When he compared it with his own memories of the safe tunnel paths, he found they nearly matched. There were a couple of small differences, but it made sense. This map was drawn heaven knows when, and the safe route he'd found was just a few months back.

Another thing matched perfectly. The tunnel he and Fei'er had traversed was marked in yellow, while the tunnel he'd heard the strange beast howl was marked in red. It connected with a purple room that had a word written in it. Houtian?

Did it mean he had to be in Houtian Realm to go there?

His gaze traversed to the Inheritance Chamber he had broken into, and it was marked in purple too. There was no word written in it.

This made sense. The Inheritance Chamber he'd stepped into was for initial inheritance, and it only had the cultivation art that reached Houtian Realm. So, once he reached Houtian Realm, he had to go back and obtain the next part of Five Elemental Way Qi Cultivation Art.

Now it made sense why no one had found these chambers. First, these paths were dangerous, and second, these Inheritance Chambers required special tokens. Who could beat a Houtian Realm monster in the Mortal Realm?

Unconsciously, he tapped his chest, feeling the metallic token hanging from a thread wrapped around his neck.

Yes, no Houtian Realm cultivator would come to this remote city. They had better things to do than check a ruined town. Although Houtian Realm cultivators could still live in the Mortal World, they would choose to go to the Martial World before they stepped in Houtian Realm, as the Martial Realm had abundant natural essence, and it was easier to break through.

His eyes traced through the remaining part of the map. There was no other purple Inheritance Chamber, but there were a couple of gold-colored rooms shown and marked as treasure.

In fact, there was another gold room he had seen when he'd walked out along the path Tian Yun and Du Xin had entered through. It was the first treasure room, but that made sense. Didn't Tian Yun say their patriarch went there and broke through Foundation Realm in one go?

Holy heavens. This was indeed a treasure map.

But if this was a treasure map marked in the language of the Ancient Gods, Tian clan must die. Otherwise, they would attract calamity to this land. Not that they could connect with forces in the Martial Realm and expose this thing, but he couldn't take any chances. And this map showed the positions of the Inheritance Chambers for Five Elemental Way Qi Cultivation Art. So, they had to die.

That was it. He would cultivate Five Elemental Way Qi Cultivation Art. Now, he even had Qi Initiation Fruit. With that fruit, his first step would be flawless.

But before that, he had to prepare the Poison Repelling Powder for Fei'er.

⟫⟫⟫ ⟪⟪⟪

Du Lufang scanned Du Fang's body lying on the small bed with tearful eyes. Next to him, his wife, Du Pian, slammed her chest and cried loudly, annoying him.

"I want revenge." Her eyes emitted rage and destruction, and he couldn't deny that sent chills down his legs. "I want Wu Xiodia's head on my table before I eat lunch tomorrow," Du Pian threatened.

"Pian'er. Calm down. It's Master Wu we are talking about. He is an Array Apprentice. We can't touch him, and I doubt he would do this." Had she gone mad? Implicating an Array Apprentice. How naïve. "And he is only poisoned. I've asked Doctor Mu to rush here. He will save him. Don't worry."

"No. Our son visited him, and now he is returned like a shriveled, poisoned corpse. It has to be Wu Xiodia." She gritted her teeth. "Wu Xiodia, I'll slice your throat with my hands." Du Pian continued to lash out at her husband.

Du Lufang trembled in anger, but he couldn't show it in front of her. The great family of Wang from Herb Fragrance City supported her, and their Blood Baptization Realm elder doted on her obnoxiously. How could he raise his voice or scold her? If he rebuked her, Wang clan might even destroy the whole Du clan in one go.

This was the tragedy of his life. Why had he accepted this marriage offer?

"My dear, please calm down." He rubbed her back, but she dislodged his hand with a flick of her shoulder. "Wait until I meet with Master Wu. There must be an explanation for this, and don't forget, even your family can't touch an Array Apprentice."

Wu Xiodia was an Array Apprentice, and he had the Array Society behind him. If someone dared to touch him, they would only bring calamity on their clan.

"Master Du . . . Master Du." Steward Chin rushed into the room without even knocking.

Du Lufang frowned. This steward was being insolent lately. He could put up with his wife, because she was family and had her clan behind her, but steward Chin was just a follower from Wang clan. He was a lowly bastard who dared to barge into his bedroom.

Insolent.

Pulling his whip out, Du Lufang lashed it at steward Chin. "Impudent whelp! Don't you know what has happened? And you dared to barge in."

"Master Du, please forgive this steward, but there is bad news."

Du Lufang's forehead wrinkled in black lines. "What could be worse than death of my third son?"

"Young master Xin—" Steward Chin gasped. "—he is dead. Someone murdered him."

Chapter 42

Du Lufang's Rage

Du Lufang lunged forward and grabbed steward Chin's collar, and before steward Chin could react, he shoved him against the wall.

"What did you say?"

"My lady Wang. Please save me!" Steward Chin cried, and Du Pian stepped forward and pulled Du Lufang's hand back.

This motherfucker. He dared to call his wife by her maiden name. How daring.

"Husband, listen to him first." She seemed unphased by the news.

Hearing her careless tone, he felt like someone had poured a pot of hot oil on his head. Fuck! Why would she remain unphased? Du Fang was his and Du Pian's son, and Du Xin was from his first wife, Du Sisoda, who had died just before he married Du Pian. Long since, he'd wondered if Du Sisoda had died of natural causes or was killed by Du Pian.

"Steward Chin. If you dare to spread false news, no one can save you. Not even your Wang clan." He pulled his hand back but kept his gaze firm on that motherfucker.

"My lord. The Tian clan found Du Xin's body along with Tian Yun. Tian Yun had stolen a precious treasure from the Tian clan and was running away, and someone killed them both and stole the treasure. Tian clan has issued a warrant against the killer, and they are telling everyone that they will absolutely wipe out the thief."

"Tian Fu." Du Lufang squeezed his fist. "Is he saying Du Xin stole their treasure and killed Tian Yun, that bastard?" This was serious. There seemed to be a need to teach this Tian clan a lesson. Only a few years back they'd licked the Du clan's shoes, and now they dared to slander the Du clan?

How impudent.

Steward Chin shook his head. "No. They came to us with the news first. But nothing is clear for now."

"Insolent. Aren't they indirectly saying that my Du Xin stole their treasure with the bastard from their clan?" He slammed his fist on a nearby table and shattered it. "I guess I have to take a trip to their clan. Someone has to pay for the death of both of my sons, and they can't run away anymore."

A servant rushed in his room with a fearful face. "My lord."

Du Lufang wanted to kill all of these pieces of trash. How a mere servant dares to rush into his room? First that motherfucker steward Chin and now a servant. His hand went to his whip, and he almost lashed out at the servant before he could deliver his message.

The clan patriarch had sent a message to him, and it was urgent.

Dropping his whip, he rushed outside. Once this was over, he would find the culprits and wipe out their whole families.

⇒⇒⇒ ⇐⇐⇐

Golden Ginseng, Green Venom Tree, Red Blood Fruit, One Leaf Lotus.

Li Wei placed all the rare ingredients on a clean white paper. A mix of sweet and bitter scents wafted in the air, making his mood tranquil. These ingredients were all precious, ten years old, and they contained enough heaven and earth's essence to make one feel elated.

Cutting them in five parts, he placed one part of each in a stone pot. The recipe was simple. He had to cut them and turn them into a pulp and let them dry for an hour. Although it was simple, the ingredients were costly, being ten years old. In those ten years they required a good amount of care—too much for a common family to try in their backyards—so only specialized herb gardens or pharmacies grew them.

After putting them in a pot, he started crushing them. He had bought enough to make five portions, costing him thirty gold. He only had sixty gold left.

After half an hour, a brown pulp formed in the stone pot, and he set it aside. The brown color meant it had reached the required state.

Now he had to wait an hour for the pulp to turn into a powder.

While waiting, he went through his pouch and found one Yin Yang Fruit lying there. This was one of the fruits he'd found in the secret stash of the Inheritance Chamber. The remaining fruits were inside the storage ring, so he didn't have access to them, nor could he put this one with the rest.

Hmm. Once Fei'er's issue was resolved, he must cultivate qi. This was one of the issues with body cultivators. They couldn't access storage artifacts, so they had to practice qi cultivation.

Looking at the Yin Yang Fruit, a thought came to his mind. Should he try Yin Yang Liquid art? It was an auxiliary art recorded with Yin Yang Hands, divine art. To cultivate this divine art, he needed to reach Houtian Realm in body cultivation, but he could still use this auxiliary skill, as his hands had already become Yin Hand and Yang Hand.

However, he needed an external source to form Yin Yang Liquid, and such a source lay on his palm right now.

With a thought, the auxiliary art cultivation technique and usage flashed in his mind. First came chaos and then came yin and yang. They made everything else. The five elements, sun and moon, male and female. They were the primary source of everything else. This liquid required one to find a harmony between yin and yang, and it was the highest-grade spiritual liquid found in any Realm. At the highest level, it could bring the dead back to life or give birth to a spiritual soul.

Of course, Wei didn't believe the liquid he formed would do this at all. There was a peculiar line mentioned in the usage notes, and that was about increasing the proficiency of medicinal herbs. Maybe he should try it on the four remaining portions he had and check the effects.

But there was a limit to this auxiliary skill. At the lowest level, he could only use it once a day, and it would only form a few drops if the highest quality yin yang source was used.

His fingers rubbed the Yin Yang Fruit, feeling small crevices marked on the green skin. It wasn't the highest quality fruit. It was a mid-tier Silver Grade herb, and he had seen it in auctions a couple of times. He had seen many low-tier Gold Grade yin yang sources too, but they were scarce and costed a fortune. If he'd needed to get a Yin Yang

Fruit in his previous life, he would have had to look around and borrow money from others.

But he would have a different path this time. He would earn so much that he could just be lazy and enjoy his life without worrying about it much.

Firming his resolve, he cut the fruit into two halves, held one in each of his palms, and started cultivating Yin Yang Liquid.

A warm current rushed through his palms and connected to his heart, giving birth to a wonderful feeling as soon as he started the chant.

Wow! He exclaimed in his mind and repeated the chant while observing the whole process with his divine sense. Having a divine sense helped a lot. Although he hadn't reached the manifestation stage with his divine sense, as it had only been born recently, it was useful enough for him.

When the energy from the fruit entered his palm, a peculiar thing happened. Golden and black threads emerged throughout his arms and guided that energy on a certain path. With his divine sense, he could feel the energy nourishing the threads and getting smaller and smaller as it traversed toward his shoulders. By the time it emerged out of the golden and black threads, the energy current had only retained one hundredth of the original power.

Yet it sent his remaining body in turmoil as it passed through his blood vessels and settled in his heart. When it reached his heart, it mixed with a tiny white drop formed inside his heart chamber, and the white drop grew from one tenth of a tear drop to one eighth.

But there was something else happening inside his body too. His blood flow had increased, and new blood pearls were constantly condensing inside his Yangming meridian.

What a pleasant surprise. Cultivating an auxiliary skill had influenced his body cultivation.

How awesome.

Elated, he started absorbing more energy from the Yin Yang Fruit, and his cultivation level kept increasing slowly. By the time he absorbed a fifteenth cycle of energy from the fruit, the white liquid in his heart had grown to ten tear drops, and his blood pearl count had increased by forty—almost reaching the next layer of cultivation.

Wasn't that awesome? If he had to go through the normal cultivation route, it would take him a whole day to condense fifty blood pearls, and as he advanced that speed decreased. But with this auxiliary art, he condensed same amount of blood pearls in just half an hour. If he could do this each day, he would reach Foundation Realm in a day's time, and Blood Baptization Realm in the next few days. He might reach Houtian Realm in a month's time.

No. It was wishful thinking. Cultivation was never a straight path. The more one traveled on it, the more difficult it became. These earlier realms were easy to traverse, but each layer in later realms was like climbing the highest mountain of the world and then finding another mountain waiting ahead.

It was that difficult.

Then there were large boundaries when one crossed a major realm. That was a headache in his previous life because of his Bronze Grade Spirit Root.

Anyway, he had gathered fifteen drops of white liquid in his heart, but how would he get them out? By stabbing his heart?

Chapter 43

Godly Liquid

Ten minutes. Li Wei spent ten minutes sitting inside his room, concealed by an array, thinking about how he would stab his heart to get the damn liquid out.

Couldn't it just appear out of his heart on its own?

A single thought, and the liquid appeared in his mouth.

What? What a stupid skill. It didn't even provide enough information.

He tasted it with his tongue, and it felt like nothing. There was no taste to it, no smell either.

Confused, he picked up a white ceramic bowl he used to drink chicken broth from the corner of his shabby room and poured the white liquid in it.

Fifteen drops that looked like white pearls floated over the ceramic base as if they were disgusted to touch the filthy ceramic bowl. They didn't even mix with each other.

What an arrogant attitude!

Staring at the liquid for a moment, he selected the Golden Ginseng and dropped a single drop on it.

For a minute nothing happened, and he thought it was a waste. Maybe he needed to reach Houtian Realm to make it work. The actual divine art needed him to be at Houtian Realm, so it was quite possible that the auxiliary skill too required him to be at the same realm. After all, that stupid information forgot to mention he just needed to wish to get that liquid out of his heart.

Even if didn't work, he would still practice the auxiliary skill to improve his body cultivation. With the half-hour practice, he had already touched the fifth layer of Refinement Realm.

When he was about to drift his gaze away, something happened. The Golden Ginseng moved.

No, it didn't move but actually grew.

His jaw dropped to the ground with the next change he spotted. No, it went under the ground.

It was changing color to golden brown.

How was it possible?

Although called Golden Ginseng, the herb had a different shade of gold with maturity. Only when it was planted and attached to a living stem would it have a golden color. A ten-year-old Golden Ginseng would have a golden-red color. A fifty-year-old Golden Ginseng would have a brown-gold color. A hundred-year-old Golden Ginseng would have a golden-white color. For a five-hundred-year-old herb, he didn't know the color. No one was foolish enough to raise it beyond one hundred years. Its medicinal value stopped at that age.

But right now, he was seeing a miracle. The one-fifth portion of the herb had grown twice its size and gained a color that leaned toward golden brown.

With a thumping heart, he poured another drop on the herb.

As expected, it grew another part, and its color turned browner.

What the heck? Was this liquid adding ten years to the herb? How was that possible? Could he really make it a one-hundred-year-old Golden Ginseng if he kept adding liquid to it?

Another drop, and the color changed again. After four drops, the Golden Ginseng regained its original shape, and it was smooth as ice and radiated a vitality that he could feel from a foot away. Of course, it had gained a brown-gold color indicating it had reached fifty years of age.

It was inconceivable. Each drop added ten years to the herb's age. Shouldn't this liquid be called Godly Liquid instead of Yin Yang Liquid?

Curiously, he dropped another drop on the Golden Ginseng, but nothing happened even after ten minutes.

So, this liquid stopped working after reaching fifty years of age. In fact, if it didn't, he would have freaked out.

How could there be something that increased an herb's age without any restraint?

Now he was curious how it would affect living plants. Could he really increase their age like this?

But before that, he had something important to do. He had to increase the age of the One Leaf Lotus, and he only had five drops left. Poison Repelling Powder was a common medicine, and its quality increased with the age of two herbs used: Golden Ginseng and One Leaf Lotus. If he could, he would have bought fifty-year-old herbs to help Fei'er, but that would have cost three hundred gold, and he'd had only hundred on hand.

So, without worrying about anything else, he poured four drops on the One Leaf Lotus one by one. The lotus stem he had cut apart grew rapidly, reaching its original height. Its color turned greener, and vitality exuded from it that enthralled his mind. It had reached fifty years of age. If he hadn't cut these herbs, he might only need three drops to make them fifty years old. Or two maybe. But after cutting them, he could create multiple fifty-year-old herbs.

Now he had six drops left, but he didn't use them right away. He would cultivate the skill the next day and then experiment a little with living plants. In fact, he would get out tonight and buy living plants, and he had his eyes set on a particular plant that would be useful for him.

With that herb in his hand, he could be rich in no time.

Putting all the thoughts aside, he cleaned the stone pot he'd used, collecting the powder in a small pouch. Although he could throw it out as he had newly aged ingredients, he didn't. It might be useful someday.

After crushing the new ingredients, he smashed them into a pulp and removed excess water and let it dry out. He had to wait one more hour to get improved Poison Repelling Powder.

Meanwhile, he recharged the Lesser Isolation Array once more. It only required one thousandth of the energy from the low-quality Qi Stone.

While waiting for the powder to form, he pulled the green dagger out of his pouch and scanned it carefully. It was a cursed item, and he could feel the itch. But surprisingly, it didn't affect him. After knocking out Du Fang, he'd touched it once to study and found the poison didn't affect him. It did try to suck his life force, but his strong life force resisted it easily.

His eyes lit up when he pondered the dagger. It could be useful for him. This curse didn't affect him, but it would definitely affect his opponent. Then this dagger was made up from Green Scorpion's Middle Bone and dipped in Blood Sucking Poison. No one should recognize this forbidden poison in Mortal Realm.

In fact, he could carve a couple of arrays to conceal its aura and improve its powers. Current him still couldn't do it, but he had Wu Xiodia who he could ask to do it for him. With a brush and bit of care, the old man wouldn't need to touch the dagger at all.

It made perfect sense.

After an hour, the pulp dried out and a golden-green powder accumulated in the bottom of the pot. Collecting half of it, he poured it in Fei'er's mouth with the help of water.

Then he sensed someone entering his array, and his whole body tightened.

Chapter 44

Daughter in law

With long strides, Li Shua headed to the old cabin built by his daughter in her childhood. She'd loved to have a house of her own, and then she . . .

He sighed in his old heart, remembering her face before she'd vanished from his eyes. It was one of the reasons he'd shifted the Li clan's main business to Bright Maritime City, one of the biggest cities in North Providence. Although it only had the backing of a small sect called Maritime Sect, it had great financial prospects for their clan. But the city had already had the Du clan, and they had marital relationships with the Wang clan—overlord of Herb Fragrance City—so the Li clan had had to remain dormant.

But things were about to change. The Earthly Fruit Tree had emerged in their clan territory, and it would either change their fortune or bring calamity. It was a Silver Grade herb used in Marrow Cleansing Pills, so every clan wanted to have one tree in their territory, but it was a nature's herb, so no one could plant it in their herb garden. Whenever a new tree was discovered, bloodshed followed.

Although he had brought all his clan elites to Old Martial City, he knew he couldn't protect the plant and prosper with it, so he had sent a message to Divine Fragrance Palace declaring his request to surrender the plant to them for some benefits.

After the deal was done, and elites from Divine Fragrance Palace took charge of the tree, he could sleep well.

As if this wasn't enough tension, that Du Lufang had barged into the clan compound and demanded Li Wei be handed over. Although he'd rejected the request, he had to know the reason behind it, so he came here.

Seeing the poor condition of the cabin, his heart quivered. How could that bastard Li Sua make his grandson live in such awful conditions?

"Brat, what are you doing?" He barged into the small cabin without a thought.

"Grandfather," Li Wei got to his feet and bowed his head.

At least the brat had learned to show some respect. The last time he saw this brat, he had showed no respect whatsoever. If his mother wasn't Li Shua's favorite daughter, he would have beaten this brat to half death.

"What did you do with Du Fang?"

"I knocked him down when he tried to kill me," the brat replied with a plain face.

Li Shua chuckled. "You don't even have an ounce of cultivation, and you knocked down a brat in layer three of Refinement Realm?"

Li Wei arched his brows. "Was he that strong? It didn't feel like that. I just punched him once, and he fell on the ground. Did he die or what?"

Li Shua rubbed his chin. Du Lufang must be hiding something. There was no way a brat with no cultivation could contend against a layer three Refinement Realm cultivator. If Li Wei was in the first layer, Li Shua might have given it a thought, but this brat had no qi in his body. His dantian was damaged at birth, and there was no way it could recover.

"No, he isn't. But he is poisoned, and in terrible condition. If he dies, you'll be in big trouble, brat. What were you doing inside Master Wu's shop?" He played with the ring on his finger.

"I was just coming back from market and saw a nice axe. I thought it would be useful for wood cutting."

Li Shua almost spurted blood. An artifact for cutting wood? Did he eat some bad fruit?

Master Wu was an Array Apprentice, and every weapon in his shop was an array artifact. The cheapest weapon would cost at least five hundred gold, and cultivators would die to have one. And this brat wanted to use an artifact to cut wood?

"Brat, stop messing around. If you trouble Master Wu, even I can't save you." Even a Bone Baptization Realm cultivator had to give face to Master Wu, and who was he? An ant?

While scolding Li Wei, Li Shua's gaze fell on the stone pot. It shone with a strange vitality. "Is that Poison Repelling Powder?"

Li Wei twitched and glanced at the powder. "Yes, grandfather. I bought it with money you gave me."

"But how did—"

Suddenly, the girl opened her eyes and a strong aura swept out of her.

Li Shua's heart trembled. This girl. She was in the seventh layer of Refinement Realm.

"Brat, this is your maidservant, right?"

Li Wei nodded.

"Then why is she in the seventh layer of Refinement Realm? How could a maidservant be this strong?" It was indeed a surprise. A maidservant would be so poor that stepping into the first layer would be impossible for them. However, this girl had already stepped in the seventh layer of Refinement Realm. In five years, she would cross the Refinement Realm and turn into an asset eyed by every clan in Old Martial City.

No, he couldn't let this happen. He had to get this girl married to Li Mu—his grandson. He would reach eighteen next year, and he had reached layer six of Refinement Realm. He had a great future ahead. Once Li Mu stepped into the Foundation Realm, Li Shua would use Foundation Refirming Pills and stabilize his foundation. Although he couldn't save Li Jia, Li Shua could make Li Jia's path as easy as possible. That would be a tribute to his dead son.

Yes, that he should do.

"Daughter in law, how are you feeling?" He couldn't restrain himself from asking her. "And is that a storage ring?" Li Shua's mind blew to pieces. How could a fifteen-year-old girl have a storage ring?

⋙ ⋘

Du Lufang frowned. In his hand lay a Red Blood Order. A Red Blood Order meant the highest priority of killing, and that order said to annihilate the Li clan.

It was from the patriarch, and he had just written one line: Destroy the Li clan at any cost.

Why? How? There was no answer for these questions, and he dare not ask when a Blood Red Order was issued from the Du clan patriarch.

There was another note attached. The first elder was coming to help him. That line made him gasp hard. The first elder was said to be in an unfathomable realm, and even the patriarch had to give him face.

"Steward Chin." He called the steward, and soon his annoying face showed up. His showed up with him.

"Husband, why are you shouting?"

Without answering her question, he handed the Red Blood Order to her.

"Master Du, I've received intel about the Li clan. They have found a heavenly herb in their area, and they have contacted Divine Fragrance Palace to collaborate."

"Husband, we can't let this chance pass us by. We have to eliminate Li clan before the first elder comes."

Du Lufang's eyes shone with a strange light. This was more than enough reason to eliminate the Li clan from Old Martial City. If he got his hand on the heavenly herb, with the help of the Wang clan, he could establish his authority in this city and might have time to become the next patriarch.

Yes, he had to get this done before the first elder visited Old Martial City.

"Steward Chin, contact Tian clan and ask their clan head to visit me right away. We have to do this fast." If he wasted any time, he might lose his chance to become clan patriarch.

Chapter 45

Shocking Breakthrough

Li Wei stared at the old man caressing his long white beard and shook his head. In one glance, he'd understood the old man's thoughts. He wanted to marry one of his grandsons to Fei'er, but he wouldn't let that happen. She had better prospects than anyone in the Li clan, so he would push her on the path of cultivation.

And how could he let his little friend get married to someone forcefully? Or let anyone touch that storage ring? It was a great advantage too.

"Grandfather, hold your horses." Wei interrupted. "Tang Sia, Divine Fragrance Palace's Holy Maiden, has taken her as a disciple, taught her the Nine Lotus Fragrance Qi Cultivation Art, and gifted her a storage ring. We can't touch her or the storage ring." He calmly warmed the old man.

The old man's face twitched, but his gaze remained fixed on the storage ring on Fei'er long slender finger. Greed was a pest that one could never get rid of. If Wei was in the old man's position, he might be tempted as well. If not for his two hundred years of life, he would consider this a once in a lifetime opportunity.

"Ha ha." The old man's lips jumped up and down in a forced laugh. "I just want to see what's inside. I won't take it away. There's no harm in having a look, is there?"

Wei chuckled in his heart. Greed was the evil of all men. If the old man glanced inside, he wouldn't be able to forget what he saw in there. Along with many pills, it also had a Bone Barrier Hitting Pill and that was a precious thing in Mortal Realm.

"If anything happens to her, our clan will be eradicated." Wei let a threat slip in his message, and the old man's face turned pale. The threat of clan destruction should wake him up.

"But—" The old man's hand went for the sword hanging from the belt around his dark blue robe. "It's just Holy Maiden. She is still in Foundation Realm."

Wei frowned. Would this man finally become decisive at the end of his life? All his life, this old man had shown only indecisiveness.

Brushing his fingers against the cold dagger lying inside his pouch, Wei let the tyrannical aura of the dagger penetrate his bones. If it came to it, he would flee with Fei'er after injuring this old man. Why not? Although Li Shua was his grandfather, the old man had never cared for him, nor had he come when his stepfather, Li Sua beat him so close to death that he had to run away from his home.

There were a lot of grievances from his previous life, and he didn't mind giving the old man a punch or two. Battling with his current power would invite trouble, but he could attack with fifty blood pearls and run away. That should be possible.

"Grandfather, I'll let you in on a secret. Holy Maiden Tang Sia didn't bring Fei'er with her because she was in a hurry to break through to Marrow Cleansing Realm. If she finds out about you harming the girl she put her trust in and shared a storage ring and cultivation method with, what would she do? Even if her sect doesn't do anything, she can still crush our clan and everyone else will give her face and not meddle in her revenge."

"Bone Baptization Realm at the age of twenty-one? She might reach Marrow Cleansing Realm by age thirty!" The old man choked on his breath and couldn't respond for a moment.

Marrow Cleansing Realm. Wei wanted to laugh. In the outside world there were prodigies that reached Houtian Realm by the age of twenty. What about a mere Marrow Cleansing Realm?

It was indeed true. After he left the Li clan, big news had hit the cultivation world. Tang Sia broke through to Marrow cleansing Realm at the age of twenty-four, and that shook the whole State of Zin. She was hailed as a prodigy in the State of Zin, and Divine Fragrance Palace set up a banquet for celebration. Many well-known cultivators attended it, hoping to set up a marriage alliance with Tang Zia. Of course, she rejected them, as she walked on the path of alchemy and wanted to reach the top.

Wei knew all about it because he'd tried to steal food from the banquets and was beaten up by a few disciples of Divine Fragrance Palace.

He sighed in his heart in depression. That was one of the worst days of his life.

"Fei'er show your cultivation art." Wei scanned the small girl who had just woken up from a coma and sat there, looking around, dumbfounded. Even Wei was shocked to see she had gained two layers of cultivation in her coma. Was she a monster? How could she raise her cultivation without cultivating at all?

Fei'er's eyes turned clear, and she sat in a cross-legged position and started cultivating.

With his divine sense, Wei could clearly feel heaven and earth's essence rushing toward her body. Although his grandfather wouldn't have as clear an understanding, he should feel the wood qi in the surrounding area. Only Divine Fragrance Palace practiced a wood cultivation art, so that should be proof of her being a disciple of the sect.

More and more heaven and earth's essence gathered around Fei'er, and he couldn't resist but send his divine sense into her body. With two hundred years' experience, he knew how to check someone's Spirit Root level. He just couldn't use it before because of his fragile divine sense.

"Damn, freaking mother!" he shouted and suddenly found Fei'er and the old man staring at him with weird eyes. He smiled sheepishly. "It's nothing, I was checking her pulse, and all is well." His words sounded normal to his ears, but he was freaking out on the inside. This girl was a monster. Her Spirit Root was a Human Grade Spirit Root.

How was it possible? Human Grade was a grade after Earth Grade, and this had never happened in the Mortal Realm before. Although he had an Earth Grade Physical Root, it was still a low-tier Earth Grade. This girl had a high-tier Human Grade Spirit Root. In the future, her cultivation would always surpass everyone around her. Even with his two hundred years of knowledge, he might not catch up to her.

He thought he should pass the Human Grade Divine Wood Qi Cultivation Art to her. In his previous life, he'd gotten it from a man who'd defaulted on his debt.

Above Earth Grade was Human Grade and then Heaven Grade, Heaven Grade being the highest grade he knew of. But in two hundred years of life, he had not seen anything that belonged to Heaven Grade. It was a Human Grade cultivation art, and he'd planned to cultivate it if he hadn't gotten his dantian repaired and also got his hand on Five Elemental Way cultivation art. This Divine Wood Qi Cultivation Art was the highest-grade cultivation art he knew of in his whole lifetime.

This was inconceivable.

"Forget it. It's not wise to go against Divine Fragrance Palace when we are about to get help from them. Having Fei'er with us might even help us in negotiation."

Business with Divine Fragrance Palace? What kind of business was the old man trying to conduct?

"Don't roam around anymore. I'll talk with the Du clan and set things up. There can't be any mistakes now. We can't attract their attention . . ." He turned back and then paused at the open doorframe. "I'll get a small tent patched up next to the cabin and get this door fixed. It's not good for a man and woman to stay in the same cabin. I'll also ask Li Ti to stay guard so no one from the Du clan dares try anything."

Wei's forehead wrinkled with black lines. If Li Ti guarded his door, how was he going to get the other herbs he wanted to experiment on?

Chapter 46

Qi Initiation Fruit Upgrade

"Uncle Li Ti, I'm going to sleep. You can go sleep too." Li Wei waved his hand to Li Ti sitting on a chair hundred feet away from his tent, looking tired. From the tent his shabby room looked so good and comfy, and it even had a new bed, a new door and delicious food brought by a servant.

And here he was, lying inside a patched up brown tent that stank with heaven knows what. The uneven ground pricked his ass through his old, thin bed roll, as there were few plants growing here that Li Ti had cleared to set up his tent.

Damn that old man. Couldn't he at least give him a nice soft bedroll? And wasn't he supposed to be the young master, and here his maidservant was being treated like a young lady of the house?

Sighing, he closed the tent flap and started changing his clothes. While settling into his tent, he had set up a Lesser Isolation Array so no one would find him cultivating in the night, and he had also carved a Persona Amplifying Array on his gray robe. It was a modified version of Armor Fortification Array, a low-tier Silver Grade array he and his friend Dian Ju had modified to create this simplified version.

Those were the days, and Dian Ju was a beast. That guy was a genius and a lecher. In fact, his brain had worked in a weirdly creative way. Persona Amplifying Array was Dian Ju's brainchild, and Wei had brought it to life. Dian Ju used it to fake a higher presence and slip away from the sect at night and do heaven knew what. Armor Fortification Array used a two-layered array structure to gather heaven and earth's essence from the surroundings and enhance a base artifact's powers. It was mostly used by the State of Zin military higher ups to increase their battle powers by at least three layers of Blood Baptization Realm. Three layers could change the tide of battle.

However, Armor Fortification Array had a drawback. Due to the two-layer array structure, it needed a minimum high-tier Bronze Grade artifact as a base and an Array Adept cultivator to carve those complex structures. So only high-level officers in the military could afford that array. But this Persona Amplifying Array didn't need a two-layer array structure, nor did it require a Power Enhancing Array, so it could be carved on a simple robe. Instead of a two-layer array structure, it used a simplified version of Power Enhancing Array and faked high realm cultivation.

Yes, it faked it. And it faked it so well that, with a tap of a low-quality Qi Stone, a layer one Refinement Realm could fake the cultivation of layer nine Foundation Realm.

Wei had a perfect use for it. With this array, he could get away from the Li clan and roam around doing his work. No one should bother him.

But before he could do anything, he had to step into the first layer of Refinement Realm to activate this array.

"I wish I could activate it using my body cultivation." Wei sighed in his heart as he lifted the Qi Initiation Fruit from his cloth pouch. As soon as he removed the purple cloth from the fruit, the scent of vitality rushed into his small tent. Thanks to the Lesser Isolation Array, he didn't need to worry about Li Ti finding out about his covert operation.

Elated, he dropped five white pearl-like drops on the fruit one by one.

The fruit started shaking as soon as the first drop entered it, and it grew in size. After the fifth drop entered, it grew thrice the size of the original. An overwhelming fragrance emitted from the fruit and permeated his senses when the fruit absorbed the fifth drop. It was so intense that his senses stirred when he inhaled it, and he felt like a divine might eased his muscles and bones. His whole body felt light as a feather, and his divine sense was enhanced a tad.

But that was nothing compared to the changes he felt in his dantian. It quivered like a thirsty bird waiting for rain in a desert.

Wow! If it could stir his dantian, what would happen once he ate a piece?

Unable to wait anymore, he cut the fruit in six parts and quickly ate one piece. That one piece equaled almost half of the original fruit, so he should get good benefits out of it.

The Qi Initiation Fruit piece melted after entering his mouth, and a stream of pure qi rushed into his body, heading toward his dantian. Along the way, it nourished his internal organs and pushed out impurities that had accumulated for sixteen years.

A smile grew on his face. He was finally stepping into Refinement Realm. In Refinement Realm, one would cleanse their body and clear their qi channels to form a qi path. Every other cultivator found their body resilient, improving in this realm, and their health improved by a huge margin. Compared to a mortal body, even a layer one qi Refinement Realm cultivator would have better life expectancy. They would fall ill less, they would have improved stamina, and so forth.

Although body cultivation also had similar realms, their real meaning differed a lot from qi cultivation. They even differed vastly among themselves. For example, his Firmament Fire Body Cultivation Art helped one to increase fire type essence capabilities of their body in Refinement Realm. It refined one's body so one could go through torturous methods to cultivate the next realms. Even his Blood Essence Body focused on his blood instead of his whole body. It was clearing his meridians, making his blood stronger and storing vitality in it.

In fact, after cultivating both cultivations to the peak of Refinement Realm, the benefits he would receive would be far superior than cultivating only one. But cultivating both at the same time would increase his overall cultivation time and the resources needed, and it was almost impossible.

Even thinking about the resources needed in future throbbed his mind. Anyway, he had the advantage of two hundred years of experience. Once he reached a higher cultivation, he would choose all the fortuitous encounters that would make it easy to obtain and gather those resources. After all, he wanted to be a lazy immortal, not a fool who always lived on the edge of life and death. He couldn't care less about those fools.

The stream of pure qi continued entering his body for an hour. As pure qi moved through his body, he cleared one qi channel after another and pushed his impurities to his skin.

Suddenly the pure qi stopped, and he realized he had refined one piece of fruit already.

How was it possible? In his experience, a twelve-year-old kid would take as much as two days to absorb a piece of fruit. Worried that something went wrong, he spread his divine sense throughout his body and then into his dantian, but there was no change. His dantian looked like a barren land. When a cultivator stepped into Refinement Realm, his dantian wouldn't store a lot of qi, and all the qi one absorbed would be used to connect qi paths. Initiation was the step to connect various qi channels to form a qi path.

Frowning, he grabbed another piece of fruit. Apparently, one piece that equaled half the original fruit wasn't enough for him to step into layer one.

Actually, it made sense. One piece equaled half of the original fruit, so he might not break through in one go. Some needed one slice, some needed two, and some even needed a whole fruit. It was rumored that Tang Zia ate a whole fruit to break into the first layer when she initiated her cultivation.

Pushing those stray thoughts away, he picked up another piece and stuffed it in his mouth to once again go through the feeling of bliss. Fifteen minutes later, the pure energy stopped traveling through his body, so he ate another piece. Then one more after ten minutes, and then one more.

When his hand reached for the last piece, he stopped.

What was going on? Theoretically, he had eaten two and half Qi Initiation Fruits, and yet he hadn't broken into the first layer. What would he do if he couldn't break through even after eating the last piece?

Chapter 47

Qi Initiation Layer

Li Wei gritted his teeth, unable to decide. On top of that, the creepy night outside the patched tent dimmed his resolve further.

Should he eat the last piece of the Qi Initiation Fruit or not? Would he break through or fail?

His gaze traced over the last piece of the fruit, observing the leaking vitality. If he kept it like this, it would only go to waste, and it smelled so nice. How could he resist the temptation?

He couldn't increase the fruit's age by pouring more Yin Yang Liquid, so there was no use trying. Five was the limit.

However, to confirm the fact, he poured one more drop on the fruit piece. Nothing happened. The fruit continued emitting the same amount of fragrance it had emitted earlier, and it remained the same size.

So, five drops was a hard limit for herbs.

"Dammit." Why the heck did his dantian look like a desert, even after eating five of these damn pieces?

Rubbing his chin for a minute, he tried to think of any place where he could get Qi Initiation Fruits, and the only place he could think of was Fragrance Herb City's auction house.

No, that wasn't an option for now. He lacked money and status to get through the front door. Fragrance Herb City's auction house only allowed participants with status. Although the Li clan would have a slot, why would that old man give it to him, a mere junior of the clan?

"Whatever. Worse case, I'll fail to initiate and have to find some other way. It's not like there isn't any other method to do this." He knew at least three of them, but they would require him to break through Foundation Realm in body cultivation first.

Shua!

With a flick of his palm, the fruit shoot into his mouth, and pure qi rushed through his throat and into his dantian, spreading a warm current in the deserted dantian and changing it subtly. His dantian walls were getting a little luster here and there, a sign of him advancing into the first layer of qi Refinement Realm.

Finally.

Suddenly heaven and earth's essence energy rushed from the heavens into his body. It was a phenomenon every cultivator experienced when one broke through major realms. This only occurred for qi cultivators. It was called

Immortal Endowment. It was the purest of the energy one received from the heavens, and one had to convert it into qi to get the most benefits out of it.

Greeting his teeth, he recalled the first layer of Five Elemental Way and practiced it, but he stopped when he noticed the changes happening inside his body.

What the heck was happening? He was distracted, and that was bad. When the Immortal Endowment happened, one had to be clear of any worry or distraction, but he was unsettled because the essence energy he'd received from the heavens was behaving on its own.

No. Actually, it was gushing in his Yangming meridian like a stream cascading over a cliff. It was nourishing his Yangming meridian, turning it dark red with every passing moment. At the same time, his blood pearl count increased, and as he was only ten pearls away from forming the five hundredth drop, he quickly passed this stage and suddenly his body rumbled, his bones cracked and his Taiyang meridian hummed in response.

Wow! He'd broken through into the fifth layer of body Refinement Realm like it was nothing. In fact, he'd expected he would be stuck at this layer, as this was a middle stage that perfected his Yangming meridian and opened his Taiyang.

One . . . two . . . ten . . . fifty . . . one hundred . . . one hundred seventy. Finally, his blood pearl count stopped increasing, and he stopped in the late period of the sixth layer of body Refinement Realm.

What the heck was happening? How could he breakthrough in body cultivation when he'd initiated qi cultivation? Wasn't it too bizarre? He now had six hundred and seventy blood pearls in his body and could rival a layer seven or eight qi Refinement Realm cultivator with sheer physical strength.

In the short period of five minutes, he had gained one hundred and eighty blood pearls. It was even faster than when he'd practiced Yin Yang Liquid auxiliary art. In fact, he'd stopped feeling bad about losing essence energy from the Immortal Endowment. However, this also led to a deficit in his qi cultivation, so he needed to cultivate to first layer as soon as possible, or he might suffer qi deviation and all his qi would go berserk, and fall back to his previous state. From there, it would be difficult to re-initiate the qi cultivation. So, he regrouped his thoughts and activated the token he had obtained from the Inheritance Chamber. It had a Qi Transformation Array carved on it, and it would gather heaven and earth's essence from nature and convert it into pure qi that any cultivator could absorb. It was a Gold Grade array, and quite precious even in the Martial Realm.

At least he didn't have to worry about exposing it in the Mortal Realm, as he believed no one here would know about it.

After activating the array, heaven and earth's essence started gathering around the metal token. After entering the token, it was purified and refined and came out as a wisp of pure qi from the other side. This array also eliminated the foul essence energy from the absorbed one and only converted the purest of essence into pure qi. So, he didn't have to worry about refining foul qi inside his body.

Unlike body cultivation art, qi cultivation art worked differently. Body cultivation art was mostly about making one's body stronger and firmer, while qi cultivation art regulated essence flow through one's body and then stored it in the dantian as qi corresponding to the Spirit Root attribute. Before reaching Houtian realm, one could use their qi to nourish their five internal organs, bones, and marrow, but they still needed to convert essence energy into qi using their dantian. This set up their foundation for higher realms. In contrast, body cultivators used essence energy to make their whole body strong.

Nourishment and increasing strength were two different things!

Anyway, this was the path a normal cultivator would take. For Wei, it was a totally different scenario. His Qi Transformation Array was converting essence energy into pure qi, and he had to push it into his dantian and circulate the qi using Five Elemental Way's first layer.

Wisps of pure qi drifted out of the Qi Transformation Array, and he straightaway inhaled it, pushing it toward his dantian. Passing through his dantian, pure qi rushed through the qi channels in his body and then re-entered his dantian through the connecting qi channels.

His body grumbled from inside as his qi paths were formed between various qi channels. This meant he had stepped onto the path of qi cultivation. Currently his qi path only had a hair's width, and with every revolution it would start getting wider. Although he absorbed a lot of pure qi coming out of the token array, most of it was used to clear impurities from his qi channels present in various internal organs. Besides clearing impurities, it also nourished his internal organs. So, theoretically, if he pushed 100 units of qi out of his dantian, only 1 or 2 units of pure qi came back after one revolution. But the returned qi would have his mark embedded in it, and it would act according to his will.

Once he reached Foundation Realm, the amount of qi used would increase, and so would his qi path width. This would continue happening until he reached Houtian Realm. That's when his actual qi path would be established. After reaching Foundation Realm, his dantian would convert qi into the attribute his Spirit Root belonged to. In Refinement Realm, every cultivator would only cultivate pure qi, and only after reaching Foundation Realm would they start converting it into their attribute. That's when one would give birth to Wisp of Soul power, enabling them to walk on the paths of alchemy, arrays, artifact refining, or formations.

But Wei didn't face that issue. He had an intact divine sense, born and strengthened from interaction with a Soul Stone. He could very well practice these other paths of cultivation anytime. In fact, if he was in ancient times, he would need not walk on the path of qi, as those masters used their soul powers to do everything one needed qi for.

However, all these heaven-defying techniques were lost to time. So, he had to walk on the path of qi cultivation in his second life too.

Wei continued clearing his qi channels of impurities and connecting them to form a qi path. Suddenly, he felt bloated, and couldn't absorb any purer qi into his dantian. Any more, and he might burst, so he stopped cultivating. It was within his expectations. He had just initiated his cultivation, so he couldn't store too much qi in his body. It would take time, days, to reach the first layer of qi Refinement Realm.

Wait, what? How could there be sunlight coming through the holes on his tent?

Chapter 48

Li Guan

Cold sweat broke out over his back when Li Wei realized the sun had set, and he had cultivated for the whole night. His stomach growling confirmed his discovery.

He had cultivated for twelve hours straight.

Suddenly he smelled something rotten, and when he looked down, he couldn't control the awe in his heart.

"Dammit! How can it be?"

A small puddle of black liquid had formed around his body, dirtying his whole bedroll, and he didn't dare sniff himself. He reeked like he'd just climbed out of a garbage hole.

How could he exude this many impurities? If someone else saw this, they might think his body was made of impurities instead of fat.

"My stomach!" he shouted when his gaze fell on his almost flat stomach. Had he really carried impurities instead of fat? Because if not, how could he explain the fat loss from all over his body?

"Brat, why are you shouting so early in the morning?" The old man's voice reverberated around the tent as he stepped in only to run back out like a dog bit his rear.

Wei followed him out quickly and then rushed to the bathing area without looking at the old man.

After cleaning himself thoroughly and changing into a new set of clothes, Wei walked back toward his tent but found it was gone, and a few maids were spraying scented water over the place.

"Brat, what did you do in there? How could you lose your bowels and shit that hard? It was like you packed it in for a couple of years and then let it all out in one go." The old man hesitated for a moment before stepping close to him.

"Grandfather, I didn't . . ." A firm palm gripped his shoulder.

A tall youth walked out of the woods and snickered. "Ha ha. I didn't know brother Wei's excretion skills had improved so much that even maids are pinching their noses." Li Guan wore a dark blue robe and his long hair fluttered over his shoulders. He liked it loose, unlike others who kept it tied in a bun.

Wei's eyes narrowed into a slit. "Li Guan. Why are you here?" Li Guan was Li Tang's foul-mouthed son. In the Li clan's young generation, he had the best cultivation, and he liked to beat up everyone around him. Whenever he came to Old Martial City, Wei fell for his tricks and got beaten up.

"Ha ha. It seems like you forgot the beating I gave you last time."

Wei frowned. He had nearly forgotten that incident. It had been half a year ago that Li Guan beat him like a dog, and he was bedridden for ten straight days. But given that he had lived for two hundred years and reincarnated since then, why would he remember such an insignificant event? It didn't matter to him anymore, nor did Li Guan matter. He just had to treat it like a fart.

"Grandfather, greetings." Li Guan cupped his hands in front of the old man. "I'm here to meet little sister Fei. I heard she is a beauty, and I want to take her out to roam this small city. Please allow me."

Wei's frown deepened. Li Guan must have learned about Fei'er's connection to Divine Fragrance Palace by now, and he must be here to win her favor.

In his dreams.

"Li Guan." Wei stepped forward, blocking Li Guan. "Isn't it important to settle our scores whenever we meet?" This was the exact line Li Guan had used before beating him every time they met, and no one had stopped him.

The old man squinted his eyes. "Wei'er—"

"Young master." Fei'er ran out of Wei's shabby room but stopped when she spotted Li Guan standing near him.

Her blue eyes glared at Li Guan sharply.

Li Guan squirmed when he glanced at Fei'er sharp gaze, then shifted his focus back to Wei. "Grandfather, this trash wants to get beaten," he boasted while slapping his chest. "Please don't stop me from teaching him a lesson. As an older brother, I've taken responsibility for this trash." He had a cold smirk plastered over his face.

Wei chuckled in his mind. Li Guan must think to step on him and win over the beauty, but he didn't know Wei had broken through two layers in one night. And even if he hadn't, his body cultivation was enough to beat Li Guan to death.

"Guan'er, you—"

"Grandfather. Please let us spar for a moment. I want to see if brother Guan still pees his pants when he gets beaten up." Wei remembered this from his childhood, that Li Guan used to pee his pants whenever he was scared.

The old man just shrugged, once again showing his indecisiveness.

Li Guan growled. "Li Wei. Don't spout nonsense. I never peed my pants."

Li Wei snickered. "Take a heart oath and clear the air."

Li Guan flushed red, nerves popping out from his neck. "Bastard. You are courting your death. I'll slap you with my fist technique. Sleeping Dragon Fist." Pulling his elbow back, he thrust his fist at Wei.

Wei chuckled. "It's not even a dog's fart, and you call it sleeping dragon." This was a very basic martial skill anyone could obtain with a few gold in the State of Zin. It only had one level, and it couldn't even exert the full pressure of a martial artist. Using it would only deteriorate one's powers.

In other words, it was trash. If Wei took it head on, it wouldn't even bend a hair on his body.

Wei side-stepped and let the fist fly through empty air.

Li Guan stumbled and almost fell on his face. "What are you doing? If you are a man, then take the fist head on," he shouted and turned back to send another fist at Wei.

"You are hilarious." Wei bent at the waist and dodged the fist. Although he wasn't a strong battle artist in his previous life, Li Guang was a frog. He couldn't even attack like the wolves Wei had faced in the tunnel. "Li Guan, are you trying to catch a fly? Why are you dancing like a monkey?"

"You—" Li Guan roared and dashed toward Wei, but Wei just stepped aside and let Li Guang fall flat on his face. Unfortunately for Li Guang, he fell right where Wei's tent had been and muddied his face with soil and dust.

Suddenly, the suppressed smell of impurities rose in the air, thrashing everyone's noses.

Fei'er couldn't hold her laughter anymore and snickered loudly. "Good job, young master." She even clapped loudly.

Li Guang got up and turned back with his blackened face, and Fei'er exploded in full-blown laughter. Even the maids watching from the sidelines couldn't hold back.

"Enough. Wei, what are you trying to show here? If you want to fight, then fight like a man." Li Tang's voice rang out.

Wei glared at his bastard uncle, wondering if he could kill him in one shot if he burned his blood pearls.

Maybe not. Although he was catching up with his uncle's cultivation, a whole realm's difference was too much to cross. He'd wait until he stepped into Foundation Realm, then it wouldn't be an issue.

Li Guan shot at him with his fist extended. "Fire Beast Palm." A tiny fire enveloped Li Guan's palm and struck forward viciously. Fire Beast Palm and Fire Beast Sword Art were two martial skills the Li clan practiced.

Now that he thought about it, everyone in the Li clan was born with a fire-attributed Spirit Root, so he must have inherited his attributeless Spirit Root from his father. Pushing that stray thought away, Wei struck with his palm.

The fist and palm attacks collided. One was backed with the half-assed Sleeping Dragon Fist skill from layer six of qi Refinement Realm, the other with a combination of layer six in body Refinement Realm and layer four in qi Refinement Realm.

Who would win?

With a cracking sound, Li Guan staggered backward; his eyes held shock, dissatisfaction.

And then he started shouting in pain.

"Father, Li Wei broke my bones." He flopped on the ground and started crying loudly.

The old man's eyes nearly popped out of his skull when he saw Li Guan rolling on the ground. "Brat, you—"

"Grandfather, this junior reached layer two of Refinement Realm recently." Wei had a smug smile plastered on his face.

Chapter 49

Forbidden Technique

"Brat, you—" The old man gauged Li Wei like one might a monster. If his eyes popped out any more, they would fall out of his skull.

"Grandfather, this junior reached layer two of Refinement Realm recently," Wei answered calmly. Although he didn't like this old man much, he had to show some respect, as he was still in the Li clan compound.

Shock was evident on the old man's face.

"You, brat. How did you dare to hit my son? Are you tired of living?" Li Tang pulled his son up to his feet, checking his condition.

A small smile played on Wei's lips. "Uncle, where were you when he beat me half to death a few months back?"

The old man ignored Li Tang. "Brat, how did you cultivate?"

"He must have hidden the benefits he got from the pit he pretended to fell," Li Tang said forcefully, pulling a pill out of his pouch and stuffing it in Li Guan's mouth. Li Guan continued crying as he bit down on the pill.

"And what does that have to do with you, uncle?" This bastard uncle of his was getting in his head now. First Li Tang had almost killed him, and now—rather than being guilty for his action—Li Tang was coveting things from him. When Wei had returned to the compound, he had planned to take care of this uncle of his, but it seemed that he would have to do it earlier than he'd thought.

"Father, let's capture this brat and interrogate him. He is definitely hiding something, otherwise how could trash like him break Guan'er's arm with one palm attack. I think Jia'er died because of him."

Wei chuckled. This uncle of his was now building a palace in the air. Did he think everyone around them was stupid like him?

"Brother, how can you say that?" Li Ti stepped forward. He had come along with Li Tang. "Li Wei took you to the pit where he obtained the Body Refirming Pill. In doing so, he has done a meritorious service for the clan."

Li Tang flushed red. "Now that I think about it, he must have lured Jia'er in there and got him killed." He stroked his short beard. "Yes, that has to be it. Now I remember, this brat kept saying there was no danger, and Jia'er stepped in unprepared and died. This brat wanted to send us to death and then enjoy the benefits."

Li Ti shook his head; he didn't seem to buy Li Tang's lie.

"Uncle Tang. Are you afraid I'll let your secret out, and that's why you are trying to frame me?" Wei chuckled in his mind, but in reality, he maintained a furious face. This bastard uncle of his wanted to die today. What could he do about it?

"Brat, what secret are you talking about?" The old man rubbed his chin.

Wei blinked at his uncle. "Uncle, shall I let out the secret?"

"You impudent brat. You dare talk back to me, your uncle? You are insolent like that bitch sister of ours. She had already ruined our clan by giving birth to you without marriage, and now you're doing the same. If you have guts then go—"

"Tang'er," The old man shouted, and Li Tang swallowed his own words.

"Father, this bastard stole benefits from the clan and hid his cultivation to injure our Guan'er. We can't let him go. We must punish him." He panted heavily. "I say we execute him right away. We have to eliminate a rude brat from our clan before he brings a calamity to our clan." Pulling his sword out, he dashed toward Wei.

Wei frowned. Li Tang had reached layer five qi Foundation Realm. A whole realm above him. If Li Tang attacked him, he wouldn't stand a chance to retaliate, even with his strong body. The gap between their cultivation was huge.

But if he used that forbidden technique, he would stand a chance to injure Li Tang and keep his life too. It was called Essence Burning Art. Anyone that stepped on the path of qi cultivation could use it and get battle prowess equal to one realm higher than their current realm.

However, he could only use it once in every realm until he reached Houtian Realm. And using it would burn his life essence, his cultivation would regress to level zero of his current realm—so he would have to cultivate all over—and breaking into every layer would be twice as difficult as normal.

But if it came to it, he had to take that chance. And he had just reached layer two of Refinement Realm, so using it would only regress him to level zero. Other than his life essence, he wouldn't lose much.

"Li Tang. Stop." The old man flicked his palm when Li Tang passed near him, and Li Tang was pushed ten steps back.

"Father, you . . ."

"Yes. I've advanced into layer seven." The old man smiled, but his smile seemed to be weighted. "Ti'er. What did the Ten Thousand Miles Pigeon bring you?"

A Ten Thousand Miles Pigeon was a Ferocious Beast that could travel ten thousand miles in a day, and it could be petted to carry letters or messages. If it came, that meant something big had happened.

"Father, a special envoy has come from the Martial Envoy Sect of the Great Martial Empire. They plan to recruit a few disciples from North Providence. Shall we send Li Guan and Li Pi to take part in the recruitment drive in Fragrance Herb City?"

Wei squinted, thinking. This was weird. Great Martial Empire was one of the five great empires of the Mortal World. They governed thirty percent of the whole Mortal World, remaining four empires governed fifty percent while remaining twenty percent were ruled by their vassal kingdoms. Their own kingdom, the State of Zin, was a vassal force of Great Qlin Empire, and they remained neutral with other empires. Normally, sects didn't participate in the worldly affairs of mortals. They generally stood aloof, backed by sects from the Martial World, so empires didn't dare to go against sects. But this Martial Envoy Sect was different. They were the force behind the Great Martial Empire, and their force coming to Fragrance Herb City had great implications for their State of Zin. This single event initiated a war between Great Qlin Empire and Great Martial Empire.

But he wasn't worried about the war. It was run across the border, far away from Fragrance Herb City. And , nor could these forces invade territory governed by Divine

Fragrance Palace. They had backup from the Divine Alchemy Hall from the Martial World, and they were renowned in alchemy, so no one dared to enter into conflict with either of these sects.

However, this event also marked the annihilation of the Li clan in the timeline.

In his previous life, he had talked with three different people, and everyone said the Li clan faced a calamity after the Martial Envoy Sect arrived in Herb Fragrance City, that the Du clan's Bone Baptization Realm elder killed everyone.

This was bad. This meant the Du clan's Bone Baptization Realm cultivator would be here any day, and Wei had to get Li Chi and Ki Fei out of here as soon as possible.

"Let's talk about it once the leader from Divine Fragrance Palace visit us." The old man turned to face Wei. "Wei'er, walk with me."

"But father, how can you—" Li Tang began but was stopped by the old man's raised hand.

"Enough." The old man grunted, and Li Tang stepped back with frustration plastered over his ugly face.

Wei snickered, but his face remained gloomy as he followed the old man into woods. The old man had lied to Li Tang. He hadn't reached layer seven, but layer eight of qi Foundation Realm. How could he hide it from Wei's divine sense? The old man hid his real strength from his own son.

Green trees covered their path, and soon they were out of anyone's reach. Spreading his divine sense, Wei checked to see if anyone followed them. But they were alone.

"Little Wei. When was the last time you saw your mother?" The old man asked in a choked voice.

Wei was startled. He thought the old man would reprimand him for beating his favorite grandchild, but he suddenly asked about his mother instead. What was going on?

"I remember," he continued without waiting for Wei's answer. "You were just four, and she . . ."

Sadness crept through Wei's mind. He too remembered that day. He'd been searching for his mother to ask for food when he heard his stepfather shouting at someone, and then news came that his mother had died in a battle.

"I loved Min'er the most. Even more than my three sons." His grandfather sounded old and fragile. His eyes stared at the horizon, his expression turning solemn. But he couldn't fool Wei. Wei knew him well.

"If you loved her, why did you force her to marry Li Sua?" Wei snapped. He didn't want to hear doctored words from this old man. No matter how much he tried to be benevolent, Wei wouldn't fall for his flowery words.

The old man didn't reply for a minute. Or he couldn't. How could he refute Wei's words when Wei knew he was in the wrong here? He sighed, a heartbreaking sigh. "I was forced to. I had to do it to save your life. I just hoped you'd live a normal life."

Wei snorted. What a joke. "A normal life where my stepfather beat me every other day? A life where I wasn't even given a single pill to heal my dantian?" In his previous life, when Wang Zia had sealed his leaky dantian using an array, she'd cursed his clan for not giving him a pill to heal his dantian when he was born. She'd said they could have fixed it with a simple pill. Thankfully, he'd managed to heal it on his own. Otherwise, he would have had to live with a sealing array that ultimately limited his dantian's capacity by fifty percent.

"I couldn't. That was a condition for your life. How could I choose between your cultivation and your life?" His voice choked. "Min'er begged me many times, but even if I'd found a Gold Grade pill, how could one heal the injury given by them?"

"Are you saying someone injured my dantian on purpose, that wasn't a birth defect?" This was serious news. In his previous life, he'd always thought he'd had a birth defect and cursed his destiny. And the Li clan was exterminated by the time he got back. So, how could he know the truth?

But listening to his grandfather, it seemed there was a scary truth behind everything.

What was it?

Chapter 50

Stepbrother?

Li Wei and the old man stepped on a trail that led to a mountain adjacent to the Li clan's compound. White clouds covered the mountain peaks, and the whole base of this small mountain was the Li clan's property. Many clans living in Old Martial City had settled their compounds near mountains, using the slope to cultivate herb gardens. Even the Li clan had done the same.

Although these herbs were only low-tier Bronze Grade, they made up the Li clan's side income.

The herbs' fragrance shrouded them soon, and they entered the herb garden. Wei's eyes gleamed for a moment before turning back to look at the old man. He had been quiet for ten minutes and hadn't answered his question yet.

"Old man. Why aren't you answering my question?"

The old man stopped below a pine tree that had popped up in the middle of the herb garden. It seemed odd to have a towering tree at the middle of the garden. He picked up five nearby stones and placed them on certain points by counting his distance and the angle of the tree.

What the heck was he doing? Was he playing a kid's game with those stones?

Wait. Wei's mind stirred when he detected an undulation of energy through those five stones. No, it wasn't coming from the five stones, but the array lines connecting those source points. In his divine essence, those lights flickered like a bright sun before dimming once more.

Damn, how did the old man carve an advanced array on this place?

The old man stepped forward and tapped on the tree trunk, hitting five points again that matched the stone pattern he'd placed around the tree.

Wei felt goosebumps raising over his whole body.

It was indeed an array, and an advanced one. This wasn't a two-layer array, but a twofold array. Each side balanced the other, and none could be activated without following a proper sequence. This was a far more advanced concept than normal arrays which could be broken by tapping on a few source spots.

Wow!

A small portion of the tree trunk in front of the old man's face caved in, and a keyhole appeared. The old man fumbled through his pouch and took a storage ring out. Out of that storage ring, a rusted green key popped out.

When the key was exposed to the air, it shone with a golden light and, like a snake shredding its old skin, it shed the rusted green color and turned into a pure gold key.

Wei frowned. This wasn't a Mortal Realm artifact, nor a Martial Realm artifact. It had to be an ancient artifact that the old man had gotten his hands on.

But why was he showing this to Wei?

The old man put the key in the keyhole, and a golden circle wrapped around the keyhole, and it vanished, replaced by a small hole.

Wei's eyes widened. It had to be another array, but he didn't remember seeing anything like this in the Inheritance of Array Masters.

How could it be possible?

"Your brother left this with me. He said if you even step on the path of cultivation, this should be your gift from him." The old man pulled a small pendant out of the hole and handed it to Wei.

"What is this thing?" Wei rubbed his fingers on the green pendant-like object. It was colder than normal, and it glimmered when he touched it. "Wait, what? A brother?" Wei's head jerked up, his mouth wide open. When did he get a brother?

The old man sighed. "He isn't your real brother, but a stepbrother. Your father's son from another woman."

Wei chocked on his saliva. What the fuck was wrong with his family?

Were they crazy for sex? His father had another wife and a son, his mother had married another man and gave him a stepfather. "What the heck is this thing, old man?"

"Maybe a storage object. Your brother said you would find its use if you reached Houtian Realm. But you have to bind it with your blood."

Wei rubbed the strange green pendant, feeling the intricate design carved on the green stone embedded in the golden ring. Touching it made him remember a strange stone he'd seen in a secret dimension in his previous life. That stone was called a Bloodline Stone, and it was formed from the blood of primordial beasts that were extinct. People went crazy for such a thing, as it could enhance their own vitality. Was this stone the same thing?

It didn't look like one, as it had some patterns carved on it.

Thinking about something, he poured a bit of his divine sense in the pendant, and it was sucked in. Okay, he didn't expect that to happen.

Now he wanted to know origin of this stone and why his brother left it for him.

Curious, he cut his finger open and let a drop of blood fall on it. It was sucked in right away. The pendant emitted a green light and hovered in the air and then wrapped around his neck on its own accord. A piercing pain emerged from his neck when the pendant cut through his skin, and a strange suction force emerged from it, sucking in his blood.

Cursing loudly, he tried to pull the pendant out, but to no avail. The pendant stuck to his neck like a leech. He could feel his blood entering the pendant like a river entering the sea.

"Wei'er, what happened? Why's your face so pale?" The old man asked, sounding worried.

Damn this old man. Did he give him some kind of cursed item? Why the heck was this pendant pulling blood from his body? With his divine sense, he could feel his blood being sucked into the pendant, and his total blood percentage was decreasing rapidly.

Fuck it.

Dropping on the ground, he sat cross legged and circulated Blood Essence Body Cultivation Art. If the pendant was trying to suck him dry, he would overcome it by feeding it more than it could take in.

Broom!

Heaven and earth's essence rushed through his mouth and moved toward his Yangming meridian and began generating new blood in abundance. After stepping into Refinement Realm of Blood Essence Body, generating new blood was child's play. Of course, that didn't mean he was invincible or that his body could regenerate limbs. But if he faced anything that sucked blood from his body, he didn't have to worry about it.

Or so he'd thought.

At first, he could replenish as much blood as he lost. But as time passed, the suction force increased, and it became difficult to maintain the balance between suction and creation. After ten minutes he was failing miserably and could only generate fifty percent of the blood that was sucked away.

This was bad. Sweat rolled down his face, and he could feel his heart throbbing with pain as he pushed it to work harder.

Ten minutes later, the blood suction force increased by a factor of two, but his creation speed remained the same. So, he was only refilling a quarter of the blood he was losing, his blood level was hitting rock bottom, and that started affecting his bodily functions.

Damn, what the heck was this thing? Was it a trap to kill him? If it was someone else, he would have died ten times by now.

When his blood level dropped to fifteen percent, he wrapped his palm around the pendant and readied himself to burn his blood pearls to boost his power and pull it away from his neck.

However, he didn't need to. When his blood level reached ten percent, his blood pearls started dissolving automatically, refilling his blood quickly.

The pressure on his heart vanished, and his tense muscles eased. Now his blood was refilling at a speed higher than the suction force, but he was burning his blood pearls faster. If this continued for an hour more, he would run out of blood pearls.

And then he would die.

Chapter 51

Trap or gift?

A cold wind blew across the green herb garden, but it didn't ease Li Wei. As his blood pearls continued burning, imminent immense danger gripped his heart. If this continued, he would definitely die.

However, after ten minutes the sucking stopped. Thanks to the heavens, he didn't have to burn all the blood pearls from his body.

Yet he'd had to burn 280 blood pearls. If he hadn't reached layer three, he would have died.

After the suction stopped, the pendant loosened from his neck and dropped into his lap. Its color had changed from bright green to blood red. It even emitted a bloody aura that sent a shiver across his legs.

Sweat broke out all over his body. If he'd been below layer three of body Refinement Realm, he would have died.

"Wei'er, what is that thing? Why is it red suddenly?" The old man bent down to touch the pendant, but Wei pushed his shriveled old hand away.

"Old man, it's a dangerous thing." He stared at the pendant, unable to understand what the heck it was. He had never seen or heard of anything like it. Of course, he had heard about some Ferocious Beasts that could suck one dry in a breath's time, but those were present in the depths of the Dark Forest spread across the east of the State of Zin. It divided the State of Zin from other countries. It was an ancient forest, and no one knew how many millions of years it had stood there, guarding immeasurable secrets inside.

Well, he didn't have to worry about the blood-sucking beasts or the Dark Forest, as he had no plans to venture inside. He was trying to be a lazy immortal, not a battle-crazy immortal.

Fear still gripping his heart, Wei reached out a finger to touch the pendant. If it attacked again, he could still overcome it with his remaining blood pearls. When his finger hovered an inch from the pendant, his heart raced faster than an Iron Blood Horse, the fastest horse breed of the State of Zin. He nearly lost his courage but pushed himself and touched it.

System: Information interface detected. Downloading message.

A percentage marker popped up, and when it reached one hundred, a young man's image appeared in Wei's mind. His clear green eyes shone when he talked, and Wei realized he had some similar features like him, but he had green eyes. Deep and dangerous green eyes.

"Brother. If you are reading this message, then I assume you've reached the first step in cultivation. Houtian Realm. This pendant is special, and will help you to survive in this brutal cultivation world. You can drop some blood on it, and it will give you enough of a boost to battle across the layers. I hope you like my gift."

Bastard! This wasn't a gift but a trap. A fucking trap. That green-eyed bastard said he needed only a few drops, but this nasty thing had sucked gallons of his blood. If it wasn't for his special cultivation art, he would have been sucked dry before he could view this message.

And how could he already bound it when he hadn't reached Houtian Realm?

He couldn't trust this stepbrother of his, for sure.

"It was a gift given by our father, and he used it for a hundred years at least, and now I'm passing it on to you. I hope we will meet soon. One more thing, don't use this before Houtian Realm or it might be perilous to you."

"Damn you, bastard." Wei couldn't resist cursing. This stepbrother of his was a real jerk, and if his father had passed it on to him, then his father was a jerk too. If he ever met him, Wei would blast his ass with some explosives.

System: Usage information received.

Primordial Blood Palace

Bound to host.

Can inject a wisp of qi to increase host's cultivation temporarily by using the blood stored in it.

Current fill: 10%

What the heck was this system? It had once again shocked him to his core. It seemed this pendant was something special. This had to be a Heaven Grade artifact. Otherwise, how could it behave like this?

And the most shocking thing? After losing gallons of blood, he'd only filled 10% of this Primordial Blood Palace. If it hadn't stopped of its own accord, how much would it need to take from him?

A thin film of cold sweat formed over his neck. He had survived by a fluke. What if it didn't stop sucking blood from him next time?

No, he shouldn't use this thing unless he reached a higher cultivation level.

Putting it in his pouch, he raised his gaze to the old man.

"Old man, is my real father alive?"

After a long sigh, the old man shook his head in disdain. "I don't know. I've never met him. Min'er came back when she was pregnant with you, and then one day your stepbrother came and gave me this pendant. Only Min'er knew if he was alive or not."

Wei bit his lip until it bled. After all, his father was a jerk who'd run away and left his pregnant wife.

But why did he send Wei's stepbrother to check on a dumped woman? And why did his stepbrother agree? Even leaving this pendant behind made little sense. In his previous life, he'd never gotten to hear this side of the story. He'd just thought his mother had died, and his real father had died before he was born.

But the truth was something else, and he thanked heaven for giving him a second chance to know this truth.

This also made one thing clear in his heart: If he ever met his father in the future, he might even beat that jerk. Who cared if that man was his father? Wei hated him for leaving them behind. Why couldn't he take him and his mother with him? If he had used this pendant for a hundred years, that meant he had at least reached Xiantian Realm. If he was in Xiantian Realm, who could threaten him in the Martial World? Xiantian Realm experts were overlords of the Martial Realm, and nobody provoked them.

Then why?

"Brat. Don't ask any more about your parents. I know nothing else. Take this and step away from the Li clan, else you might die here." The old man pulled a yellow paper out of his robe and handed it to him. "At first, I wasn't worried about you because you couldn't cultivate, and if things got hard, you could leave unharmed. But you have stepped onto the path of cultivation, so this is my last option to save your life."

Wei stared at the yellow paper in his hand and couldn't control his shock. This was an Overwhelming Shield Talisman. A high-tier Silver Grade talisman that could take ten attacks from a Bone Baptization Realm cultivator.

How could the old man hand it over to him like that? And if he was giving him this talisman, that meant he was sure of the Li clan's destruction. Did he already know about the Du clan's Bone Baptization Realm elder? No, it couldn't be. The Du clan had hidden it from everyone.

Then what the fuck was happening outside?

Chapter 52

Du clan barge in

Li Tang brushed his fingers over the white ceramic cup's rim, experiencing the sharp feeling it produced in his heart. It was filled with Warm Fragrance Tea and mixed with Blood Nourishing Powder to ease the pain in his body. Warm Fragrance Tea had a tranquil and warm feeling, but mixing Blood Nourishing Powder dampened its fragrance by a tad, and that irritated him.

But he had no other choice. He had given up on that choice years back.

Back when he ate that poisonous One Path Fruit, he knew this would happen, but for his own bright future, he had to eat it and step into Foundation Realm. It had advanced him in Foundation Realm in one go, but also reduced his lifespan by half and left him with this blood poison flaring up now and then.

There was only one solution to it, and that was to step into Bone Baptization Realm before age thirty. It wouldn't give him back his lifespan, but once he stepped into Bone Baptization Realm, his lifespan would increase to two hundred years, giving him a few more years to reach the next realm even if it was cut in half.

His face darkened when someone banged on his private room's wooden door as if someone would die if he won't open the door quickly.

"Who dares to disturb my cultivation?" he roared. The calming tea had a sweet and tranquil aroma as well as a nourishing effect on one's comprehension ability. He had to settle his mind before eating a Body Refirming Pill. If he ate it while angry, the effect might not be as efficient as it would be when taken with a calm mind.

With a long stride, he opened the door and struck with his palm when he spotted a servant standing outside. His palm swooshed through the air and hit the servant's face and sent him flying backward.

"Impudent whelp. Are you tired of living?"

"Young master Tang, please forgive this insolent lowly servant, but you have to come outside else the matter will get out of hand."

"What's going on?" Li Tang asked, suppressing anger in his heart. He was already pissed off because of that puny bastard Li Wei, and now someone dared to disturb his cultivation. It was like no one in Old Martial City took him seriously. He should put everyone through a tough training regime so they would learn some discipline. Especially that Li Wei. He must die.

"Reporting to young master, the Du clan's city head is standing outside of the clan compound and beating our guards."

Li Tang furrowed his brow. Had Du Lufang gone crazy? Or did he not know his father, Li Shua, was in town? How could a mere layer four Foundation Realm ant dare to cause trouble in the Li clan compound and beat their guards? Of course, he wasn't worried about the Li clan guards—he would often beat them himself—but someone else beating them was like not putting the Li clan in their eyes. It was a slap in the face. How could Li Tang take it lightly?

Without issuing any punishment for the impudent servant, he dashed out to the front area of the Li clan compound. It seemed he needed to teach Du Lufang a lesson today. Although the Li clan couldn't go against the Du clan wholly, beating a mere city head of the Du clan wouldn't bring any trouble. Then again, Du Lufang had struck first, so it should be okay if he taught Du Lufang a heavy lesson.

And once they received support from Divine Fragrance Palace, why would he fear the Du clan? Heck, he wouldn't even fear the Wang clan—the Du clan's ally by marriage.

When he reached the main area, he saw that Du Lufang had knocked two of their Refinement Realm guards unconscious. He was even daring enough to hit a Li clan elder that had come with them to Old Martial City, and that elder was in layer two of Foundation Realm.

"Du Lufang, you're crossing the line," Li Tang shouted, rage bursting through his roar.

"Li Tang, call your father. I don't talk with minor characters." Du Lufang snickered and continued hitting their guard.

"Du Lufang, if you don't stop and give me a proper explanation, don't blame me for being merciless." Li Tang pulled his sword out. If it came to the blows, he wasn't afraid of Du Lufang. With his cultivation realm and advancement of sword martial skills, he could suppress Du Lufang.

"Li Tang. It seems I have to teach you a lesson first before your coward patriarch will come out."

Li Tang's nerves on his neck popped out, and he charged forward with his sword raised in the air. "Earthly Sword Strike." It was an exclusive skill cultivated in the Li clan, and he had reached level three of the same, overshadowing his peers. One time he had fought two layer-four Foundation Realm cultivators simultaneously and the fight had ended in a draw. In front of him, a single layer four Refinement Realm cultivator was like an ant.

"Overbearing Boulder Sword." Du Lufang brandished his sword and swung it upward. Like the Li clan, the Du clan too practiced the sword, and they were famous for this Overbearing Boulder Sword. It was a high-tier Silver Grade martial skill and had greater might than the Li clan's Earthly Sword Strike, but it couldn't surpass cultivation layers and beat someone. So, Li Tang wasn't worried about this overbearing skill.

"Suppress him!" Li Tang roared as his sword bore down on Du Lufang.

However, contrary to his expectation, Li Tang's sword strike didn't suppress Du Lufang. Instead, Li Tang felt like his joint in shoulder was crushed when their swords met.

Sparks flew and Li Tang's sword flew back. The pressure Du Lufang executed was much higher than Li Tang's sword strike.

"No way." Li Tang shook his right hand, trying to shake sudden numbness in his arm. "You've reached layer five of Foundation Realm. Impossible."

Du Lufang let a smug smile cover his whole face. "Call Li Shua out, else your whole clan will be in trouble today."

Li Tang gritted his teeth. This was inconceivable. With layer five cultivation, Du Lufang could suppress the Li Clan's Old Martial City branch easily and they might have to swallow their pride.

But would that happen? With Li Tang reaching layer nine Foundation Realm, even if Du clan's patriarch came, he wouldn't have to worry too much about it.

"Du Lufang, don't be arrogant with just layer five Foundation Realm powers. My father has already reached layer seven in Foundation Realm. Once he takes action, you'll be reduced to a mere ant." A small smile crept on his lips. For now, he would let his father take charge, and once he reached layer seven with the pills he had, he would take the remaining two Foundation Refirming pills and reach layer nine himself. Then he wouldn't have to worry about small fries like Du Lufang.

"Let him come too. I'll crush him today and even crush your ancestor if he dares to come out."

Li Tang frowned. What gave Du Lufang such assurance to call out their ancestor? The ancestor was a figure in layer eight of Foundation Realm who always remained in seclusion in their main city. But this time he had come out because of the Earthly Fruit Tree matters.

"Who in the Du clan juniors is pretentious enough to curse this ancestor? Even your patriarch doesn't dare to raise his voice in front of me." A powerful voice reverberated in the surroundings, and the Li clan's ancestor, Li Tim, stepped out of the clan compound.

"Senior Li Tim. Today is the day you die." Du Lufang chuckled. "Brother Tian Wu, how much longer are you going to hide behind the trees?"

Li Tang felt his heart quiver when ten people belonging to the Tian and Du clans stepped out of the woods. It seemed like this was going to be a tough fight.

Chapter 53

Tier 4 clan?

Li Wei and Li Shua were on their way back from the herb garden when a servant came running for Li Shua. A little cloud of dust rose around his feet as he halted abruptly a few feet away from them. Sweat poured down his face and merged with blood leaking from a sharp wound on his chin. Disheveled, he looked like he'd run a mile or two.

Wei licked his parched lips and wondered about the reason behind the servant's poor condition. Had someone beaten him up? Internal fighting?

No, he smelled trouble. It couldn't be internal fighting, as that would invite the wrath of the old man. He was quite particular about internal fighting.

"Patriarch, forgive this lowly servant for talking without asking, but the Du and Tian clans are causing trouble at the main gate and even the ancestor has emerged from his seclusion," he sputtered in one breath.

Wei frowned. Was this the same trouble the old man mentioned before they left the herb ground?

"Ancestor Uncle Tim took action?" The old man's body trembled. "Wei'er. Go back and leave through the back of the mountain and head toward Fragrance Herb City." He sounded resolute and firm.

Wei understood the meaning behind the old man's words. This was indeed the trouble he'd spoken about.

"Old man. What's the highest level of cultivation in the Du clan's local branch?"

"Layer four Foundation Realm," the old man replied with wide eyes. "Brat, I ordered you to go. You've just stepped into Refinement Realm, and in an expert's eye you can't even compare to an ant. Do you not get it? If you die here, what will I say to Min'er when I meet her again?"

Wei was touched. This old man's behavior contradicted the impression Wei had held in his heart for him. In one day, it had gone from bitter stinky jerk elder to someone who was a bit warm in nature. Earlier, this man had given him a treasure (or trap) that his stepbrother had left, and then the old man even gave him a Silver Grade talisman that could save his life once.

Didn't this convey warmth from the old man's heart?

Maybe the old man wasn't as bad as Wei had thought. Now he wondered how many things he'd missed in his previous life due to running away from his clan. After he left, the Li clan had vanished from the Mortal Realm, stripping his chance to know the other side of his family.

Of course, Wei hated Li Tang, and he must die, but that didn't mean Wei should let the whole Li clan vanish from the Mortal Realm. At least not when the opponent was merely in Foundation Realm. Although he himself was just in Refinement Realm, how much time would it take him to step into Foundation Realm with his body cultivation? When he'd dealt with Li Sua, his stepfather, he'd failed, but that was because of his lack of vitality and cultivation. He'd inherited this body in the lowest possible condition and couldn't even cultivate a strand of qi. How was he supposed to go against a Foundation Realm cultivator at that time?

"Grandfather, you are right. I'll head back and run away with Fei'er. You should stabilize the situation outside first." He had decided to call the old man grandfather going forward. He'd earned his respect.

Disappointment flashed through his grandfather's eyes before he nodded and rushed toward the main gate.

Wei waited and observed his grandfather's old back and wondered if he could hold back the calamity with his own hands. His grandfather had stepped into layer eight of qi Foundation Realm, and ancestor Li Tim should also be in the eighth layer of qi Foundation Realm, but as per information he'd gathered in his previous life, one of the Du clan's elders in Bone Baptization Realm had obliterated the whole Li clan in one go.

"Hmm. It means they are hiding behind the veil." Currently everyone thought that the Du clan only had their ancestor in layer nine of qi Foundation Realm, that they were a Tier 5 clan. But with a Bone Baptization Realm elder in their ranks, they would qualify to be a Tier 4 clan. And there was a big chance that their ancestor had also stepped into Bone Baptization Realm. If the Li clan knew this, how would they fall so suddenly?

The State of Zin was divided into four provinces, and Old Martial City was in the North Province. The power level in the North Province was quite low. It was divided into clan territory. Sects had their own power system, and they didn't fall under imperial influence, but they also disdained partaking in normal people's affair, so unless one provoked them, they wouldn't take part in worldly affairs.

All the clans in the State of Zin were divided into a tier system ranging from Tier 1 to Tier 5. North Province only had Tier 4 and Tier 5 clans. It was a simple system. If a clan only had Foundation Realm cultivators, they were a Tier 5 clan. A Bone Baptization Realm cultivator would qualify them for Tier 4, and so on. Currently, only the Wang and Fu clans were considered Tier 4 as they had Bone Baptization Realm cultivators in their rank.

But he didn't get two things. First, why did Du clan hide their achievements? Advancing one tier would bring them more benefits and improve their standing in the province. Second, if they had a reason to hide their powers, why would they reveal them now?

What kind of treasure did the Li clan possess for them to reveal the powers they'd concealed for so long?

Chapter 54

Essence Burning Pill

Li Wei moved through the thick forest adjacent to the compound. He jumped through an unguarded area and then headed toward the main gate under the veil of thick trees. His divine sense spread out in every direction, detecting every change in his surroundings. Be it a withered leaf falling to the forest floor, a rat digging in the black soil, or bees humming around a Blue Dragon Flower, everything was recorded in his mind.

When his divine sense detected a person, he stopped and hid behind a tree and watched the action unfolding nearby. There were two parties in confrontation. One was a group of Li clan people standing in front of the main gate. Their eyes were full of rage, ready to devour anything that came at them. Opposite them were ten Du and Tian clan people forming an impenetrable line in front of the main gate. With his divine sense, he instantly sensed their cultivation realms. Du Lufang was in layer six of qi Foundation Realm, while Tian Wu was in layer eight of qi Foundation Realm, and all the others behind them ranged from layer two to layer four of qi Foundation Realm. Comparing their overall strength, the Li clan were not outmatched. Li Tang was in layer five, Li Shua was in layer eight, and Li Tim was also in layer eight of qi Foundation Realm. There were two other elders present from the Li clan as well who had reached layer four of qi Foundation Realm.

The Li clan's combined strength surpassed that of the Du and Tian clans' party. But where was the Bone Baptization Realm cultivator? If they had a Bone Baptization Realm cultivator with them, as they'd had in the version of the conflict Wei had learned of in his past life, the Li clan wouldn't survive.

Wei searched a large area behind the Du and Tian clans' party, but he didn't see any trace of a Bone Baptization Realm cultivator anywhere. If he had found one, Wei had planned to take the Li clan's juniors with him and run away.

That was the only option to save the Li clan's heritage.

In his previous life, he didn't even look at Bone Baptization Trash's, but right now fighting a Bone Baptization realm cultivator with his current cultivation would be suicide.

It seemed that the Bone Baptization Realm cultivator wasn't here yet, so this party must have been just a vanguard sent to test the Li clan's strength.

Then what did the Du and Tian clans have with them to rely on?

Wei narrowed his eyes when he spotted a lustrous white pill appear in Du Lufang's and Tian Wu's palms.

Essence Burning Pills.

This was indeed a perilous situation for the Li clan. But it also meant he still had a chance to act.

* * *

Li Shua's face darkened when he spotted the lustrous white pill exuding a medicinal fragrance on Du Lufang's palm. It was an Essence Burning Pill. How could he not know what that pill could do?

"Senior Tim. Do you recognize this pill?" Du Lufang asked arrogantly.

"Junior. It is an Essence Burning Pill." Ancestor Tim took a long breath before continuing. "You're a Foundation Realm cultivator. You should know the aftereffects of this pill. You will be bedridden for three months. Do you want to take that risk?" he said, tapping the ground with his leather shoes. It was a signal for Li Shua to prepare for battle. "Shua'er," Ancestor Tim whispered in a low voice that only Li Shua could hear. "If this junior eats this pill, we will take charge and let your sons run away and survive. An injured dog is better than a dead tiger."

Li Shua's heart became heavy. The message was clear; the ancestor wanted to sacrifice their lives to let their descendants survive. If he put himself in the ancestor's shoes, this was the best option available for them. Essence Burning Pills were expensive medicinal pills that allowed a cultivator in Foundation Realm to burn essence stored in their dantian's walls and increase their cultivation exponentially. If Du Lufang and Tian Wu both ate that pill, they would have prowess equal to layer nine of Refinement Realm, and that would put the Li clan in danger of extermination. Foundation Realm was easy to reach, but harder to master. When one reached the peak of layer nine, they would be invincible in Foundation Realm. With those pills, Du Lufang and Tian Wu could easily obliterate the Li clan. Only he and his ancestor uncle could hold them for a few breath's time.

But the situation need not be so grim. If it came to it, he could expose his own trump cards.

"Du Lufang. Don't go overboard. Do you think the Li clan doesn't have those pills?" Li Shua pulled out a small pouch. It also contained two Essence Burning Pills. A few days back, Divine Fragrance Palace had given these pills to him in exchange for securing the deal with the Earthly Fruit Tree. He had kept these pills with him in case of calamity, but he didn't expect that calamity would come so soon.

Ancestor Tim's gaze shifted to the pills in his hand, and a grin turned up the corners of his lips.

Du Lufang chuckled loudly. "Li Shua, you don't seem to understand the situation yet. We won't be eating these pills, but other elders will consume them and destroy your whole clan. Then, when the time comes, Tian Wu and I are enough to deal with you two." He pulled a bottle of Essence Burning Pills out and shook it in front of them. "If you show me this many pills, then I'll leave and won't return again."

Li Shua's heart stuttered. His face turned deathly pale. This was inconceivable. How could Du Lufang produce eight to ten Essence Burning Pills? The Li clan would have to give up a month's income to buy one, and this bastard had produced a bottle like it was a dirt-cheap thing. It was like slapping the Li clan with money.

The situation that had seemed balanced instantly turned into a one-sided massacre.

"As expected, brother Lufang." Tian Wu laughed. "You are hitting the dog with money. I bet even if they sold the entirety of the Li clan's properties, they couldn't buy this many pills in one go."

Li Shua squinted. "Tian Wu, how ruthless. Why are you siding with this bastard?" He couldn't contain his anger anymore. He wanted to tear these two bastards apart right now.

Tian Wu chuckled and stood next to Du Lufang, stroking his small mustache. "It's the rule of the world, Li Shua. The strong always bully the weak. Who told you to obtain wealth when you can't protect it?"

Li Shua suddenly understood what this was about. It was the Earthly Fruit Tree that had brought calamity upon him. As soon as Li Ti had told him about the tree appearing in their forest, a sense of looming danger had emerged in his mind. That's why he had contacted Divine Fragrance Palace to make a deal. The tree was something he could never protect with his own prowess.

And now this calamity befell his clan.

Could they survive?

At least that brat Li Wei had agreed to walk away. When the brat said he would walk away, Li Shua felt disappointment in his heart, but now he knew that the brat had made the perfect decision. If Wei was killed here, what would he say to Min'er when he met her in the afterlife?

Although he hadn't been able to give her safe refuge, he could at least save her son.

"What if I help the Li clan?" A deep voice echoed in the surroundings, followed by the appearance of a tall man with an unending aura and a black head cover walking out of the trees. "If I eat one of those pills, can you bunch of idiots survive this battle?" The strong aura of a peak

Foundation Realm expert descended upon them like a hundred-ton boulder falling from the sky. Although it was just a single layer, the difference between layer eight and the peak of layer nine was as vast as heaven and earth.

Chapter 55

Li Wei's master

Du Lufang knitted his brows when an aura stronger than anything he had felt before crashed into him, sending quivers across his body. With the pressure he felt, he instantly recognized the cultivation the hooded man possessed.

The stranger was at the peak of Foundation Realm, or a half step into Blood Baptization Realm.

When did the Li clan hire an expert like this? His lungs constricted as he observed the mysterious gray-hooded man. From just a glance, he could tell the mystery man was an unfathomable existence, and even his big brother, the clan's second elder, Du Kun, might not be able to take on this person.

His big brother was at the peak of Foundation Realm, but even he had never shown Du Lufang the kind of pressure this mystery man gave off.

A bone-breaking chill ran through his heart when two dark eyes stared into his soul.

"Brother Lufang." Tian Wu clenched his fist. "If he helps the Li clan, we might be in trouble."

"Shut up." Du Lufang grunted. Of course, he knew that. If a peak Foundation Realm expert ate an Essence Burning Pill, he could rival even a Bone Baptization Realm expert. With that person holding down the fort for the Li clan, they had no chance to eliminate the Li clan today. "Senior, you don't seem to be from the Li clan." His voice quivered under the uncertain pressure the mystery man exuded.

The mystery man neither denied or confirmed.

Du Lufang suddenly saw a glimmer of hope. "Senior. It must be taxing to come here to help the Li clan like this. How about you help us, and I'll offer you twice the benefit the Li clan is offering? This way, your trip won't be wasted."

The mystery man didn't reply. He just stared back at him, his aura diminishing a little.

Du Lufang felt a cold breeze rushing through his mind. The mystery man was retracting his aura, so he was interested in Du Lufang's proposal.

"Senior. If you're not happy with twice the compensation, how about thrice? You can judge my riches by checking this pill bottle." He flaunted the pill bottle in his hand. He'd been buttering up his wife for years so she would get some good quality pills from her maternal clan, and she had bought this pill bottle for him. This was all he had when it came to his own money, but he didn't believe the Li clan had promised this senior a hefty price like Essence Burning Pills. If needed, he could sell a couple of these pills and pay triple the amount the Li clan promised to this senior. With the senior expert on his side, he might even have a chance to get a greater share of the wealth from the main branch.

Yes, that should be easy. Li Shua and Li Tim had bewildered expressions on their faces, and that meant their relationship with this senior hadn't stabilized yet.

The black hooded senior laughed. "You can't offer me what the Li clan has offered me."

Du Lufang frowned but changed his expression instantly and put a benevolent smile on his face. "Senior, what can the mere Li clan offer? An artifact? Gold? Qi Stone? I can offer thrice the amount they offered. You must be aware that the Du clan has always surpassed the Li clan financially." Even if he had to sell four of these Essence Burning Pills, he would buy enough treasure to pull this senior to his side.

"They offered me a life. Can you do that?"

A life. Was he asking for his life?

No, the Li clan must have offered someone else's life.

Aha! Like a flickering light, an idea formed in his mind. This senior hid his face, and he had this deathly aura around him. The senior must be a demonic cultivator. That had to be it. Only demonic cultivators used others' lives to cultivate. "Senior, I can also offer you ten lives." He shook his head. "No. I can offer you all of the Li clan's lives. You can cultivate as much as you like."

The gray-hooded senior paused and looked at the Li clan members who had wary expressions on their suddenly pale faces.

"Li Shua opened his mouth but no words came out.

"Senior, see? The Li clan is not capable of the things I can offer. If you want, I can offer you a hundred more slaves on top of the Li clan's lives." He had many useless slaves in his manor, and he would happily give them to this senior.

"Du Lufang, you're overestimating yourself," the senior said in a chilly voice. "Who said I want the lives of others?"

Du Lufang felt sudden death coming at him, like he'd missed something in their conversation. Then it hit him. This senior was a demonic cultivator, but he didn't want to expose his true path of cultivation. Of course. There were so many people present here, and if anyone exposed this, the senior might be in trouble."

Du Lufang suddenly felt how brilliant he was. "Senior. I'm sorry for the misunderstanding I caused. I didn't mean you need others' lives. I know you are a righteous person and look down on others who take lives. I'll just use my slaves to please you. You can use them as your servants." He was even ready to offer virgin boys. Once, his clan elder had told him about a demonic clan that stole pure yang from virgin boys to cultivate.

⇛⇛ ⇚⇚

Li Wei wanted to smack Du Lufang's face. What the heck was going on? Why was he suddenly pushing slaves at him? Did Du Lufang think he could sway Wei's thought by offering a few dozen slaves?

Was something wrong with that blockhead? First Du Lufang offered riches, and then he suddenly started offering slaves. All he wanted was to scare these bastards away. The Persona Amplification Array he had crafted on his robe was slowly vanishing. The ink he had used seemed to have some other blood mixed into it. So, the array was fluctuating, and he had to maintain it by imbuing more qi into it through the low-quality Qi Stone he had.

It was such a waste.

Damn that Wu Xiodia. He called himself an Array Master, yet he sold mixed blood in his shop. This was a big taboo among array carvers, and if it was exposed, his shop wouldn't sell a single thing afterward.

"Du Lufang, shut up. If you dare say one more word, I'll kill you," Wei shouted, using his divine sense to pressure Du Lufang more. If Du Lufang lingered for ten more minutes, Wei might lose his facade of an expert.

"Senior, why don't we step away and discuss our terms? I'm sure I can satisfy them."

Had Du Lufang gone mad? Didn't he hear his big fat no?

"Du Lufang, get the fuck out of here, else I'll eat an Essence Burning Pill." He reached for the pills in his grandfather's hand.

"Senior . . ." Du Lufang stepped back. "Please think about this. I will come back tomorrow. If you want, I can offer you virgin boys as well."

A thin layer of perspiration formed on Wei's forehead. Was this guy a sicko? First money, then slaves, and now virgin boys. What was wrong with him?

"Li Shua, give me that pill. If I don't kill this brat today, then I won't show my face in the outside world." He blurted nonsense as the array slowly disintegrated from his robe.

"Senior, what about virgin girls?"

"Fuck off!" He stomped, raising a cloud of dust in the air.

Du Lufang sighed visibly but retreated. "Senior. I'll come back again. Please let us talk privately. I believe we can come to an agreement."

Wei's blood boiled. What more could he do? If he had the strength, he would have smacked this bastard rather than trying to scare him off. This was utter humiliation.

Thanks to the heavens, Du Lufang walked away with his underlings and Tian Wu.

"Senior . . ." Stepping forward, his grandfather bowed, almost touching the ground with his head.

Wei felt a speck of guilt enter his mind and take root. He'd wanted to help his grandfather, not make him bow down before him.

"Patriarch Li Shua, you don't need to show any courtesy. I did it for my disciple."

"Disciple?" Li Shua's head shot up, his eyes spanning wide.

"Yes, your grandson," Wei replied, maintaining his fake hoarse voice.

Ancestor Li Tim cupped his hands. "Senior. Thanks for your help. If it wasn't for you, my Li clan would have suffered a great calamity." His gaze jumped to the houses in the Li clan compound. "Li Guan, Li Pi, you bastards! Why did you hide something like this from your ancestor? Are you trying to embarrass me to death?" His voice echoed through the whole compound. Although he showed anger, Wei knew that the old ancestor's mind was full of joy.

"It's Li Wei." Wei answered hoarsely.

Ancestor Li Tim couldn't believe what he was hearing, and he rubbed his ears harshly. Every other Li clan member present had a dizzy look in their eyes.

Only grandfather Li Shua had a calm expression. "So that's how that brat fixed his dantian. Senior, I guess it must be you who helped him. The brat had this fortuitous encounter and didn't even tell his grandfather."

The Persona Amplification Array pulsed, its energy down to half. Wei had to leave, else he would give the game away.

"Patriarch Li Shua, trust Li Wei with your whole heart —" "Wei cut his sentence in half as an ominous feeling gripped his heart. Something was wrong.

Looking in the direction Du Lufang and Tian Wu had gone, he spread his divine sense forward.

A bunch of figures flashed through the forest and entered his divine sense's radius.

Fuck! A Bone Baptization Realm expert led that group, and that meant the Du clan elder had made his way to Old Martial City.

Something he feared for had already knocked on his door.

Chapter 56

Du Su

Li Wei gritted his teeth and looked around helplessly. Calamity was already here, and he had no option but to give in to the situation.

The Bone Baptization Cultivator's strong aura rushed toward them, and his heart palpitated. He wasn't afraid but knew he was helpless. His fingers clenched in a tight grip, and he only noticed it when blood leaked from his palm.

Hopelessly, he looked around.

There were five Foundation Realm experts around him, and only two had reached level eight. The rest were layer one to layer four. Although there were two layer-eight qi Foundation Realm cultivators, they didn't add up to one layer two Bone Baptization Realm cultivator. They could hold up for some time, but that was it. They would die in the end.

How was he supposed to face a Bone Baptization Realm expert with his insignificant cultivation?

A man appeared atop a long Rua tree. His golden robe fluttered with the north wind, and he jumped down like an emperor. "Li Shua, we meet again." His white beard reached his waist, and he looked to be in his late forties. But that couldn't be his real age. He must be at least fifty years plus, but his cultivation had reached Bone Baptization Realm, giving him a youthful look. A long black sword hung on his back, and his pea-shaped eyes scanned everyone in the vicinity, malice leaking through them.

"Du Su," Grandfather Shua replied, but his voice lacked confidence. "How could it be?" He must have recognized the opponent's cultivation level.

"I know what you're thinking. You must be wondering how I reached Bone Baptization Realm, while you—a talent of our generation—remain stuck in Foundation Realm." He laughed, stroking his beard with his left hand.

"It . . ." Grandfather Shua had an unsightly expression on his face, like he regretted being powerless.

"You were a prodigy, and you ended up being trash. What an irony. Now, look here, Li Shua." A red glow appeared behind Du Su's head like a crown.

After stepping into Bone Baptization Realm, cultivators could form a phenomenon behind their bodies, and the red aura was a common phenomenon many Bone Baptization Realm cultivators formed.

"Du Su, when did you break through?" Ancestor Tim said. He seemed to age suddenly by a decade. "I can't believe you used to play with Li Shua once." He sighed, helplessly.

"Li Tim. Shouldn't you call me senior, as I've already surpassed your cultivation?"

Ancestor Tim had an awful look plastered on his face for a moment, but it turned into a self-mocking smile. "You're right, senior Du. You're indeed a senior I should look up to."

"Ha ha. It's good that you didn't forget your humble nature, Li Tim." Du Su smirked.

Wei gnashed his teeth. Arrogance had slipped into Du Su's very bones, and he had the urge to smack him to the ground.

"There's no point in hiding from you, Li Tim. I broke through a decade ago and was in closed-door cultivation. Recently I reached Bone Baptization Realm layer two and thought of coming out." A proud smile played on his lips. "But then I thought of meeting an old friend to see if he'd achieved a breakthrough as well, but I didn't think he would prove unable to reach the peak of Foundation Realm."

"Senior Du, what's the point in hiding this information? If you've reached a Tier 4 clan, then say it so we can act accordingly." Ancestor Tim's voice faded like the end of a flute song.

"Li Tim, why should my Du clan tell a dog about our achievements?" his voice turned icy as frost. "A dying clan doesn't need to know about it."

"Du Su. State your demands." Grandfather Shua said in a hoarse voice, his emotions leaking through. "We can compensate you for your loss. As for the Earthly Fruit Tree, that information has already been passed to Divine Fragrance Palace. You're free to take it away if you have the guts."

Grandfather Shua shivered in humiliation, but he couldn't do anything.

The speed of Du Su's beard stroking increased. "Give me one hundred low-quality Qi Stones and Li Wei, your grandson. Then hand over the coordinates to the ancient treasure you obtained. Then I shall consider leaving a few of your young generation alive."

Grandfather Shua's face tightened. "Don't talk nonsense. We don't share enmity. Why would you kill us? If we've offended you, then we will make compensation. Don't make it hard on us. Remember, a wounded wolf always bite harder. I can offer you fifty low-quality Qi Stones in exchange for fifty years of truce. There should be no conflict between the Du and Li clans. As for the coordinates, we don't have them." He looked pained to part with that much profit, but he had no other choice.

What were these coordinates this man wanted, Wei wondered but couldn't think of anything that the Li clan in his previous life had known.

Du Su stepped forward like a gust of wind and slapped one of the Li clan's Foundation Realm elders. It was one slap, but the elder died miserably.

Everyone's faces turned grim, and their killing intent rose. Their faces were red, and they looked like they could burst in anger anytime.

Wei stood a bit apart from the Li clan members, but he couldn't control the gnashing of his teeth. This was insane. After a lifetime, he got his family back, but he had to see them facing humiliation again and again.

Although he didn't care about most of the Li clan members, a family humiliation was family humiliation.

Was he going to see without doing anything?

"Consider that a warning," Du Su said. "There will be no negotiation. Coordinates, one hundred Qi Stones, and that brat Li Wei. I want to tear his tendons apart and offer them to my personal disciple, Du Xin."

Wei's throat went dry. How could this bastard know about him killing Du Xin? Had he missed something that led to him? Then he suddenly remembered Du Xin threatening him with his master's name. So, this was that bastard master of his.

"Du Su, don't go overboard," Grandfather Shua replied hurriedly. "My grandson is a cripple, and you know it very well. He can't even cultivate. How can you believe he killed your grandson?"

Du Su's face wracked with a strange expression. "I used a Spirit Severance Talisman to confirm it from my disciple. He spoke one name, and that was your grandson, Li Wei."

Wei felt as if a bolt of lightning had struck his brain. How could he forget about this talisman? If one found a remnant of a recently dead person, they could use this talisman to initiate a conversation.

Damn, why had he left their bodies behind? If he had hacked them in tiny pieces and fed them to wolves, this situation could have been avoided.

"Should I believe it simply because you say it, Du Su? Don't even think of touching my grandson. You want one hundred low-quality Qi Stones, I'll give you one hundred, but you must give up on that dream of yours."

Tides of overwhelming emotions flooded Wei's heart. His grandfather could have sold him out, but he didn't. Instead, he tried to protect him. This man didn't show it on the surface, but he cared in his heart.

No matter what, Wei had to save his grandfather today.

"Then I shall destroy your Li clan and unearth that brat."

"Father, why are you not giving that bastard to Du clan?" Li Tang opened his mouth and vomited vile shit. "That bastard is nothing but trouble."

Wei's gaze turned cold. Even if he died, he would kill this bastard Li Tang.

Chapter 57

A rare hope

Li Shua's heart thumped in turmoil. His back was drenched in sweat, and his nails almost bore inside his palm. But his face remained calm as an evening lake in an empty land.

"Du Su. Don't push me too hard." His clan was in danger, and a single display of weakness would lead to destruction faster than anything else. Somehow Du Su had dashed into Bone Baptization Realm, and that had already affected the morale of his clan. If they crumbled under pressure, it might leave a shadow in their heart forever.

However, Du Su was a true Bone Baptization Realm cultivator, and the gap between them was too large to surpass.

How was he supposed to save his clan? And this bastard also wanted his grandson, Li Wei. After he'd failed to save his daughter, a heart demon had stuck with him, and it had stopped him from reaching Bone Baptization Realm. Heck he couldn't even reach the peak of Foundation Realm because of that heart demon. Whenever he tried to breach that barrier, he failed miserably, so he'd been stuck at layer eight for so long.

Now he just wanted to let Wei'er live a normal life. So even after Li Sua, Min'er's fake husband, beat Li Wei up, he didn't act upon it because he knew he couldn't harm Wei'er no matter what.

Du Su flicked his sleeve. "What if I do? Are you going to threaten me?"

A man came running out of the woods, his chest heaving like he ran a thousand-mile race. "Elder Su, you are here." It was Du Lufang, and two Foundation Realm cultivators followed him. "Elder Su, why didn't you tell us before coming here? Please forgive me for not attending to you directly."

Heaviness gripped Li Shua's heart. Du Lufang joining the fray meant more trouble for him. Suddenly the Li clan's chance of survival reduced by a huge margin.

"Do I, Du Su, have to inform you when I come to your wastrel city? Have you broken through Bone Baptization Realm?" Du Su mocked Du Lufang heavily.

"Elder Su . . ." Du Lufang shivered and then prostrated on the ground. "Ancestor Su, please accept my apology and punish me for not seeing mountain Tai with my lowly eyes."

Li Shua furrowed his brow. Even Du Lufang hadn't known about Du Su breaking through to Bone

Baptization Realm. It seemed like the Du clan had hid it pretty well, and Du Su didn't want anyone else to know for some reason. But as Du Lufang was already nearby, it was impossible for him not to notice Du Su. After all, everyone had spies around everywhere.

"Lufang, you failed to protect my disciple, Du Xin, so I'll deal with you later. But first—" His vicious gaze turned toward the Li clan, and Li Shua felt chills.

A Bone Baptization Realm cultivator was not something a Foundation Realm cultivator could hold out against. If it came to that, he had to rely on his final trump card and leave everything to ancestor Tim.

"Ancestor Tim," he whispered, so low that only the ancestor could hear what he was saying. "If it comes to it, I'll utilize that pill and then you take everyone away."

Ancestor Tim's face stiffened. "Shua'er. Give that pill to me. If it comes to it, I should eat it. My old bones should have already turned to dust, but I kept using Life Extension Pills for this purpose. I should eat it and turn to dust." Despite his words, his voice was heavy and reluctant.

Li Shua had a complex expression on his face like he was stuck between a rock and hard place. What should he do? His trump card was a demonic pill he'd ransacked from an ancient cultivation vault. It allowed a Foundation Realm expert to break through once. If he or ancestor Tim ate it, they could breakthrough to Bone Baptization Realm right away, but it wouldn't last long. In ten minutes, they would die from blood explosion. But if they held Du Su off for ten minutes, it could save all the other clan members from this calamity.

"Patriarch Li Shua, are you talking about Blood Berserk Pill?" A voice rang in Li Shua's mind, startling him.

"Who is this?" Li Shua looked around but couldn't see anyone talking to him. Was it a ghost?

"Li Shua, have you already lost it?" Du Su chuckled as he pulled his sword out. "I haven't even started massacring your clan, and you've already lost your wits. How pathetic. I despise myself for being friends with you once."

Li Shua steeled his heart. "Du Su. I guess you don't see how high the heavens are." He flipped his hand, and a blood-red pill appeared on his palm.

"A Blood Berserk Pill. Li Shua, where did you get your hands on that?" Du Su's face turned grim for a moment. "Did you collude with demons and receive this pill?"

Li Shua laughed. "Du Su, you don't need to know anything, just like I need not know anything about your mysterious breakthrough. But if you force my hand, I'll fight you with my life on the line, and you know when you provoke a nasty beast what you will get in return. I might not be able to kill you, but giving you a heavy parting gift won't be difficult once I eat this pill."

Li Shua didn't want to do this, because if he ate this pill he would die. But if he didn't, then he'd die too and his entire clan alongside him.

Du Su looked bewildered by the sudden change of situation but then pulled a wooden disc out and swirled it in his hand. "Do you think you can pull one over on me? I came prepared this time." He laughed.

Li Shua's face fell. It was a Yin Yang Disc, a Du clan Spirit Artifact. It was said that it could even go against a hit from a Marrow Cleansing Realm cultivator, so what could a Bone Baptization Realm expert do?

This was bad. No, worse than bad. "Ancestor Tim. Go with the young generation. If heaven permits, we will meet in the afterlife." He brought his palm to his mouth and threw the pill in his mouth.

However, before the pill entered his mouth, a hand grabbed it. "Patriarch Li Shua. Who said you have to eat a Blood Berserk Pill to enter Bone Baptization Realm? There's another way that won't take your life. Are you interested in knowing that?"

Chapter 58

Forbidden Technique

Li Wei scanned the black and white wooden disk in Du Su's hand. It looked like a child had painted it for fun, but that wasn't the case. It gave off an ancient aura, and as soon as the disk appeared, the surrounding space turned sluggish and dark. Scanning the others' faces, he realized they might not have noticed it, but his divine sense could feel a strange suppression.

His eyes lit when he spotted a shiny, strange symbol marked in the center of the disk. It wasn't a normal martial artifact found in the Mortal World. In fact, the Mortal World shouldn't have this thing in it. In the wrong hands, it could turn very nasty.

It was a spirit artifact. While martial artifacts were classified from Bronze to Heaven Grade, there was another type of artifact present in this world: spirit artifacts. Those were artifacts left behind by ancient people, and every artifact had a heaven-turning power embedded in it. But only a few people in the Martial World had a spirit artifact.

How did it end up in the Du clan's hands. This was inconceivable.

Anyway, it exuded a familiar aura: A Yin and Yang aura. He had sensed it from the Yin Yang fruit, and when he sensed it again, he itched to snatch it from Du Su's hands.

But before that, he had to change his grandfather's mind. The old man was going to suicide by eating a Blood Berserk Pill. It was a tyrannical pill made of demonic blood and would overload one's meridians with baleful qi, elevating their power to a higher realm for ten minutes.

But it killed the user. It absolutely killed that person, and there was no way around it.

He couldn't let his grandfather eat it, not after realizing his grandfather cared for him.

"Patriarch Li Shua." He sent with his divine sense. "Who said you have to eat a Blood Berserk Pill to enter Bone Baptization Realm? There's another way that won't take your life. Are you interested in knowing that?"

"Who are you?" Grandfather Shua seemed startled for a moment, but he regained his composure. "Senior, please tell me what you are planning."

"I'm your grandson's, master. Don't worry. I'm using a secret method to communicate so this Du Su won't hear us talking."

"What method you are talking about?" Grandfather Shua asked, his voice lower than previously.

Wei took a deep breath and explained a forbidden technique he had found in his previous life. When he found this, he was already a high-realm cultivator, and this technique didn't work after Houtian Realm, so it wasn't useful for him. It was a strange technique where one used lots of medicinal pills and a strange cultivation pathway to boost their cultivation to a new level. Unfortunately, these powers would wane after an hour, and they would be weakened for a period and fall back to the base layer of their current cultivation. For his grandfather, that would be the first layer of Foundation Realm.

"Use two Essence Burning Pills to stimulate your qi flow like this." He imparted the strange qi flow to his grandfather and also passed it to ancestor Tim. "You won't die if you use this technique, but there's a caveat: your cultivation will fall to Foundation Realm layer one after an hour, and it will be twice as difficult to raise it back to the previous level."

Ancestor Tim's eyes widened when he looked at Wei's disguised appearance. "Senior, does this thing really work?" He shook his long face in disbelief.

"It won't kill you to try," Wei replied through his divine sense. It was better than eating the Blood Berserk Pill. Although the spirit artifact in Du Su's hands looked powerful, if they had two Bone Baptization Realm cultivators, escaping shouldn't be an issue.

"Shua'er. Let me try it out first and see if the artifact is really as formidable as the Du clan claims." Ancestor Tim had a definitive look on his face, and then he stuffed two Essence Burning Pills in his mouth.

Du Su was watching them, and when ancestor Tim ate the two pills, his hideous face broke out in a smug smile. "Li Tim, have you gone mad because of your age? Or are you trying to impress your ancestors in the afterlife with how you died heroically?"

"Ancestor is wise. He saw through a fool's motive in a single glance." Du Lufang joined the laughter. "Li Tim thinks to raise his cultivation to Bone Baptization Realm by using two pills." He took a step back and put on a mock-fearful expression. "This lowly one is afraid. It seems to be a new technique developed by the Li clan to exterminate themselves. We might as well just end our lives."

Other Du clan elders joined in the laugh. Their eyes lingered on ancestor Tim like they were waiting for a good show to happen. It was given. If a person ate two Essence Burning Pills, they should explode and die.

A powerful aura gushed out of ancestor Tim, and his cultivation jumped to layer nine of Foundation Realm.

"Look brothers, I'm about to die now." Du Lufang laughed, clutching his stomach with one hand. "If he breaks through, I'll eat stones."

Just wait, you fool. The corner of Wei's lips lifted upward, and he chuckled in his mind. When ancestor Tim broke through, would these fools eat the stones?

Ancestor Tim roared in pain, his eyes almost popping out of his eye sockets. He looked to be on the verge of death, like he might explode at any moment.

"Look, he is exuding so much pressure. He is about to reach Bone Baptization Realm," one of the Du clan elders shouted, and everyone from the Li clan fell deadly silent. Even grandfather Shua couldn't hide worry on his face.

But ancestor Tim didn't explode. Instead, his cultivation continued pushing forward.

Du Lufang stopped laughing. "How is that possible? How did he break past the peak of Foundation Realm? He is almost at Bone Baptization Realm." The color drained from his face, and he staggered back and fell on his ass.

Boom! Ancestor Tim's clothes fluttered, and an even stronger aura gushed out of his body, instantly pushing him to layer one of Bone Baptization Realm, and the pressure he gave off was higher than Du Su.

Du Su's face turned grim. "How did you— That's genuine Bone Baptization Realm cultivation."

"Ancestor Su, did he really—" Du Lufang crab-walked backward, scuttling across the ground. "It's impossible. How can he?"

Ancestor Tim pulled his thick brown sword out, and bright red fire gushed out of his body, enveloping the sword. "Junior Su, come, let me test the might of your artifact. I don't believe you have enough powers to use its full might." And then he charged forward like a cheetah, dashing through the air and reaching Du Su instantly.

"You're courting your death," Du Su roared and brandished his sword to counterattack. Their swords met in midair, sending sparks everywhere. The impact was so fierce that it generated a shockwave, sending one of the Du clan elders staggering back.

"Good attack. I haven't felt this alive in the last two decades." Ancestor Tim laughed haughtily. "Du Su, come fight with me." It seemed that he liked this feeling of power.

Chapter 59

Fire Beast Explosion

Du Su grunted heavily. The strike from Li Tim had pushed him back a step. If he hadn't dug his heels into the rough ground, he might have been pushed a few steps more.

This was inconceivable. His heels had left a furrow several inches deep on the tough ground.

"How could you eat two pills and reach Bone Baptization Realm? It's impossible."

"Again." Li Tim's sword came for him again, and he had to take it head on. He was once again pushed a step backward.

Impossible. There had to be some trickery involved.

Li Tim might have already reached Bone Baptization Realm and hidden his cultivation like Du Su had for a decade.

Yes, that had to be the case. Otherwise, how could one explain this? But how had this never come to light when they had spies inside the Li clan? It didn't make sense, unless Li Tim hadn't told anyone but the patriarch.

"Li Tim. Don't overestimate yourself. I haven't used my martial skill yet."

A crafty smile appeared on Li Tim's lips. "Neither have I."

Roaring, Du Su activated Roaring Tidal Sword, the Du clan's famous sword skill. A thread of qi rushed out of his dantian into his arm and then into his martial artifact. Before Houtian Realm no one could use their qi directly, and only martial artifacts allowed them to use it somewhat.

When his water qi entered his sword, his sword shone with a blue color, and a thin layer of water formed around its blade. When it met with Li Tim's sword, the water flowed like a river and pushed Li Tim back. "Li Tim, I underestimated you, but if you think your layer one cultivation can go against my layer two, then you're courting your death."

"Du Su, stop talking and take my sword." Fire jumped out of Li Tim's hand and covered his sword, turning it into a fiery beast. "Fire Beast Roar." He struck with his sword, and like a beast, his sword roared, rippling the water film on Du Su's sword. When their swords met, Du Su was pushed back, and the water film on his sword was vanquished by the fiery beast.

"You." Du Su's hand went numb when the impact passed through his sword into his wrist and then into his arms. "You even have a low-tier Silver Grade artifact. How is this possible?" Even after becoming a Bone Baptization Realm cultivator, he'd only received a high-tier Bronze Grade sword, and it hadn't even had an array carved on it. So many times, he'd gone to master Wu's workshop, only to have his request declined. He wanted to smash that old bastard with his palm, but he couldn't. An array cultivator wasn't someone to trifle with.

But how could the Li clan have a Silver Grade artifact?

Was the rumor true? Did they really emerge out of the Imperial Capital?

Du Su stomped on the ground and regained his composure. "Roaring Tidal Sword." Pushing all the unnecessary thoughts to the back of his mind, he used the second level of his Tidal Wave Sword Art. It consumed one third of his qi and increased the intensity of the water swirling on the sword blade. The fire on Li Tim's sword was extinguished in one strike.

"Li Tim, although you have a higher-grade weapon, don't forget I've yet to use my Icy Hell Disk. You're nothing but an ant in front of me. Today I'll eliminate your clan and then bury them in this same ground so no one will dare to go against my Du clan." Rage burned in his heart, and he attacked again.

"Fire Beast Strike." Li Tim responded with similar vigor and his sword swiped down at Du Su.

Fear gripped Du Su's heart. This was the second level of the Fire Beast Sword Art martial skill of the Li clan, and it was said that it could increase a martial artifact's might by a minor layer.

It seemed there were many things about the Li clan he didn't know.

Had he made a mistake by coming here alone?

No, this couldn't be happening. If this continued, he might get injured and have to retreat, maybe even lose his life.

Li Tim pushed forward, his sword attacking Du Su from seemingly everywhere. Although old, Li Tim had fought many battles, and he had much more experience than Du Su, and Du Su realized it quickly. If this continued, he would fail because of his lack of experience.

"Li Tim, you're pushing me to do this." Slipping his hand in his pouch, he pulled one white pill out. It was a Qi Expansion Pill that allowed one to raise their cultivation by two minor layers for two hours. It would leave some medicinal effects in his body, but he could slowly push them out.

Of course, he could use the Icy Hell Disk and finish this quickly, but it would consume a medium-quality Qi Stone, and he didn't want to waste that yet. If he could, he wanted to eliminate the Li clan using his cultivation alone and tell the patriarch that he'd used it. That way he could gain double benefits.

But if the fight continued like this, he would have no choice but to use their clan artifact.

"Du Su, you need to eat a pill to go against a cultivator of a lower realm than you? How shameful." Li Tim stomped his feet and charged forward like a wild beast, his long white hair fluttering on the wind, giving him a solemn look.

Du Su smirked and initiated Flowing Tidal Sword, the third level of their martial skill. It was his limit—he couldn't learn the fourth and fifth level yet—but no one could underestimate the might of the third level. It was unparalleled in the same cultivation realm. Water rushed like a heavy tidal wave and swept over Li Tim's sword in a speck of a second, pushing Li Tim back.

Li Tim staggered back and spat a mouthful of blood. A deep bloody wound appeared on his chest.

"Li Tim. I've already reached layer four of Bone Baptization Realm. Kneel and cut your own head, and I'll leave your corpse intact. You can't win."

Du Su's gaze burned with fury as he got up and charged forward with an undying attitude.

But Du Su wasn't afraid of it anymore. He had a cultivation realm advantage, and nothing could overcome that. Definitely not a tiny ant like Li Tim. Today he would wipe out the Li clan and snatch the coordinates.

In ten minutes, they clashed forty or fifty times, but every time Li Tim ended up with new wounds. Finally, he fell on the ground and didn't get up.

His body littered in wounds, and he looked like a withered tree on the last stress of its life. Seeing him like that, every other Li clan person went dead silent. They couldn't watch their ancestor's humiliation, but they couldn't do anything about it either.

Du Su chuckled. This was the effect he'd wanted. In fact, he could kill them all quickly, but he was afraid only Li Tim and Li Shua knew the coordinates of the ancient treasure trove, so killing them meant he wouldn't get them.

That wasn't he wanted, so he chose to humiliate them and make them surrender.

"Ha ha. I told you, Li Tim. You can't win. Just give up and die."

"Ancestor . . ." The Li clan members came forward but stopped when they spotted Li Tim pushing his sword into the ground and lifting his body with help of it.

Du Su narrowed his eyes. This old bag of bones surprised him. Even after fighting with him to this condition, he had some energy left to stand up. It seemed like he'd gone too soft, considering the old man's age.

"Du Su. I'll fight you with my life." Raising his sword, Li Tim dashed forward.

Du Su chuckled and readied his sword to take Li Tim's life, but suddenly an inexplicable fear gripped his heart, like death was watching him from the shadows.

"Fire Beast Explosion." Fire leaped out of Li Tim's sword and enveloped his whole body.

"Crap!" Du Su shouted and hazily retreated. Li Tim had directly used the fourth move of Fire Beast Sword Art, and it was a forbidden move. It pushed a cultivator's qi in a strange manner, and it exploded out of their body. If an opponent fell under the effect of the explosion, he would die.

Chapter 60

Still Alive?

Fire exploded out of ancestor Tim's body and swallowed a three-foot area around him. Du Su was in there too. It was like a miniature sun going nova and burning everything in its path.

The explosion rang in Li Wei's ears, making his heart quiver.

Dust and stone flew everywhere, hitting a few Li clan disciples. They cried in pain. A few of them started to rush forward, but grandfather Shua raised his hands and stopped them, his face turning grim.

A huge pit appeared from behind the curtain of dust, and Du Su lay half-buried in the middle. He didn't look good, but a wooden disk hovered above his head, spreading a strange light over his body.

There was no trace of ancestor Tim.

Li Wei's chest tightened. Demise of ancestor Tim wasn't something he thought would happen. With this loss, Li clan had suffered a huge loss.

Ancestor Tim had used the fourth level of Fire Beast Sword Art. Fire Beast Explode. It was a forbidden move that allowed a cultivator to channel their life energy into the sword, but the sword would explode after use, destroying itself and killing the cultivator. It was equivalent to a Blood Berserk Pill, but this move didn't even give ten minutes of power up. It just exploded and vanished.

"That motherfucker!" Du Su leaped out of the pit, his eyes burning with rage. His right hand hung limp when he landed outside of the pit. His right arm and half of his face was charred black, and his jaw was wrecked beyond repair. "I'll—" He tried to fix his jaw with his left hand, but it didn't work. "Motherfuckers, I'll kill you all. Each of you dies here today." With his unharmed hand, he pulled out a medium-quality Qi Stone and inserted it into the Icy Hell Disk. When the pure white stream of qi entered the wooden disk, it started revolving in the air. It floated in the air like an emperor, spreading its might to the whole world.

"Yang Domain," Du Su shouted, and icy cold energy burst out of the Icy Hell Disk. It descended like an icy apocalypse in a hundred-foot area around the Icy Hell Disk, and the temperature dropped sharply.

A few Du clan and Li clan disciples fell under the Yang Domain, and they cried in pain. Wei too felt the chill penetrating his skin and reaching his bones, but with a shake of his blood it vanished. Grandfather Shua had stronger cultivation, and his expression didn't change, so he must've shaken it off too.

However, within seconds the temperature dropped again, and the cold air turned into an icy hell, forming a thin film of ice around people caught in its radius. It was so cold Wei felt his internal organs on the verge of freezing. He was only in layer six of body Refinement Realm, and he couldn't sustain himself without using his cultivation art. Firming his mind, he began to absorb essence energy from nature and kick-started his cultivation art. As soon as the essence energy entered his Yangming meridian, the cold was pushed back. With every new drop of blood undergoing the transformation, a stream of vital energy rushed out of his meridian and suffused his entire body, easing the pain and coldness. This was one of the unique properties of his Blood Essence Body Cultivation Art. Blood was everything, and blood was above everything. It was said that blood would resolve every ailment in one's body.

Wei's eyes gained clarity when he circulated the essence energy through a fifth cycle, and he didn't feel cold anymore.

From the corner of his eyes, he spotted grandfather Shua circulating his fire qi and fending off a thin layer of ice that had formed on his clothes.

But not everyone could do the same. Two peak Refinement Realm experts that were caught within the icy domain couldn't resist the cold, and their bodies froze in a blink of an eye. The thin film of ice around them expanded and formed an ice sculpture of those disciples.

"Sha!" Grandfather Shua patted one of the frozen disciples' back, and fire jumped out of his palm, melting the ice, but by the time ice melted away, the disciple had died.

"Die you bastards," Du Su shouted again, sending another pulse of cold energy out of the Icy Hell Disk.

Wei retreated. He had nothing but his own blood to fend off this energy, and he wasn't sure how long he could survive the assault.

But grandfather Shua didn't retreat. Instead, he pulled two Essence Burning Pills out and ate them in one go. "Senior," he whispered in a soft voice. "I've placed a small note in my grandson's pocket. It bears the coordinates of a secret treasure trove. If you think it's enough compensation, please escape with a few of my Li clan's young generation and take them to Dabuio City. The Lord of Dabuio City is my friend, and he will help them settle."

"Grand—" Wei bit his lip. He understood his grandfather's motive. He was going to perform the same action ancestor Tim had and die for the Li clan's survival.

No. Wei clenched his fists and wracked his brain to think of a solution, but there was none. If his grandfather didn't fight Du Su, there was no way the Li clan could survive. A wise choice would be to leave everything and run. A half-wise choice would be to take the young generation of the Li clan with him, and the worst choice was to try saving his grandfather.

What choice should he take?

Chapter 61

Third Choice

Wei chose the third option.

In both of his lives, he'd had no one he could call a blood family. All his close friends had had their own families, and he'd envied them. Maybe he felt a little jealous too. While sitting by himself under a tree, drinking tea, he always wondered why he felt like that when he hated the Li clan.

Yet despite hating them, he still returned to Old Martial City after he'd gained power, looking for them, and when he learned the Du clan annihilated them, he went after the Du clan and took revenge.

Wasn't that a form of belonging? Now the same thing was happening with the Li clan. How could he let it?

Flipping his hand, he pulled a Qi Burning Pill from the storage ring and put it inside his mouth. For activating the forbidden technique to break through, a realm needed a powerful medicinal pill. What could be better than a Qi Burning Pill?

Boom! The pill's medicinal energy exploded inside his stomach and rushed to his dantian. It gushed in like a roaring river meeting the sea and formed a small whirlpool of thick qi that swirled inside his dantian. It rushed through his tiny qi path, destroying all the impurities in its wake and clearing a wide path for itself. It pushed his qi path to the limit, and then he felt his cultivation realm breaking through.

His cultivation level rose sharply. Layer three, layer four, and then it paused when he reached the peak of Refinement Realm. The whirlpool inside his dantian pulsed, and a tide of pure qi flashed through his qi paths, pushing his cultivation to layer one of Foundation Realm. After he reached Foundation Realm, unlike others, he didn't gain any attributed qi. That worked to his advantage. For others, when they absorbed pure qi, they had to convert it into their attributed qi, and caused a loss of some percent of the qi in the transformation process.

But he didn't.

When pure qi rushed through his meridians, he felt an impeccable power pulsating through his body, like he could break a hundred kg stone with a single punch. But this wasn't enough. If he wanted to fight Du Su, he had to reach the peak of Foundation Realm.

He had to power up once more, else he couldn't beat that bastard.

A sharp cry made him open his eyes, and he found his grandfather trying to make his way to Du Su, but with the Icy Hell Disk sending undulations of cold energy, it was quite difficult. Cold energy continued pushing him back and assaulting his body, wounding him. Freezing him.

This was bad. He had to stop him, but he couldn't go and fight. With his current powers, he was nothing but an ant in front of Du Su and his spirit artifact.

But he had a ray of hope shining inside his heart. He had the strange Primordial Blood Palace, and it could elevate his powers.

How much, he didn't know, but he was about to find out.

Activate. He pushed a bit of his pure qi inside the green pendant, and it hummed in response. A stream of pure blood qi rushed out of the cold pendant hanging around his neck and entered his body, rushing toward his dantian. It was blood qi, a rare-attributed qi that only appeared in the Demonic Serpent Blood Clan of the Martial Realm.

Wei arched his brows. This could be troublesome. The Qi Burning Pill he'd used provided pure qi that could be easily assimilated by anyone, as it didn't clash with their innate attributed qi, but if one received a different attributed qi, a clash was inevitable. Fortunately, he had attributeless qi, so it shouldn't fight with blood qi to the bitter end.

But the result was yet unknown. He could only wait until the blood qi reached his dantian.

Boom!

Blood qi gushed inside his dantian and overwhelmed the pure qi whirlpool, turning it red. In the blink of an eye, the white whirlpool transformed into a blood-red, giant whirlpool that sent streams of blood qi to his whole body. New power rushed through his meridians, pushing his cultivation up, and he once again began breaking through madly.

Layer two. Layer three. Layer four. Layer six.

When his cultivation reached layer six, the blood qi whirlpool stopped sending more qi to his meridians, and his realm stabilized at layer six Foundation Realm.

Wei grunted. This was short of what he needed to reach. Only after reaching the peak of Foundation Realm would he have a chance of defeating Du Su with the sword he had crafted Strength Expanding Array on.

Another cry sounded, and when he turned back, he found three Li clan disciples frozen dead on the ground. They had hundreds of wounds on their bodies, all frozen, and one of them was Li Guan.

Emotions flooded him, and his hand went to his sword. No matter what, he had to fight today. He couldn't live with a guilt inside his mind, even if it meant his death. This was his martial way. A lazy martial way.

Pulling the sword from his back, he marched forward, taking in the icy feeling emitting from the Icy Hell Disk. It still exuded the icy domain, but it didn't affect him the same as it had previously. First, he had backup from his layer eight body Refinement Realm, and second, he now had reached layer six of qi Foundation Realm.

Wait, how did he reach layer eight in body Refinement Realm? When did that happen?

Spreading his divine sense inside his body, he checked his Yangming and Taiyang meridians. Both of them were on overdrive, absorbing the blood qi rushing out of his dantian and producing new blood pearls. Upon reaching layer eight, he should have obtained eight hundred pounds of strength.

What? Was this an intended effect of the Primordial Blood Palace?

He didn't know why, but it was awesome. With his cultivation increasing in Blood Essence Body, he could feel power rushing through his muscles and tendons. It gave him a feeling that he could break a large boulder with one punch.

"Senior, why— are— you— not— retreating?" An exhausted voice reached his ears, as grandfather Shua was pushed back and fell next to him. "I can't hold— on much — longer." He spat a mouthful of blood. He looked like a fallen warrior on the verge of dying in his tattered clothes, soaked with blood from countless wounds. Even his vitality had taken a big hit. Wei could feel it from a few feet away.

Wei's eyes turned bloodshot, and his mind screamed, *Kill*!

"Patriarch Shua, stay here and let me handle this for you." Lifting his chin, he glanced in Du Su's eyes. With half of his face charred black, he looked like a demon from hell, but his eyes remained intact. He was in bad condition and couldn't possibly sustain the spirit artifact. If Wei didn't kill him and take control of the artifact, a catastrophic event would occur.

Kill! His mind roared, and he rushed forward with his sword extended to hit. Every step he took, cold energy penetrated his skin, trying to freeze his blood and muscles, but his meridians were on overdrive, converting heaven and earth's essence energy into his muscles and bones and everywhere. Whenever his blood touched the icy energy, it evaporated. This was his blood, and it could destroy anything.

When came within twenty steps of Du Su, Du Su's bloodshot eyes stared at him in disbelief. Pulling another medium-quality Qi Stone out, he inserted it into the Icy Hell Disk, and a huge undulation of cold energy swept through the spirit artifact and turned Wei into an ice sculpture.

"Break!" Wei shouted, and a stream of energy rushed out from his dantian. The icy feeling vanished from his body. The thick layer of ice formed on his body melted like it had been placed on a hot stove.

"Du Su, is that all you got?" Wei snickered and dashed forward with his sword aimed at Du Su's heart.

Chapter 62

Heaven's Suppression

Du Su pulled another medium-quality Qi Stone and pressed it into the Icy Hell Disk spirit artifact.

"Heaven's Suppression."

"Heaven's Suppression? He's gone mad!" Grandfather Shua cried. "That will suppress everyone's power in a thousand-foot area by at least thirty percent and kill the young generation." His dire words exploded in Wei's mind.

Ten feet. Nine feet.

However, before Wei reached five feet's distance, a strange undulation of power shot into his body, suppressing the qi whirlpool inside his dantian and restricting his body cultivation by fifteen percent.

How was this possible? But then he realized he was fighting against a spirit artifact made by an ancient civilization, and anything was possible when it came to spirit artifacts. They went beyond the Martial World's senses, and that's why they were highly dangerous in a fool's hands.

After Wei's cultivation was suppressed by thirty percent, he struggled against the cold energy thrashing against his whole body.

His body cultivation art failed to expel the icy energy invading his body, and soon he was covered in thin film of ice.

Damn! He hadn't even reached fucking Du Su, and he was restricted.

"Whoever you are, give up. I'll not stop before killing everyone in the Li clan today." Du Su's ugly voice reverberated inside his ears, and his mind jolted awake.

"You think so?" Snorting coldly, Wei spread his divine sense inside his body, monitoring everything carefully. Although the icy energy had penetrated his skin, it had stopped before reaching his muscles. It wasn't impossible to resist this energy.

Gritting his teeth, he marched forward, maintaining a slow pace. But every step forward was like walking against a thousand kg of pressure that tried to push him back.

One step.

The icy energy broke through his chest and entered his muscles, but he was ready and moved a blood pearl to counter against the icy energy. When the icy energy and his blood pearl collided, his blood pearl overwhelmed the icy energy and expelled it from his body. But in doing so he consumed the blood pearl.

Not bad.

Second step.

The icy energy broke through his stomach, and once again he sent a blood pearl to expel it as soon as it entered. Too bad he couldn't form a protective shield of these blood pearls outside his body, else he could have saved a lot of trouble.

Third step.

Fourth step.

Fifth step.

Pausing, he took a deep breath and collected his composure. This was exhausting. If he had reached Foundation Realm in body cultivation, this would have been easier.

"How can you—" Du Su's ugly voice struck his ears, and he spotted Du Su panting. Using a spirit artifact wasn't a small task. Only high-level cultivators could make full use of its abilities, and Du Su was merely in Bone Baptization Realm. He was powering the artifact with medium-quality Qi Stones, but how could a spirit artifact be used by a low lever cultivator at all? Every extra second he spent with the spirit artifact meant he spent a lot of his life force.

If Wei could hold on a little bit longer, Du Su would naturally die of exhaustion. He was already injured, and he couldn't possibly hold on much longer.

"Du Su, I know you're dying. But wait for my sword." Smirking, Wei pushed forward.

"You're courting your death. Give up." Du Su panted hard.

Sixth step.

Seventh step.

Eighth step.

Ninth step.

Tenth step.

When Wei reached ten steps away from Du Su, Du Su pulled out another medium-quality Qi Stone.

"Don't." Wei watched Du Su's body wavering like a wooden pole in a whirlpool. If he continued like this, he would die, and that meant no one would be controlling that damn spirit artifact. It would go berserk.

But Du Su didn't stop. He shoved the medium-quality Qi Stone into the spirit artifact.

The spirit artifact shuddered, and a thick film of white ice swept out of it. It was so thick, Wei was sure he would lose half of his abilities if this continued.

Damn!

The icy energy gushed through his skin like a roaring sea and penetrated into his muscles from all over. Although he had his divine sense spread around his body and used his blood pearls to resist the icy energy, how many places could he protect at once?

But he couldn't give up, so he spread his blood pearls thin and sent them everywhere inside his body, rushing inside the muscles and bones and fighting against the biting icy energy. His body turned into a battlefield, and everything became a mess.

A complete mess.

Yet it couldn't stop him, so he took another step. Albeit slow and painful, he took that step.

Eleventh step.

Twelfth step.

Thirteenth step.

The icy energy became more tyrannical, and Wei struggled to press forward, but when he spotted Du Su, lying on the ground at death's door, he bit his tongue and gave another strong push.

Spirit artifacts had their own will, and if they went berserk, they could destroy a whole city until they powered down. So, powerful sects had put strict laws in place for their use, and only the strongest cultivators dared to use them. But this fool had awakened a spirit artifact and was about to die. The fallout might destroy Old Martial City entirely.

Wei endured and pushed forward with all his might.

Fourteenth step.

Fifteenth step.

The icy energy penetrated his heart this time and threatened his life, but he utilized the blood qi from his dantian to fight against it. Of course, the blood qi was just a borrowed power, and it couldn't fight like his blood pearls, which had his vitality stored in them, but it could at least protect his vital organs.

Wei's blood-red eyes gawked at Du Su's sorry figure. His eyes had turned black, and Wei could see red vital energy gushing out of him and entering spirit artifact.

This was bad. That fool had lost control of the spirit artifact, and it was feeding on his vitality. Wei had to kill him and take control before the spirit artifact went berserk.

"Consume. Break for me." Wei's body flared with a bright red light, and he burned one hundred blood pearls instantly. This was the highest number of blood pearls he had ever consumed. If he was still in layer six, he wouldn't have dared to do this, but with layer eight of body Refinement Realm, he took the gamble.

Immense energy rushed inside his body, like he'd eaten a hundred ginsengs at a time. With this newfound power, he raised his leg and took another step.

Sixteenth step.

Seventeenth step.

Du Su's body quivered a final last time, and his eyes went glossy as the last strand of vitality rushed out of his body, entering spirit artifact.

Dread filled Wei's heart, and he dashed forward with all his might. If he couldn't restrict the spirit artifact in a breath's time, everything would be over.

Eighteenth step.

Nineteenth step.

Stretching and straining toward the artifact, he tapped on the control point while stabbing the sword into Du Su's heart with the other hand, ending his final connection with the spirit artifact.

But he was too late. Tyrannical ice and fire energy burst out of the spirit artifact and enveloped him in the blink of an eye.

Chapter 63

Fire and Ice

Li Wei felt like his whole body was trapped in a thousand-year-old glacier. It was so cold his thoughts turned sluggish, and the air in his lungs froze. Every tiny part of his body revolted against the cold, but nothing worked. Everything froze and refused to obey his command.

While he tried to fight the bone-breaking cold, a mad rush of fire burned at his soul, giving him the experience of the ninth hell.

Rage built inside his heart, but there was nothing he could do. He couldn't even cry out, as he couldn't feel his mouth. Everything had turned dark around him, and the only sensations he felt were ice and fire. A foreboding intuition occupied his mind; if he couldn't overcome this, his mind would collapse, and his body would become soulless.

But a tiny purple flame flickered inside his mind, and when he focused on it, the sensations of ice and fire vanished for a moment, giving him a brief glimpse of clarity.

However, when he tried to focus on the purple flame, it vanished, and he was once again drawn into the abyss of ice and fire. It was an unending abyss, and he had no hope of surviving it.

How could one survive when trapped in thousand-year-old ice while burning up inside from hellfire?

Was he going to die, accomplishing nothing? Was his new life going to end in a void like this?

Maybe he deserved this because he couldn't save his family in his previous life. Maybe it was the retribution of heaven that made him go through the whole cycle only to see his family destroyed with his own eyes.

Sigh!

In the end, he'd lacked courage. In his previous life, he'd lacked the courage to do what needed to be done, and in this life, he'd lacked the courage to gain absolute power. If he gave himself an excuse like he had been reincarnated only for a few days, then he would be looking down on himself. That wasn't an excuse he would give a rat's ass in his final breath.

He had failed to live.

Grrrr!

The last speck of air vanished from his lungs, and the feeling of breathlessness jolted his body awake.

System: Host body is in danger. Activating . . .

No, he couldn't fall unconscious. The last time this message appeared, he'd lost consciousness for an entire night.

Before his final thought vanished, the purple flame appeared again, and he gained another moment of clarity.

Break!

An undulation of power erupted from the purple flame and spread through his mind, and everything around him changed. The unending ice-fire abyss melted away, and he appeared in a barren world with a gigantic beast standing a few hundred feet away. The beast had a body of fire and ice, ten legs, a serpent's body, and a dragon's head.

Realization struck his mind. This was a soul space. A legendary space every cultivator created after reaching an unprecedented realm. But it wasn't his own soul space, as he had not reached that cultivation realm yet. When a cultivator formed a soul space, a new entity was born out of it: their divine sense. Wei having a divine sense without a soul space was a miracle in itself.

Tapping with his leather shoes, he tried to feel the surface below his feet. The land hovered between real and unreal, air that one could breathe but couldn't smell, entities one could see but couldn't touch. This was indeed a soul space.

But it wasn't his soul space, instead it was the Icy Hell Disk's soul space.

A smiled curled on Wei's lips as he stared at the beast standing in the middle of this soul space. It was a snake with ten legs and the mouth of a dragon. It was a Yin Yang beast, as half of its body was made up from ice and half from fire. That explained why he felt similar pressure from the spirit artifact.

Wei couldn't help but chuckle. That stupid Yin Yang Beast had pulled him into its soul space to fight a war and regain control.

How naïve. It had dug its own grave.

Spirit artifacts were left behind by ancient people, and people had spent thousands of years studying them, but no one could unlock the mysteries behind them. But that didn't mean they'd failed completely. With the passing of time, humans had unlocked many mysteries of spirit artifacts. They knew that ancient people had sealed a high-level Ferocious Beast's soul inside each spirit artifact, and because of that the spirit artifacts normally had their own will. This was also the reason why spirit artifacts went berserk. If the beast soul sealed inside gained control of the spirit artifact, it could cause massive destruction, or just fly away to an unknown place.

This Icy Hell Disk was trying to do the same. It was trying to wrestle out of his control.

That also meant Wei had established control at the final moment. This eased his mind a little. Because after entering this soul space, he had lost connection with his body, so he didn't know what was going on outside. What if the spirit artifact had already destroyed the whole Li clan?

But that didn't seem to be the case. It would have to obey Wei's commands in the outside world, since he was its master. That's why the stupid beast had brought him here to fight.

When Wei stared at the beast, he couldn't control his laugh. This stupid beast might have thought it could pull in a mere Refinement Realm cultivator's soul and consume it in one shot.

But it had underestimated Wei's prowess when it came to soul.

Space collapsed when the beast opened its eyes, and an impeccable force locked onto him. One icy blue and one fiery red eye stared at him with resentment.

Shaa!

A wall of fire emerged out of the fiery red eye, and an arrow of ice shot out of the icy blue eye. In the blink of an eye, it appeared in front of Wei, sending a shiver down his legs.

The attack was strong. Stronger than he'd expected.

"Six Directional Shield Array," Wei shouted, and six array diagrams floated around him, one in each cardinal direction, one above him, and one below his feet. It was a complex array formation he had learned in his previous life. To perform it in the outside world, he would require precious materials that could be only found in the Martial Realm. Some of them were so expensive that one couldn't buy them with money and could only trade for them with equally valuable treasure. On top of that, he couldn't carve it with his current powers.

But inside a soul space, everything could be manipulated. Whoever had stronger soul power and divine sense ruled in this world.

The wall of fire and icy arrow crashed into the arrays around Wei, but they failed to make a dent before vanishing completely.

The beast paused for a moment as if it couldn't understand the change, and began a powerful torrent of back-to-back attacks at Wei. They were all made up of fire and ice and an unbound might that could destroy a mountain.

Wei smirked, and with a thought, a hundred-foot-tall golden sword appeared in his hands. It exuded a heavenly might, and everything in a thousand-foot area trembled. Be it a stone, a speck of dust, or the Yin Yang Beast.

The sword was his divine sense. The divine sense was born from the soul, and in a soul space, it was the best weapon.

"Three Layered Beast Subduing Array." A three-layered array appeared on the golden sword. Five arrays formed one after another and carved themselves into the divine sword's blade. When they appeared on the divine sword, an intricate pattern shone with a bright gold color, and the sword's might increase one hundredfold.

Break!

Wei swung his sword vertically, slicing down the attacks sent by the beast. Copies of the sword instantly appeared in front of the myriad attacks and sliced them in half.

The beast seemed to be startled and ceased its attacks. But the sword didn't stop.

Just before the divine sword pierced the beast's forehead, it grew larger, changing into thousand feet avatar of itself, and using one leg, it pinned down the divine sword.

"Spirit Trapping Array," Wei shouted, and the array on the divine sword transformed into a huge array that seemed to cover heaven and earth. It flickered brightly and then enveloped the beast, trapping it in a huge net. The divine sword pulsed with a strange white light and shot for the beast's forehead. Wei intended to finish the fight in one go.

For the first time since the fight started, the beast seemed to fear the sword. Its whole body shook and shrank back to its original size. A boundless might emitted from the beast's body, clashing with the white light coming out of the divine sword, but no matter how hard it tried, the beast couldn't resist the might of the divine sword.

"No!" A thought appeared in Wei's mind just before the sword pierced the Yin Yang Beast's forehead.

Excitement gripped Wei. He had branded a soul mark on the beast, and that meant the spirit artifact belonged to him. With his understanding of spirit artifacts, it would be easy to sweep through the whole Mortal World and live the life of an emperor.

He was drooling with greed when a phantom of the Divine Worms appeared next to him, and golden and black threads shot from their bodies.

"Wh—" Before Wei could get even a single word out, the threads had split the beast in half and sucked it dry.

What the fuck?

Chapter 64

Path of Immortality

Something cold fell on Li Wei's nose, bouncing and entering his parched lips. That little bit of moist sensation sent a waking signal through his mind.

When he opened his eyes, his shabby room welcomed him. The fragrance of wet soil and rain hung in the air, and he could see drizzle outside through the holes on his roof.

It was kind of the same feeling he'd gotten when he'd reincarnated.

He sighed in his heart. It was good to be back in his room. Although shabby, it was his room. He had a strong sense of belonging here.

Briefly, he forgot everything that led to this moment, losing himself in the memories of his past. But that tranquility was disturbed when he heard footsteps running toward his room, and when he spread his divine sense, he sensed Fei'er, a hundred feet away, running toward him.

Strange. How could his hearing have improved?

Pushing his palms on the ground, he tried to get up, but a sharp pain reverberated through his body, and he lost the will to rise. Only then did he realize his body was wrapped with soft white bandages, and lingering pain pulsed through every inch of his flesh.

"Young master, you're awake," Fei'er's warm voice reached his ears, swiftly followed by her icy orchid fragrance. Then the little lass's dainty face leaned over his body. "Thank heavens. I've been praying for you day and night." The corners of her eyes turned moist, and she choked on emotions.

"F—"

"Don't speak, you're too weak. Look what I got from old master Shua. A Flesh Nourishing Pill. He said you can eat it once you are awake." She pushed the tiny blue pill into his mouth and forced it down his throat.

Wait. He didn't need that pill. But before he could speak, the pill had entered his stomach, and a refreshing medicinal energy spread through his body.

Closing his eyes, he spread his divine sense inside his body, investigating his current condition. A moment later he opened his eyes in shock. How could this be true?

"Young master, did it work?"

Saying nothing, Wei closed his eyes again and began refining medicinal efficacy from the pill while his divine sense inspected every inch of his body. This was shocking. When did he reach layer two of body Foundation Realm?

He quickly checked his dantian, but as expected, the tiny bit of qi he had cultivated had vanished. That meant he had descended back to layer one of qi Refinement Realm. Although he didn't need to do qi initiation again, he would expend twice the effort to cultivate back to his previous state. But that was fine, as he was only at layer two qi Refinement Realm before using the forbidden technique.

But breaking through Foundation Realm in body cultivation. How did this happen?

When he used the dual boost from the forbidden technique and Primal Blood Manor, his body cultivation had jumped to layer eight Refinement Realm. So, even if it didn't descend back to layer one, he shouldn't have broken through and opened his Taiyang of bladder meridian.

In Blood Essence Body Cultivation Art, every realm required him to open two meridians in his body. The Refinement Realm opened the Yangming of stomach and Taiyin of spleen meridians. Those belonged to the Earth Constellation of the human body. The Foundation Realm opened the Taiyang of bladder and Shaoyin of kidney, making the Water Constellation. Bone Baptization Realm, in body cultivation, would open the remaining two meridians of his lower body, Jueyin of liver and Shaoyang of gallbladder. Once he completed the Wood Constellation, he would have had mastered the whole lower body Constellation, and that's when he would learn the first major divine ability associated with Blood Essence Body. This was another reason he had chosen this cultivation art. It had innate divine abilities that other body cultivation arts lacked.

For initial levels, Blood Essence Body didn't supercharge his activities or make his skin tough like iron. It only provided him raw strength and healing ability. But it had special constellations he could get help from. Now that he had completed the first Constellation, he could get help from the earth to enhance his strength—something he would have to dig deeper for inside himself.

Sighing in his heart, he spread his divine sense into his meridians. Although he had broken through the Taiyang meridian, his internal organs were still in disarray, and the blood pearls inside his body only numbered about two hundred. To reach peak physical condition, he had to condense twelve hundred blood pearls. Although every realm had nine layers, the start of the next realm could be counted as the tenth layer. So, his body should have condensed one thousand blood pearls when he broke through to body Foundation Realm. There was one more thing he noticed: His blood had thickened. It had lost its thin, watery state and turned into a thick liquid. Every blood drop looked much bigger than what he'd had in Refinement Realm.

His heart raced with excitement. Once he regained his vitality, his every punch could exert over one thousand pounds of strength. He could hardly wait to test it out.

This new knowledge came from the depths of his mind. Some cultivation arts were like this. Unless one cultivated it to a certain stage, they wouldn't receive thorough knowledge.

Anyway, getting back to peak condition seemed like a tedious task, and heaven knows how many months he would need. Although the Flesh Nourishing Pill was good medicine, for him it only mended some parts of his flesh. His vitality would recover once he regained at least half of his total blood pearls.

"Fei'er. How did I get here?" He groaned in pain. Just getting these four words out made his mouth dry and his body quiver. "How long have I—" He stopped and took a deep breath. "I was unconscious?"

"Yes, for five days."

A firm knock sounded on the door, followed by his grandfather Shua's old figure slowly walking into the room. Surprisingly, he smiled, and his cultivation had reached layer four of qi Foundation Realm.

"Grandfather, how did you regain your cultivation?" Wei couldn't resist asking.

"It was all thanks to your master. If he hadn't taught me the secret art, I wouldn't have gone a step forward into

Bone Baptization Realm. After regressing to the bottom, I gained comprehension about the path forward, and using Foundation Refirming Pills, I broke through easily. If I get a few more pills, reaching the peak of Foundation Realm won't be difficult." Grandfather Shua's face turned grim. "But I don't know what happened with your master. I hope he survived."

"What really happened?" Wei frowned.

"Shouldn't you tell me that?" Grandfather Shua squinted; his eyes full of suspicion. "I don't even know when or how you rushed in there to save your master. When the bright light ended, we found your naked body lying on the ground with a green dagger and a wooden disk."

"That—" Wei closed his eyes. "Now I remember. When he killed Du Su, I went in there to help him, but I got stuck in the aftermath of their battle and was injured." It was good that he hadn't been exposed.

"Brat, don't do something stupid like that again. I know you've filial respect for your master, but you shouldn't endanger your life."

Warm feelings filled Wei's heart. It eased his pain more than the pill he'd just eaten. "This grandson should follow your command, grandfather." He blinked. In fact, that was all he could do right now with his broken body. "Grandfather, how many losses did we suffer?" The image of Li clan members dying flashed painfully in his mind. "And what happened to the wooden disk?"

"It's with Divine Fragrance Palace's seventh elder. He is inspecting it."

Wei regretted losing that disk. It was a spirit artifact, not a roadside disk. It would be impossible to get it back until he reached a higher cultivation realm. Anyway. "How much did the Li clan suffer, and did the Du clan retaliate?" Wei asked. He had a feeling the Du clan had two Bone Baptization Realm cultivators.

Grandfather Shua's face darkened. "Yes. Du Tenjua came knocking on the door." He sighed. "Thanks to Divine Fragrance Palace's seventh elder, he couldn't do anything. Instead, he was scolded by the seventh elder."

Wei licked his lips, bringing some moisture to them. Fei'er leaned over and pushed a spoonful of chicken soup inside his mouth. "Young master, elder sister Sia came, and she wanted to take me back to the sect. She was happy with my progress. But I refused."

"What?" Wei wanted to get up and smack the little girl's forehead, but his body didn't listen to him. "Why?"

"Don't worry." Grandfather Shua chuckled, and his eyes flashed for a moment when he looked at Wei and Fei'er. "I asked Holy Maiden Sia to rest for a few days in our clan, so you can talk with Miss Fei and convince her to go to Divine Fragrance Palace."

"Thank you, grandfather." He glared at the stupid lass. She didn't know that being acquainted with Tang Sia would change her destiny. In the future, Tang Sia would be known not only as the fierce leader of the sect, but also well known for taking care of her people. It would be best if Fei'er could cultivate diligently and reach Houtian Realm someday so she could live a carefree life.

"Grandfather, what about the Li clan? How much damage have we suffered?"

Grandfather Shua sighed dejectedly. "We lost twenty people, and two of them were in Foundation Realm. Our Li clan is reduced to dregs."

Sadness gripped Wei, but now he had a short-term goal. He would use his powers to make the Li clan overcome this tribulation and rise like a phoenix. Suddenly he found his purpose. He'd wanted to become a lazy immortal, but he didn't know what he needed to do to get there.

Now he had the answer.

Or, at least the first step. The path of immortality required a calm heart, and a calm heart required a safe and peaceful family.

Warm soup entered his mouth and soothed him. "Grandfather, don't worry. I'll help you build our strength faster than anyone can imagine. My master has taught me many things." This time, he would do all in his power to help his clan. He didn't want to have any regrets, and he would make sure he didn't.

Dear Reader,

The fun is not over. Li Wei has only stepped on the path of Lazy Immortal and there is lot to come.

The next book is available for purchase

Inheritance (Path of Lazy Immortal Book 2)

Sign up for my Wuxia Sect to get latest update, and sneak peeks.

Patricia's Cultivation Sect

Chapter 65

Cultivation Realms

Realms of cultivation in the Mortal World (Body and Qi cultivation share the same names)

Mortal Realms (Where a person's body is still considered a mortal body.)

Refinement Realm

Foundation Realm

Blood Baptization Realm

Marrow Cleansing Realm

Boiling Blood Realm

Heart Blood Realm

Houtian Realm

...

Meridian List for the Blood Essence Body Cultivation Art

Lower body Constellation

Refinement Realm (Earth Constellation) - 1) Yangming of stomach 2) Taiyin of spleen

Foundation Realm (Water Constellation) - 1) Taiyang of bladder 2) Shaoyin of kidney

Bone Baptization Realm (Wood Constellation) - 1) Jueyin of liver 2) Shaoyang of gallbladder

Grades of everything (Divided into three tiers. Low, mid, high)

Bronze

Silver

Gold

Earth

Human

Heaven

...

Array Realms

Array Carver Realm

Array Apprentice Realm

Array Adapt Realm

...

Martial skill completion levels

Early Completion

Middle Completion

Late Completion

Peak Completion

If you like cultivation novels, don't forget to check below facebook groups to find out more books in cultivation genre.

Western Cultivation Stories

Cultivation Novels

Printed in Great Britain
by Amazon

38462812R00245